Deadly Devotion

Candle Sutton

Prologue

Night crept in with a predator's stealth. He welcomed the cold embrace of darkness, which felt far warmer than that of the woman who held his heart.

Light leaked from the windows of the house across the street.

He tried not to think about what was going on inside, but found himself consumed with little else.

How long had they been in there? Minutes? Hours? It felt like it had been days since she'd started a movie and closed the drapes.

The front door opened and a man stepped out, the circle of the porch light illuminating him. Tall, broad, dark hair. Beyond the man, he caught a glimpse of her. A smile engulfed her beautiful face and she stepped into the man's arms.

The little slut!

He longed to look away. Yet he couldn't even blink.

She was practically making out with that jerk.

And on her doorstep no less! It was bad enough that she rubbed his nose in her unfaithfulness, but now she was flaunting it for the whole world to see.

How could she do this to him?

His fingers curled around the smooth ivory handle of the antique hunting knife resting on the seat beside him.

He'd teach her a lesson, one she'd never forget.

After one final kiss, she flitted her fingers in a small wave – meant as yet another cruel taunt solely for his benefit, no doubt – and closed the door.

The dark haired man walked down the porch steps, an idiotic grin on his face and a bounce in his stride.

What a chump. He better enjoy it while it lasted because with her, it wouldn't last long.

It never did.

Part of him wanted to jump out of the car and plunge the blade into the man's chest, but none of this mess was that guy's fault. He likely didn't even know she was using him as her pawn. Just another victim of her heartless games.

The loser climbed in his car and backed out of her driveway.

As soon as the taillights disappeared around the corner, the man threw open his door and stepped into the balmy evening air.

He glanced up the street. The night was as still as death.

Weed-filled cracks littered the path leading to her front door. Further evidence that she wasn't the woman he'd thought she was. The lack of care for her property reflected the carelessness in her heart.

Tremors vibrated down his fingers as he pushed the doorbell. Chimes echoed inside.

He stepped into the shadows to the left of the door.

A chain rattled. The lock clicked. The door opened.

"Back so soo–"

He slapped a hand over her mouth and thrust her inside, kicking the door closed behind him.

A scream slid past his fingers as she stumbled. He caught her arm and jerked her to her feet, pressing the flat part of the knife against her neck.

The scream died in her throat.

Her eyes flicked down, futilely trying to see the blade she could feel against her skin, before resting on his face. Tears glittered like broken glass.

Shaking in his fist, she looked so small, so weak and helpless.

How could he feel sorry for her after all she'd done? He'd given her his heart and she'd thrown it to the dogs.

"Please don't hurt me." The breathy words spilled from her perfect lips.

Was that repentance he heard?

Maybe. But it'd take a heck of a lot more than a simple "I'm sorry" to smooth this over. She needed to know, to truly appreciate, exactly how much she'd hurt him.

Let her be scared for now. She deserved it.

"Please. Don't hurt–"

"Shut up!"

She clamped her lips together.

"Down. On your stomach." Growling the command, he lowered the knife and pushed her back a few steps.

"Wh–what do you want?"

"I said shut up. On the ground. Now!"

She dropped to the floor. Her body quaked. A sob hiccupped, the sound echoing off the polished hardwood beneath her.

"Hands behind your back."

The sob morphed into a soft wail.

"Shut up!"

Kneeling beside her, he set the knife aside, pulled a roll of fishing line from his pocket, and lashed her hands together. He grabbed her arms and pulled her to her feet.

"Here's how this is gonna play out. You're coming with me. You make one sound and I'll slit your throat, got it?"

Light danced up the edge of the blade as he held it up. Her wide eyes rested on the weapon before focusing back on him.

She nodded.

Pressing the knife against her back, he shoved her out the door.

The street appeared deserted, but that didn't mean someone wouldn't turn the corner at any second. Not to mention the threat of being seen by one of the neighbors.

They needed to hurry.

Opening the driver's door, he pushed her toward his car. "All the way across."

She crawled in, falling over the center console, and landed sideways on the passenger seat. Not waiting for her to right herself, he slid into the driver's seat and cranked the engine.

Ragged, shallow breaths shuddered from her, the noise drowning out the hum of the tires on the asphalt.

Five minutes passed before she broke the silence. "Whe–where are you t–taking m–me?"

Frankly, as much as she liked to talk, he was surprised she'd waited so long to say something. "Someplace where we can talk without being disturbed."

"Ta–talk about what?"

Was she serious?

He whipped around to look at her. "You and me. Him. The future."

Fresh tears scrolled down her cheeks. "Why me? What did I ever do to you?"

"What did you...?" He fought to keep his attention on the road, but couldn't stop his eyes from straying to her. "How can you ask me that? After that scene back at your house?"

"Scene?"

She couldn't be serious. "Oh come on! You know what I'm talking about. Your infidelity. You didn't even try to hide it!"

"Infidelity?"

"Yes, infidelity." Was she acting dumb just to irritate him? If so, it was working. "I saw him leaving your house. Did you seriously think I wouldn't find out?"

"I don't even know you!"

Don't. Even. Know. You.

The words ricocheted inside his mind as he stared at her. "Why would you say that?"

"I've never seen you before."

Aiming for the curb, he jerked the wheel to the right and

slammed on the brakes. She flew forward, her body slamming into the glove compartment before crumpling to the floor. A yelp escaped.

Good. Served her right.

The pain she felt was a fraction of what she'd inflicted upon his heart.

She struggled to get back on the seat, but lacked the leverage to do so. With her back against the door, she drew her knees to her chest and stared at him.

"I don't know what kind of game you're playing, but it's over. A connection like ours–"

"There is no connection!"

The words knocked the air from his lungs. No connection? It was like he didn't even know her.

Maybe he didn't.

Maybe she'd been putting on a show this whole time. Maybe the woman he loved didn't really exist behind the false front she'd shown him.

The dome light blinked on and she tumbled out of the car.

No! Somehow the little tramp had managed to get the door open.

He grabbed the knife as she stumbled to her feet.

"Help! Help me!"

The screams bounced off the empty buildings lining either side of the street. Too bad for her the businesses had long since closed and no one ventured into this area after dark. The only witnesses to what was about to happen included a delivery van, tractor trailer, and graffiti-covered dumpster.

It was a good place to die.

One

The scream severed the silence.

Paul Van Horn jerked his head up. Another scream followed the first, slamming him like a fist to the gut.

The raw fear in the woman's voice evidenced greater terror than most people experienced in a lifetime. Certainly more than he'd ever known. And he'd been through a lot.

The noise choked off as abruptly as it had started.

He paused. The echo faded, but it sounded like it might be one or two blocks to his left.

He ran.

Not away, although that might've been the smartest thing to do, but toward the source of the sound. He'd never claimed to be a genius anyway.

A boarded-up business flew by on one side. A graffiti tagged warehouse on another. A pawn shop with bars on the windows, a paper manufacturing plant, a mom-and-pop deli. All closed.

In fact, there was no sign of any living person. Except the unknown source of the scream.

The woman needed help; unfortunately for her, it looked like she was stuck with him.

He rounded a corner.

Two blocks up, headlights illuminated a figure kneeling over something on the sidewalk.

As he neared, he saw that it wasn't something. It was someone. His gut told him it was the woman who screamed.

That same gut told him that the figure leaning over her wasn't trying to help.

The creep touched her.

"Get away from her!" The words rumbled through his chest before he'd thought them through.

The man jerked his head up. Hesitated. Then bolted toward the car.

This guy wouldn't get away. Not if he could help it. Paul charged down the block.

The car door slammed.

Even as Paul's brain told him that the guy was going to escape, his feet kept carrying him closer.

He had to at least try to stop him.

The engine roared. The headlights swept him as the car whipped a U-turn and sped down the block.

Dang it!

He faltered, watching the taillights recede until they were pinpricks in the darkness.

If only he hadn't yelled. Maybe he could've gotten the drop on the guy. The guy had been so focused on the victim… the victim!

Paul snapped his attention to the still form on the ground.

Was she alive?

She was perfectly still. Too still.

And there was so much blood. Pooled beneath her. Coating the exposed skin on her arms and neck. Staining her pink shirt.

Even the bare feet poking from under her long skirt were etched with red scratches.

It was hard to believe all this blood had come from such a small woman.

In spite of the Florida humidity, a shiver rocked his body.

Images flashed through his mind, a slideshow of one of the worst days of his life, the only other time he'd seen so much blood firsthand. The day he'd almost watched a friend die.

Focus. She might still be alive.

Forcing the memories back into the recesses of his mind, he jogged toward the woman, careful to avoid the blood and spatter surrounding her. Midnight hair tangled around her head. Eyes stared sightlessly at the black sky, her mouth frozen in a silent scream.

He didn't need to feel for a pulse to know she was dead.

Still, he knelt beside her and pressed two fingers against her neck. His stomach pitched as the fingers slipped in the blood smeared on her skin. Fighting the instinct to rip his hand away, he moved his fingers to the right spot and felt for any flicker of a heartbeat.

Nothing. The woman was long gone.

Blood ringed Paul's fingernails. He rubbed at it, as he had so many times in the past hour, but the color seemed tattooed on his skin.

The hard curb hurt his tailbone, but he couldn't find the energy or motivation to move.

At least *he* could still feel pain. That woman–

"Paul?"

The voice poured over him, warming him like fire, even if it didn't completely chase the chill from his bones.

She'd come.

Of course she'd come. She'd told him she would. And in the year since he'd met Milana Tanner at her father's church, he couldn't think of a single time she had failed to keep a commitment.

Just one more trait on the already long list of things he loved about her.

Police lights bathed her in a blue and red glow as she

approached, the colors dancing on her olive skin and shiny black hair.

He pushed to his feet and enveloped her in his arms. "Sorry I disrupted your night."

"Don't be. This isn't your fault."

True. But choosing to call her, knowing she'd give up whatever she had going on to help him, was his fault.

He hadn't considered calling anyone but her. Even if she hadn't been his first choice, she was probably the only person he knew who wouldn't be completely horrified by what he'd witnessed tonight. Years of working for the US Marshals' service guaranteed that she'd seen things like this before.

Probably much worse.

"You okay?" Her words muffled into his shirt.

"Yeah." As much as he didn't want to, he released her and stepped back. "Better than her."

Both of them turned to look at the body, not that they could see much. Between the police, medical examiner, and distance, the body was little more than a speed bump. But he didn't need to see her. The woman's pained face burned his mind.

He looked down at his blood-stained fingers.

"It'll wash off." Lana's soft words carried a wealth of compassion that brought tears to his eyes. He forced them back.

She was right. The blood would wash off his hands. But would he be able to wipe it from his memories as easily?

"There was so much blood."

"Usually happens with a stabbing."

That explained a lot. The amount of blood, the tortured scream. Not to mention the lack of a gunshot.

He looked up, meeting eyes so dark they appeared black. "She was stabbed? How did you…?"

"I listened to the police scanner on my way over. What were you doing down here anyway?"

"I was walking back from the police station."

"What happened?" Her eyes narrowed slightly, intensity

shining in their depths. "And why were you *walking*? Where's your car?"

"Some punks slashed the tires." The night swirled in his head.

If he'd known what kind of day today would turn out to be, he would've stayed in bed. Not that avoidance would've prevented any of this from happening.

"So you went to the police station to report the vandalism?" Confusion laced her voice.

"I wish. Austin was arrested." The words cut like a knife to the heart.

"Gangs?"

"It always is with him. He was part of a drive-by tonight. Thank God no one was killed." He rubbed the back of his neck and sighed. "I failed him."

"Hey, you did everything you could. It's hard to help someone who doesn't want to be helped."

The truth didn't make him feel any better. "I don't know what I'm gonna tell the other kids."

The faces of the kids in his group home filled his head. At sixteen, Austin was one of the oldest and, when not around his gang buddies, a pretty good mentor to the younger kids.

"How about the truth? That there's right and there's wrong, that choices have consequences, and that those consequences can last a lifetime. It's never too early to learn that lesson."

Didn't he know it.

Here he was in love with someone way out of reach because of mistakes he'd made in the past.

"I guess you're right. But it's not going to make the conversation any easier."

"It never does." She turned to look at the cluster of police surrounding the body. "Have they taken your statement or said when you'd be free to go?"

"They took my statement, but didn't say much after that."

"Let me see if I can take you home."

Home sounded nice. Especially considering the headache

building behind his eyes.

She pulled her badge from her pocket and strode across the asphalt. Several heads turned as she made her way toward the detective, but none of the uniforms moved to stop her.

At only a little over five feet tall, it amazed him that she could command the authority she did. Heck, half the kids in his home were bigger than her and yet, here she was, moving through a sea of cops as though she called the shots.

Then again, a high level of confidence was probably a necessity in order to be taken seriously in what was still largely a man's world. Especially since she looked a whole lot younger than thirty-seven.

As she stopped beside the detective, Paul sank back to the curb and rested his head in his hands.

Man. What a day.

After today, he'd probably be on a first name basis with the cops at the local precinct.

He drove the events of the day into the background and focused on more pleasant things instead. Like Lana. Her quick smile and slightly upturned nose. The way she smelled like mangos. How she always dropped everything to support the people she cared about.

"Okay. Let's get out of here."

He jerked, his eyes flipping open to find Lana a few feet in front of him, looking every bit as good as she had in his mind.

"Hey. You okay?"

"Uh, yeah." Pushing up from the curb, he tried to smile. "I think the long day's getting to me, though. So we're good here?"

"They want you to come to the station tomorrow for a formal statement, but he said you can go for tonight."

Yay. Another trip to the station.

He fell into step beside her as she led the way around the police tape to where her white Toyota Corolla waited. As she started the car, his eyes fell on the clock.

"Aw, man." 11:03 p.m. "I should've called Dale to let him

know what was going on."

At least it was summer. Dale and Annie Webber, his live-in staff, wouldn't need to be up early to get ready for school. Sometimes it paid to be a teacher.

"You can fill them in when we get there."

"Yeah, but Dale gave me a lift to the police station. He was expecting me to call him when I finished up so he could come get me, but I was so keyed up I decided to walk."

Funny how such a seemingly small decision could so dramatically impact his life.

He leaned his head back against the headrest. "I bet Jason and Stef will still be there, too."

"They were there when the police told you about Austin?"

"Yeah."

"I take it they haven't figured out who they want to adopt yet?"

"Not yet." The Pools had been getting to know his kids for a few weeks now and were always over helping out.

Which was fine by him. Not only was it nice to have an extra set of hands, the more adults who invested in those kids, the better.

"You should've called me. I would've gone with you."

"Like I'd make you drive halfway across town to help me deal with one of my kids. It's bad enough I called you for this."

"You can always call me. You know that."

"I know. But you've got your own problems to deal with." The last thing she needed was to absorb all his issues, too.

She pulled to a stop in front of the group home and quieted the engine. Silence fell for a few seconds before she broke it, her voice soft and serious. "The police think this is the work of that serial killer."

Serial killer?

The truth tore through him like a flash flood. What were they calling him? "That Jacksonville Ripper guy?"

"That's the one. And you're the only witness."

Two

He snorted. "Some witness. I didn't get a good look at him."

"He doesn't know that." She hesitated. "We need to talk about protective custody."

Protective custody? They'd lock him away in some safe house. Every move would be watched by a team of gun-toting agents. He'd have no access to his kids.

It would be like a death sentence.

No. Protective custody wasn't an option.

"Thanks, but no thanks."

"Believe me, I get it. My brother was a witness once. It's not fun. But you have to take precautions. Tonight's victim makes four women that he's killed–"

"Exactly. Women. He's obviously too much of a coward to pick on someone his own size."

"We don't know that. And if he thinks you can ID him, he might feel threatened enough to come after you."

"Or maybe not. Look, either way, I can't leave my kids."

"You also can't put them in harm's way. What if he came after you when one of them was around?"

"So you expect me to abandon them? Like their parents already did?" A few of his kids were orphans, but most had been rejected by their parents, removed from their homes by the state, or had parents in prison.

He couldn't leave them, too.

"Of course not. It's only for a short time. We'll explain that to them."

"Oh, that'll be a great conversation. 'Hey kids, I saw a serial killer stab a woman to death, so I'm gonna hide out for a while, but don't worry 'cause he'd never look for me at my own *home*.' I'm sure they'll feel much safer without me around."

Lana's sigh seemed loud in the suddenly silent car. "Just think about it, okay? You've got a lot of dark-haired little girls in there that might catch this guy's attention."

Could that happen?

Images flashed in his mind, only instead of the woman from earlier, he saw the faces of his kids. Brittany. Tess. Maria.

The thoughts sucked the oxygen from his lungs.

No. They'd be okay. The Ripper had never gone after kids. Not even teens. His girls would be safe.

He tried to see Lana, but very little light penetrated the darkness surrounding them. "I should head inside so Dale and Annie can get some sleep. You wanna come in for a while?"

Even though he couldn't see her, he sensed her hesitation. "Let's continue this conversation tomorrow. You need time to process everything. Sleep on it–"

A humorless laugh slid out before he could stop it. "Sleep? Yeah, right."

The pause felt heavy. "I could hang around for a little while."

He was a jerk. What was he thinking anyway?

Lana had to work tomorrow and he had the gall to ask her to stay up with him so he wouldn't dream about the dead girl. "Look, don't worry about it. I know you've gotta get up early and–"

The dome light popped on.

She flashed him a smile as she stepped out of the car. "That's why God gave us coffee. Come on."

While he knew he should argue, the words stuck to his tongue. "Thanks."

He led the way to the historic mansion he called home. Years of neglect in a declining neighborhood had allowed him to pick the place up for a steal and he'd been slowly fixing it up.

Unlocking the front door, he pushed it open and scanned the living room. The secondhand furniture – 2 sofas and 2 chairs – were empty, although a glass of lemonade sat on one of the end tables.

Movement from the twin staircase on the far side of the room, the one that led to the girls' wing, snagged his attention.

A small face surrounded by dark curls poked between two of the rails.

Anyone but Maria would've received a playful scolding for being up so late, but his most damaged child required an extra gentle touch.

He crossed the room and crouched in front of her. "Hey, kiddo. How come you aren't in bed?"

Solemn eyes fixed on him, but she didn't say a word.

Not that he was surprised. Maria wasn't a big talker. So he spoke for her. "Bad dreams?"

She nodded.

"You wanna stay up with us for a little bit?"

Another nod.

"Not too long though, okay?" He held out his arms and she came to him, wrapping her arms around his neck.

Good thing she was small for a six year old. He picked her up easily and walked back to where Lana watched, a sad smile on her face. Lana didn't know all the details about Maria's past – heck, he didn't even know everything – but it didn't take a psychologist to see that Maria had been severely abused.

Even though Maria should be in bed, part of him was glad she'd been waiting for him. It effectively ended all talk about protective custody, serial killers, and dead women.

Not to mention that it was nice to feel needed.

Footsteps echoed down the hallway seconds before Stefani and Jason stepped into view. The Webbers were only a few steps behind.

"I told them I heard voices, but they all thought I was hearin' things." Stefani playfully elbowed her husband in the ribs before smiling at Lana. "Lana here knows what I'm talkin' 'bout. If men would just listen to us once in a while…"

Jason held up both hands. "Hey, Paul was supposed to call when he was ready for a ride home, so I thought it couldn't possibly be him."

"Yeah. Sorry about that." The apology was meant to cover much more than not calling, but Paul felt too drained to put it all into words.

Jason shrugged. "Looks like you got a better offer. Can't fault you for that."

"So'd y'all get this mess squared away?" Annie spoke up, the corners of her dark eyes pinched.

"No." Paul's gaze slid down to Maria, who had her arms wrapped around his neck too tightly to have fallen asleep. He didn't want to say too much with her right here, but the Webbers loved Austin, too; they deserved a little more information. "Let's just say it's looking like he'll have plenty of time to think about what he wants from life."

Moisture sparkled in Annie's eyes and her dark fingers covered her lips. "The poor little thing. You think they'll let him out on bail?"

"It doesn't matter if they do."

"You wouldn't pay it?" Surprise tinged Stefani's words. "If it's 'bout the money, we could always help out, right hon?"

Money was the least of his worries. The substantial trust set up in his name ensured it would never be about the money, but the Pools didn't know that. Lana and the Webbers didn't even know that. "Thanks for the offer, but it has more to do with setting a precedent. Bailing him out tells everyone that no matter what they do, I'll fix it."

"Besides, maybe this will be the wake-up call he needs to get his act together." Jason stuffed his hands into the pockets of his khaki shorts.

One could only hope.

Sometimes it was crazy how closely he and Jason thought, especially since they couldn't be more different. Jason was educated, successful, and dressed like a pro golfer. Seriously, how many polo shirts could one man own?

"Hon, we should probably get going." Stefani placed a hand on Jason's arm.

"Hey, thanks for staying you guys. Sorry it turned out to be so late."

Jason waved off Paul's concern. "No big deal. I don't have any clients coming in until eleven tomorrow morning, so I'll go in a little later."

Ah, the benefits of being a partner at a law firm.

Too bad Lana didn't have any such luxury.

"Well, I think we'll turn in." Dale put his arm around Annie's shoulders. "It's been a long day."

The couple made their way to the bedroom under the stairs to the girls' wing.

The door closed softly behind them, the latch the only sound in the now silent living room.

Lana glanced at Maria's face. "I think you lost her."

The limp arms around his neck validated her words. "Good. Maybe the rest of the night will be better for her."

Lana's gaze lingered on the Webbers' closed bedroom door. "They just break my heart. I can't imagine going through everything they have."

"Me either." The Webbers had lost their son after an expensive and prolonged illness which had drained their finances and put their house into foreclosure. While God had worked it for good – he couldn't run the house without them – he often wondered how they could look at the kids and not thing about what they'd lost.

As the Pools' car pulled away from the curb, Paul turned to

Lana. "I'm sure you've got an early morning. I better let you go so you can get some sleep."

The words were exactly the opposite of what he wanted to say.

If he had his choice, he'd tell her to stay. And never leave.

The way she studied his face told him she'd picked up on his hesitation. Hopefully she'd tie it more to the day's events than to the emotions that he battled whenever she was around.

"You sure?" Her gaze slipped to Maria before returning to him. "You've had a trying day. If you need to talk it out, I can stick around for a while. I've functioned on less sleep than this."

She had no idea how tempting that offer was.

He almost agreed, but managed to force the selfishness aside. "Thanks, but I think I'm okay now."

"All right. But if you need anything, you call me. Tonight was traumatic. It'll come back to you when you least expect it and when that happens, I want you to call."

"Will do." He shifted Maria's weight slightly. The girl didn't move.

Faint crinkles appeared in Lana's forehead and her lips curled in a small frown. "I mean it. Any time, day or night."

"I will." Even as the words left his mouth, he knew he wouldn't. It'd have to be pretty bad before he'd disturb her during the night. "Thanks again for coming. I didn't know who else to call."

"Always happy to help, you know that."

He followed her across the living room to the front door, wishing now that Maria hadn't been waiting up for him. If his arms weren't already full, he'd grab Lana and pull her to himself.

Maybe it was a good thing Maria kept him from acting on impulse.

With her hand on the knob, Lana paused to look at him. "I'll be by after work so we can finish our discussion from earlier."

Both a promise and a warning. He nodded.

He watched until she'd backed out of his driveway, then closed the door and slid the locks into place.

"Hey, kiddo. You awake?"

No response. The rhythmic rising and falling of her body indicated she'd fallen asleep.

Good.

He'd put her to bed then see if he couldn't make a dent in the mountain of paperwork piled on his desk. While he knew he needed the sleep, he also knew it wouldn't come easily. Maybe the paperwork would help with that. If government forms could induce coma, surely they could help him sleep. Even after a day like today.

Three

The alarm shrilled in tune with Lana's screams. Paul jerked awake.

Lana! He had to save her!

The bedroom slowly came into focus. Early morning sunlight seeped around the blinds and bathed the room in a warm glow.

A nightmare.

He sagged against the mattress and worked to calm his ragged breathing.

His body ached as if he'd physically run as much as he had in the dream. Initially he'd tried to save the woman from last night, but sometime over the course of the nightmare, the screams no longer belonged to her, they belonged to Lana. No matter how far he ran, she'd always been around at least one more corner.

Failure smothered him.

No. He hadn't failed.

None of it had been real. Lana was fine. The Ripper wasn't chasing her. She wasn't being murdered just out of sight.

The arguments, no matter how sound, didn't bring any peace.

He had to talk to her. Make sure she was really okay.

That was stupid. Of course she was okay. She couldn't be hurt by his nightmare.

He peeled the sheet from his body and swung his legs over the edge of the mattress. The room tipped.

Whoa. He'd have to remember to move a little more slowly.

Sand filled his eyes. The pounding in his head made him wish the medicine cabinet in the bathroom wasn't so far away.

A shower. That would help. That and a half dozen aspirin.

Screams still echoed in his head.

His gaze drifted to the cell phone resting on his dresser.

It wouldn't hurt to call her. After all, she'd told him to, right? Then he'd know she was okay and he could get on with his day.

Besides, it wasn't the middle of the night or anything. She'd be up.

He pushed to his feet and trudged toward the dresser.

Thank God for the ability to store phone numbers in the phone because he couldn't think clearly enough to recall her number at the moment.

The ringing sounded distant. One ring. Two. Three.

"Hi Paul. How are you?"

His head and stomach felt like he'd spent the night with a bottle of Vodka, but her voice soothed his nerves. "All things considered, not awful."

"That good, huh?"

"Yeah."

"You could've called me earlier." Her voice sounded normal. A little worried, perhaps, but certainly not like she was in pain or running for her life.

Even so, he couldn't stop himself from asking, "You, uh, everything's okay, right?"

A pause. "Why wouldn't it be?"

Of course she was fine.

Dreams. Couldn't. Hurt. Anyone.

In the background, he heard voices and phones. He checked the time. Almost eight a.m.; dang, he'd called her at work. "Sorry, I know you're busy so I'll let you go. I just needed to hear your voice."

"Are you sure you're okay?"

Man, she probably thought he'd lost it. "Yeah. Yeah, I'm good. Just a, uh, long night."

"If you say so. I should be able to get away by six so I'll see you a little after that."

"Sure thing. Thanks."

"And do me a favor, okay? Keep an eye out for anything suspicious. Strangers, cars you don't recognize, weird phone calls…"

"Got it. See you later."

He terminated the call and set the phone aside. As his worry for Lana slid away, his headache stampeded to take its place. He headed for his private bathroom, fished a key from the top of the door frame, and unlocked the medicine cabinet.

The childproof lid on the aspirin bottle challenged his fingers, which didn't want to cooperate. Palming four of the chalky white pills, he swallowed them dry.

He should check on the kids, but he didn't feel like he had anything to offer them.

Not for the first time, he was glad that Dale and Annie Webber were morning people. They'd probably been up for a few hours and taken care of breakfast already.

Good thing, too. He'd needed the sleep, even if it hadn't been terribly restful.

He closed the cabinet, pausing at the sight of his reflection.

Dang. Black crescents made his eyes appear to sink into his unusually pasty face and the stubble lining his jaw looked like a layer of dirt. And he was certain he hadn't had that much gray in his hair yesterday morning, although it was a light enough shade of brown that the grays didn't stand out too much.

How could he have aged ten years overnight?

He turned away from the senior citizen in the mirror.

Maybe a shower would help. It sure as heck couldn't hurt.

Lana downed the rest of her can of soda before opening her car door. So much for her pathetic hopes that the soda's combination of caffeine and sugar would chase away the fatigue she'd battled all afternoon.

Now to put on a front so Paul wouldn't know just how much last night had drained her.

She must be getting old. What had happened to the days where she could function on just a few hours of sleep?

A blanket of heat enveloped her as she stepped into the evening humidity. Crazy how hot it could be at seven p.m. in June.

The front door opened before she reached the bottom of the porch.

Had Paul been watching for her? Darn. She should've called to let him know she was running late.

Brittany, a teenage girl with skin like dark chocolate and enough energy to power a small car, stepped into view.

White teeth lit up in her dark face. "Lana! We didn't know you were comin' by."

Lana crossed the porch. "I would've been here sooner, but I got tied up at work."

"Can you show me some more moves?" Brittany jabbed at the air, mimicking some of the self-defense moves Lana had been teaching the older girls.

"Another time, okay? It's been a long day."

As she stepped across the threshold, she saw Cody and Trevor waiting, too. Big surprise. Brittany, Cody, and Trevor were three of the oldest and almost always together.

"Hey guys. How's everything?" What she really wanted to ask was how they were dealing with what had happened with Austin, but hesitated. Not knowing what Paul had decided to tell them, she didn't want to overstep.

Trevor adjusted his glasses. "Okay, I guess. It's weird not

having Austin around, but I think we all knew something like this was coming."

Of course he had. Trevor was a bright kid. "Well, if you guys need anything, you let me know, okay?"

"So'd you catch some perps today?"

She grinned at Cody. "Perps? You've been watching too much TV."

"Hey, that's what they call 'em."

"Well, to answer your question, no. I spent today in the office."

"Oh." Cody studied her for a second.

Oh boy. She knew that look well. The next question would be a doozy.

"Have you ever shot anyone?"

And the boy didn't disappoint.

Actually, the biggest surprise was not that the question had surfaced, but that it had taken so long to do so.

Paul appeared from the direction of the kitchen and she tossed a smile his direction. None of the kids gave any indication that they noticed his approach, waiting instead to hear her answer.

She turned her attention back to Cody.

Now to figure out how to answer. She needed to be careful so it didn't sound glamorous or exciting, but conveyed the reality of what had happened. Not an easy task. Like so many things, the media did a great job of glamorizing a very serious matter.

"I have." She leaked an even breath. "And it's nothing like you see on TV. It's awful."

All three kids leaned in closer, each towering over her by several inches.

"What's it like?" Trevor's voice was hushed. Maybe he grasped the severity of the situation.

Or maybe he was following her lead. Hard to say.

Memories trickled through her mind.

The recoil of the gun in her hands. The echo of the blast.

The hot smell of gunpowder.

But mostly, the hole that had appeared in the assassin's head. The blank look on his face as he fell. All the blood.

None of which she could – or should – explain to a group of teenagers. "A part of you dies when you take a life. No matter how bad the guy is or how necessary killing him is, it's hard. You're never the same."

Silence spread between them.

She looked up to find Paul's eyes on her. No condemnation, just compassion.

"H–how'd you get over it?" Hesitation lingered in Brittany's question.

"You don't. Not completely. Everything about that night is so fresh in my mind that it feels like it happened yesterday. But it's been five years."

"How'd it happen?"

She met Trevor's direct stare. "This guy was trying to kill a friend of mine. He'd already shot me–"

"Wait." Paul stepped closer, joining the conversation for the first time. "You were shot?"

Brittany gasped. "Was it bad?"

"It was pretty serious. I think he thought he'd killed me."

"Did he shoot your friend?"

"No. I stopped him." Even now, it hurt to say she'd killed him.

"Did he shoot you in the heart?" Cody asked, his eyes traveling down to her chest as if searching for a seeping wound.

"No, stupid." Brittany elbowed him. "She'd be dead if he had."

Ignoring Brittany, Cody returned his attention to Lana's face. "Do you have a scar?"

"Right here." She pointed to a spot below her left collarbone.

"Okay, I think you guys have interrogated Lana enough for one night. I'm sure none of you have had dinner, right?"

A hint of strain lined Paul's words.

Hmm. Once the kids were out of earshot, she'd have to ask him about it. Maybe today had been rougher than she'd suspected.

"We were headed that way, but then Lana got here." Trevor rolled his shoulders in a half shrug.

"Well let's get in there. I'm sure Lana's sticking around for dinner, right?"

All heads swiveled toward her. She nodded. "Sure. I think I smell garlic."

As she'd suspected, the mention of food distracted the kids from gunshot wounds and brushes with death. The three of them headed toward the dining room.

Good thing, too. Cody had probably been half a step away from asking to see her scar.

Once the trio was out of sight, she turned her attention to Paul.

Wine rings settled below his hazel eyes, making them look small and sunken. Lines marred the skin around the edges and she doubted those lines were from smiling. While his slightly spiky hair was styled as usual, light stubble shaded his chiseled jaw and his face looked paler than usual. "Are you okay?"

"I was until a few minutes ago. Why didn't you ever tell me you'd been shot?"

He was upset about that? "It happened five years ago. Why would I bring it up?"

"It's kind of a major event, don't you think?"

"There've been a lot of major events. You want me to tell you about all of them?"

"I have a feeling that almost dying ranks near the top."

Obviously. She sighed. "It's kind of an awkward subject to bring up. Besides, I try really hard not to think about it."

Several seconds of silence lingered. "Okay, I see your point. Any other secrets you're hiding from me?"

Plenty, but none she could reveal. She smiled. "I think

that's the biggest one."

"Good. Then let's go grab some dinner before Cody eats it all."

"How're you holding up?"

Paul lowered himself into the chair opposite Lana. "Okay, I guess."

Dark eyes canvassed his face. "I couldn't help noticing you hardly ate anything tonight."

"Wasn't really hungry."

"That's unusual." The gentleness in her tone soothed his nerves. "Are you sure you're okay?"

"It's like you said earlier, I try not to think about it."

The woman's face flashed in front of him. Those vacant, staring eyes. The slack mouth fixed in an eternal scream. The metallic stench of blood. Sticky, stained fingers.

He tried to halt the thoughts, but they looped through his head in an endless parade.

A shudder rocked his body. The few bites of spaghetti he'd choked down earlier felt like bricks in his gut.

Maybe making something with a red sauce hadn't been the best dinner option.

The room spun like a carousel. He needed more air! But it seemed he was only capable of pulling in the smallest, shallowest of breaths that left him gasping for more.

"Paul. Paul, look at me." Cold fingers brushed his cheek. "Just breathe. In. Out. In. Out."

He forced the breaths in time with Lana's directions and her face slowly came into focus. Creases formed an inverted V on her forehead and her eyes lacked their usual sparkle.

Aw, dang it. He just had to have a melt-down when she was around to see it, didn't he?

Very cool. She probably thought he was a total pansy.

Blinking to clear the moisture from his eyes, he tried for a smile. "Whoa. That was weird."

Lana didn't return the smile. Her hand dropped and she slid back on the chair. "You should consider talking to someone. A psychiatrist, grief counselor, someone who can help you process the trauma."

Great. In addition to pansy, she also thought he was crazy. "I'm okay. Really."

"I thought the same thing after I was shot, but counseling and a full psych eval were mandatory in order for me to return to work so I did it. And you know what? It helped. A lot."

"Yeah, but you were the one who shot the guy. And you were almost killed in the process. Of course you needed counseling."

Yikes. That hadn't come out quite like he'd wanted it to.

"I mean, who wouldn't, right? It was a double whammy and..." Paul clamped his lips together until he was sure he could speak without rambling. "I found a body. That's it. I can handle this."

At least he should be able to. What kind of wimp was he if he couldn't?

"Don't trivialize the impact of being the first on the scene. It leaves a mark on everyone." She rested her elbows on her knees and leaned in. "There's no shame in admitting you need help. It took Reilly months to get over witnessing a murder."

"He witnessed a murder?"

She nodded. "It's what led to me getting shot."

Huh. Lana's older brother seemed to have it all together. Maybe there was something to the whole counseling idea. "I'll think about it."

"Well, let me know if you'd like any names. I know a few people who could help." She leaned back in her chair. "Have you thought any more about protective custody?"

Sure he'd thought about it. And come up with the same

conclusion he had last night. "Can't do it."

"I understand why you'd feel that way, but think about your kids."

"I am. These kids are wounded, but we're making progress. If I leave, even for a short time, it could undo all the work we've done." What he couldn't explain was that he needed these kids almost as much as they needed him.

The momentary silence screamed her disapproval. "What happens when your name leaks?"

"Leaks?"

"To the press. The police will try to keep it quiet, but in a case this high profile, I doubt it'll be long before the press finds you. Once that happens, reporters will be camped on your doorstep and the Ripper won't have any trouble tracking you down."

"Exactly why I have to stay here. If the Ripper comes here, he might hurt one of my kids. I've gotta make sure they're safe."

"How do you plan to do that?" She tucked her straight hair behind her ears. "By using your advanced self-defense skills? Or perhaps with a secret arsenal of weapons?"

Neither of which he possessed. Too bad she knew it.

"I can throw a few punches. Never underestimate the size advantage."

"You can't help these kids if you're dead."

"At least if I'm dead, they'll know I didn't choose to leave." The words burst out before he could stop them.

Not that he necessarily wanted to.

Other than a brief flicker in her eyes, her face revealed nothing to indicate his response surprised her.

Somehow he had to make her understand.

"Lana." He spread his arms. "These kids have already been left by people they trusted. You don't understand–"

"Don't you dare tell me I don't understand." The measured words and even tone belied the hurt lingering in her eyes. "I spent years thinking I'd been abandoned by my parents.

Wondering why I hadn't been worth keeping. Believe me, I get it."

"But it's not the same. You were adopted. These kids don't have anyone else. I'm it."

"They have the Webbers."

Yeah, they did have the Webbers. And the Webbers loved his kids, he knew that. But it wasn't the same. "The kids need me. Besides, someone has to take care of this place. Pay the bills. That sorta thing."

"The Webbers can handle all that. They used to own their own place, remember?"

"It's not their responsibility. It's mine. I can't ask them to take all this on."

"We're not talking about forever. Just until they catch this guy."

"That could take months. Or years! I can't do that to the kids. Just drop it, okay?"

She crossed her arms over her chest. "Well forgive me for wanting to make sure you're safe."

Seriously? She was going to play that card? "You're one to talk! Every time you walk out that door I wonder if I'll ever see you again. I bet your family does, too. But you don't hear any of us asking you to take a desk job."

Cool it. No point in attacking her. She was only trying to help.

Dragging in a deep breath, he forced it out slowly before continuing, "We trust you to take every precaution and use your head. All I'm asking is for you to do the same."

Silence stretched.

Had he gone too far? He hadn't necessarily meant to blurt all that out, even if every word was true.

Maybe he should apologize.

Her arms dropped as she deflated against the chair. "You're right. I'm sorry. I've just heard of so many situations like this that ended badly and I don't want that to happen to you."

"Hey, it's nice to know you care, but I'm sure this'll blow

over soon. Besides, that guy was about half my size and–"

"I thought you didn't get a good look at him."

He hadn't... had he? "I didn't think I had. I mean, I can't tell you his age or hair color or anything."

"Let's focus on what you do know. You said he was short?"

He stared at the wall, not blinking even as the colors blurred before his eyes, and tried to conjure up the man from the night before. "More than that, he wasn't built. Kind of a scarecrow type, you know?"

"Good. Can you remember anything about his hair? Did it blend with the night or stand out?"

Closing his eyes, he brought up images of the night before. The woman on the ground, the man leaning over her. The man jerking up when he yelled. Too far away for details. "I think he's white."

"That helps."

Not much. There were no doubt thousands of scrawny white guys in a city of Jacksonville's size.

The woman stampeded through his mind, dominating his thoughts with her blank eyes, blood-soaked shirt, sprawled body. His breath caught in his chest. How could dead eyes be so consuming?

Cool fingers rested on his hand. "Paul? Stay with me."

He rolled his wrist to grip her hand and drank in her concern.

Okay. He could do this. If for no reason other than that it was Lana who asked him to try.

But there wasn't anything else.

After he'd called out, the Ripper had run away. He'd never gotten close enough to see him... Wait!

The Ripper had passed in front of his car's headlights. And the light had reflected off his hair. "Blond hair."

"Are you sure?"

"Ye–" Wait, was he? Recalling the image, he let it run through his mind but couldn't be sure. "It might've been red, I guess. Definitely light colored."

"Long or short?"

"Short."

"Good. Did you see his face?"

He shook his head.

"Any guesses as to age?"

Right. He couldn't guess the age of someone standing right in front of him, let alone someone running away. "No idea. But he was fast. Even if he hadn't had his car waiting, I don't think I'd have caught him."

Something else popped into his memory. "His car. I saw it."

"You told the police it was dark colored."

"Yeah, but it had chrome trim and fancy rims. And a hood ornament. Tinted windows." The details fell into place like dominoes.

He'd seen a lot more than he thought.

Great.

He wanted to help the police, but the more he remembered, the more pressure Lana would put on him about protective custody.

Several seconds dragged before she spoke. "We need to contact the detective. You have his card?"

"Yeah."

When he'd stopped by the station earlier to give his statement, Detective Arlington had given him a card, along with the standard "call me if you think of anything else" line. While he'd put the card in the top desk drawer for safekeeping, he'd never expected to need it, especially not so soon. "I don't get it. Why didn't I know all this last night?"

"The brain's a funny thing. Might've been the shock or some kind of emotional overload."

Maybe. "I hate being treated like a suspect."

"It's standard. But given that you were at the police station prior to the attack, I bet you'll be cleared pretty soon."

That was something. "Do they have any leads?"

Logically, she shouldn't know anything about the investigation, but something told him she'd have an answer anyway.

"The FBI has been brought in to work up a profile. Hopefully that will help."

"You're staying out of this, right?"

"It'd be unusual for the Marshal's office to get involved in an investigation like this. We normally only deal with the criminals after they've been charged. But…" She shot him a pointed look. "We would get involved to protect a witness."

"You said you'd let it drop."

"That was before you came up with a description."

"So what? Only you and Detective Arlington will know."

"For now." A single nod accented the words. "Trust me, it's not going to stay that way. Your name will go public. It's just a matter of when."

"Maybe this time will be different." The words felt false even as he spoke them. Not only did Lana know how these things went, but in the instant-information, media-saturated world around him, few things remained secret for long.

She didn't point out the obvious. "Just pray about it, okay?"

How did she do that? She'd hit on the one thing he hadn't done that he most needed to do. "Absolutely."

She glanced at her watch. "I'd better get going. Call me if anything strange happens, okay?"

"Strange? Like UFOs and zombies strange?"

Serious eyes told him the attempt at humor had failed. "Attempted break-ins, prowlings, phone calls where the caller hangs up. Anything that doesn't feel right. Trust your gut and you'll know it when it happens."

"I'll be fine."

Her lips curved in a small frown.

"Yes. I'll call you if anything comes up."

The response seemed to satisfy her. "Good."

He followed her to the front door. The muggy evening air wrapped around him like a sweater as he stepped onto the front porch.

"Remember–"

"I'll be careful, I'll be alert, and I'll call."

A hint of a smile touched her face. "Actually, I was just going to remind you to call Arlington."

Oh. "I'll do it now."

He waved as she pulled away from the curb, but didn't move until her car disappeared from sight.

For the first time ever, he was relieved to see her go.

They'd never argued before and he didn't like it. Not at all.

Being pushy was a casualty of her job. Staying here was a casualty of his.

He'd better call Arlington before he forgot. With a sigh, he turned and trudged into the house.

At least now that they'd argued about it, maybe the issue would be settled and things could return to normal. But something told him life wouldn't be normal for a very long time.

Four

"That's him."

Paul stared at the composite sketch of the man he'd seen two nights ago. Lacking in detail, but hopefully it would help.

Vague as it was, it still brought that night back with crystal clarity. The metallic tang of blood scenting the air, the stickiness on his hands as he felt for a pulse, the taste of vomit in the back of his throat; it was all real, too vividly real for a sketch.

He swallowed with difficulty, his tongue feeling swollen inside a mouth as dry as sand.

"You're sure?"

He blinked Arlington into focus. "Oh yeah."

"And there's nothin' else you remember?"

"Hey, I never got closer than half a block. We're lucky I could see that much."

Leaning back, Arlington held up his hands. "Whoa, whoa. Just trying to see if anything else comes to mind, okay?"

Paul eased a slow breath.

Yeah, he could see why Arlington would ask.

That sketch looked like any number of men, including a cop he'd passed on his way into the station today. Blond hair, slight build, narrow face with two eyes, a nose, and a mouth. Not exactly the stuff of positive IDs.

But it was the best he could do.

Arlington shoved it toward a uniformed cop standing nearby. "Get that thing circulating. I want it in every station in the city. Make that the state. Georgia, too. Don't forget the Sheriffs, FBI, DOJ, US Marshals, ATF… heck, anyone with a badge. Media relations, too. I want the press involved."

The officer scurried out, sketch in hand.

Turning back to Paul, Arlington extended a hand. "Thanks for comin' in."

Paul pushed back his chair, but didn't rise. While he was here, he should check up on Austin. "Hey, one of my kids landed here the other night. Any chance I could see him?"

"What's the name?"

"Austin Ballew. Last I knew he was being held here."

"What'd he do?"

"Shooting. Gang related."

"Lemme see what I can do."

The hard wooden chair didn't inspire lingering. But maybe that was the point.

A bolt scraped and the door opened. Austin appeared in the doorway, shaggy blond hair hanging over an unusually pale face. He shuffled into the room and dropped in the chair.

"Ten minutes." The officer, a stocky woman who looked like she would sooner bite your ear off than shake your hand, stated before turning toward the door.

The door closed with a slam and Austin started. Dark eyes darted around the room and a tremor shook his fists.

Poor kid. He looked scared to death.

"How're you doing?"

Austin dropped his gaze to the table. "Aiight. No biggie."

Right.

"Austin." Paul waited for the kid to meet his eyes. "How

are you?"

Tears pooled in his eyes. "I wanna go home. Can you get me out?"

"Man, buddy, I wish I could. But you shot someone."

"I didn't mean to."

"You were shooting a gun! What did you think would happen?"

"I didn't think 'bout it. 'Sides, the cops said he's gonna be okay."

"But he's still hurt. What were you thinking?"

"I dunno, okay? I'm sorry. Come on, I don't wanna stay in here."

Paul rubbed the back of his neck. Part of him wished he could help, but most of him knew this was the wake-up call Austin needed to get his life on track. If he didn't come out more screwed up than when he went in. "It's out of my hands."

"What about Lana? She's a cop. Can't she do anything?"

"She's a US Marshal, not a cop. But she can't help you anyway. You made the decision to run with a gang and now you'll have to live with the consequences." Paul bit back the *I told you so* that sat on his tongue and purposely kept his tone gentle.

Leaning back, Austin crossed his arms over his chest. "Shoulda known you wouldn't help me. Being Mr. Perfect and all."

"Hey, hold up. I'm far from perfect."

Austin snorted. "Right."

"Austin, there was only one perfect man. Jesus Christ. Maybe you should try talking to Him."

"Yeah. 'Cause He's gonna come down and bail me out."

"No. But He's the only one who can save you from hell."

"Spare me, all right." Austin slapped his palms on the table. "They're talkin' about trying me as an adult! I could get the chair."

"Of course they're going to try you as an adult. You're

sixteen. And that was an adult crime you and your buddies pulled."

"I don't wanna die."

"You won't get the death penalty. Look, you've only had small brushes with the law. This is your first major offense and no one died. Yeah, you'll likely spend some time inside, but I don't think it'll be that long. Especially if you cooperate and tell the cops what they want to know. Maybe take a deal."

"You want me to snitch?"

"You think your friends will stand by you? Heck, no. It's every man for himself. They'll probably rat you out the first chance they get."

A quiver shook Austin's lower lip. "Do the other kids know?"

Man, did he wish he could spare Austin the humiliation. "I had to tell them something."

Tears leaked down Austin's cheeks. "I didn't mean for this to happen."

"I know, buddy, I know." Paul reached across the table and placed his hands over Austin's. "But you know what the best thing you can do right now is? Cooperate with the cops. Show them the respect they deserve and don't give them any attitude. And think hard about your life and what you want from it. You can come back from this. When you get out, you can make a difference in this world, but you have to choose to do it. It won't be easy."

Swallowing hard, Austin gave a jerky nod.

The bolt grated and the guard strode back in. "Time's up."

Paul walked around the table and pulled Austin to him in a tight hug. Tears dampened Paul's shirt as Austin clung to him like a life preserver in a stormy sea.

"Will you be at my arraignment?"

Paul stepped back and mussed Austin's shaggy mop. "Count on it."

Paul walked through the quiet house, his steps echoing on the old hardwood floors. With the kids playing in the back yard, the house was quieter than usual, but the quiet should give him a chance to catch up on the government forms collecting dust on his desk.

Maybe he'd call Lana before starting on those.

She hadn't called or stopped by yesterday. Not that it was unusual for him to not hear from her for a few days, but they'd never clashed like that before.

Was she mad? Holding a grudge seemed out of character for her, but she was awfully stubborn.

Maybe he should make amends. Not apologize, because he wasn't wrong, but reach out to make sure they were still good.

Of course they were good. She was probably busy.

It wasn't like her life revolved around him or anything.

But she wouldn't mind if he called. Besides, she'd want to hear about the composite he'd helped the sketch artist with down at the police station yesterday, right?

Although if she'd watched last night's news, she likely already knew.

The door to the back yard opened and Annie stepped into the hall, her eyes crinkling in a smile, her white teeth stark against the darkness of her skin.

Normally, she'd be teasing him about something. Today all he saw was sympathy.

He really just wanted everything to return to normal.

"Tell me y'all got some sleep last night, hon." Her black curls, which were actually more gray than black, brushed the top of her shoulders as she studied him.

"A little." No point in telling her that he felt even more exhausted than when he'd gone to bed.

"Well, if there's anything we can do to help, you let us know, you hear me? You carry too much on your shoulders."

"Will do. Thanks."

She disappeared into the kitchen.

Of course, Lana would've told him to show her the books and all the workings of the house so she and Dale could take over. But he couldn't do that. He needed to be here almost as much as the kids needed him to be here.

He closed the office door behind him and sat at the desk. The message light on the answering machine flashed.

Seven messages.

Dang. That was more than he usually got in a whole day. He'd deleted the old messages last night, so all of these were from this morning.

Hopefully nothing was wrong.

He tapped the button and picked up a pen.

"Mr. Van Horn."

Not a familiar voice. Paul paused, pen hovering above the paper.

"This is Jorge Esquival from channel seven news."

A reporter.

He froze, Lana's earlier words coming back to him. She'd been right; his name had leaked and now everyone would have it.

Including the Ripper.

He tried to focus on the voice coming through the answering machine's speakers.

"I was hoping to talk to you about the murder of Carmela Santa Cruz."

Carmela Santa Cruz.

No one had told him her name before, which might've been easier. Without a name, she'd been a stranger, someone he'd encountered in her final moments of life. Weird how knowing her name changed all that. Carmela had been a young woman with a future in front of her. She'd had a family, hopes, dreams, fears. And now she was gone.

Paul blinked. The reporter's voice filtered through his thoughts.

"Maybe put you on air. Hey, it'd be great publicity for your home, right? Gimme a call."

Paul hit the delete button before the reporter had finished rattling off the phone number.

The next three messages were more of the same. He deleted all of them without writing a single word.

Good thing he'd decided against cancelling his home line and using his cell or all of these calls would be going there instead.

Jotting down the contact information for the only call that was legitimate business, he deleted the rest and rubbed his eyes. How had the press found out about him? Had someone purposely released his name? Accidentally mentioned it in a casual conversation? Was the police station bugged?

The how didn't really matter. All that counted was that his name had gone public and life was about to get more complicated.

Just what he needed.

The phone rang and he stared at it. Probably another reporter. He shouldn't answer.

But what if it wasn't? What if it was someone calling about adoption?

He snatched up the receiver before he could change his mind.

"Paul Van Horn?"

The woman's voice on the other end was brusque and unfamiliar.

"You've found him."

"Abigail O'Flannigan from the Daily Herald. I understand you witnessed the Ripper in action."

Should've gone with his gut and let the machine get it. "I don't have anything to say."

"But you did see him? Because if you talk to me, we can turn the heat up on this guy and help the police catch him."

Right. "Look, I didn't see anything. I've gotta go. Don't call again."

He dropped the receiver into the cradle, ignoring the protests squawking across the line.

From now on he was screening his calls. Besides, those who were most important to him would call his cell phone.

The phone rang again and he clicked off the ringer. Now he wouldn't have to listen to it ring all day.

He'd call Lana later. Besides, he'd left his cell upstairs anyway.

He picked up a pen and slid one of the forms in front of him, trying to ignore the blinking light on the answering machine. Hopefully the reporters would tire of leaving messages and move on to more willing subjects.

Something told him it wasn't likely to happen any time soon.

The man listened to the news segment, his chest holding his breath hostage.

Paul Van Horn. The only witness to what he'd done.

According to the silver-haired news anchor, Van Horn claimed he hadn't seen anything, but maybe the police had told him to say that.

Then again, it had been pretty dark. It could be the truth.

Maybe.

There must be some way he could find out for sure.

The only idea he could come up with was to let his and Van Horn's paths cross and see if Van Horn recognized him, but that involved considerable risk. More risk than he was willing to take.

No, his best option was to keep an eye on Van Horn from a distance.

Besides, even if Van Horn had gotten a good look at him, so what? There had to be thousands of guys in Jacksonville matching his description. And the sketch he saw looked like any number of them.

For now, he'd be careful. Alert. And deal with Van Horn only if necessary.

He didn't really want to kill anyone, especially someone who'd just been in the wrong place at the wrong time, but he'd do what he had to do. And if that required killing the only witness, then the witness would die.

Five

It'd been a long two days.

But worth it, now that another fugitive was no longer on the loose.

As her computer shut down, Lana gathered up the paperwork strewn across her desk and organized it in the file. Yesterday's tip, the one that had kept her and her team working late into the night and at it again early this morning, had paid off.

Snagging her phone from her desk drawer, she noticed a missed call from Paul and dialed into her voice mail.

"Hey, just wanted to let you know that things are good here. Um, the press has been calling all day so if you call, don't use the house line, okay? And, uh, yeah. Hope you're doing okay and... and maybe we'll talk soon."

Hmm. He sounded a little off. Worried, maybe. Definitely awkward.

She needed to stop by and check up on him.

That bit about the press was concerning, but not unexpected. Too bad Paul wouldn't accept her help.

Come on. Leave it in God's hands.

Believing God was all-powerful and omniscient came easily, but why was it so stinking hard to trust him with those she cared about the most?

Maybe if she knew how the investigation was going, she'd

be able to let this go. She'd told Paul she wouldn't get involved, but it wouldn't hurt to stop by and talk to Arlington, right?

Staying abreast of the case was way different than jumping into it.

She glanced at her watch. If she left now, she could probably make the precinct by a little after six. Given that the Ripper case was so high profile, and Arlington seemed like the type who was married to his work, she bet he'd still be around.

All she had to do was convince him to talk to her.

The media circus in Paul's front yard forced Lana to park at the end of the block.

She stepped into the blanket of humidity and eased her car door closed. The last thing she wanted to do was draw any attention, although if she intended to get inside, she was likely to do just that.

Too bad she couldn't sneak around the back and scale the fence without trespassing on Paul's neighbors' property.

Half a dozen news vans parked by the curb, camera crews camped out on the sidewalk, and several people with digital cameras hovered under the massive tree at the edge of Paul's lot.

Sheesh, it looked like every news outlet in town had a representative here.

But of course they did. Serial killers fascinated and terrified the general public and Paul was the only witness to the latest one to hit the airwaves.

So. The big question was how close could she get before the vultures realized she wasn't one of them?

Actually, the bigger question was if Paul would even open

the door for her. After all, the reporters had probably rung the doorbell all afternoon and the drawn blinds ensured that no one inside would see that it was her and not another reporter.

She pulled out her phone and brought up Paul's number, glancing around to make sure no one was within earshot. The closest person was half a block up and across the street.

While the other end rang, she surveyed the crowd, looking for anyone who stood out.

If the Ripper was trying to track Paul down, what better place to blend in than with a group of reporters?

From where she stood, she counted two men with blond hair, one redhead, another with white hair, and several others whose hair was light enough that it might pass for blond in the right lighting. Any one of them could be the Ripper.

Too bad there was no easy way to find out.

"Hey, Lana." Paul's voice filled her ear. Exhaustion added an unusual huskiness to the words.

Even though no one was close enough to hear, she kept her voice low, just in case. "I'd ask how it's going, but the answer's pretty obvious."

"It's on the news, isn't it?"

"Probably, but I'm watching this live."

Silence blanketed the line for a second. "Where are you?"

She glanced around again before answering. "Across the street. Wondering how I'm going to make it inside."

"You could always pull your gun and fire a few shots."

A smile played with the corners of her mouth. "And risk a stampede? Being trampled was low on my to-do list today."

"Well, I'd suggest muscling your way through, but that's a pretty aggressive group."

Ha. Like a group of reporters could stop her. "Can you head for the door? I'll knock three times."

"You got it."

She terminated the call and crossed the street. No one gave her a second glance until she broke from the group and approached the door.

"Good luck, sweetheart, but we've been tryin' that all day."

The man's voice came from somewhere behind her left shoulder. She ignored him.

"Hey, wait a sec. You ain't a reporter, are you?"

Well, it'd lasted longer than she'd thought it would.

"Who are you?"

"Are you a friend of Mr. Van Horn?"

"What's your connection to the case?"

"What can you tell us about the murders?"

"Is it true Mr. Van Horn knew the victim?"

Knew the victim? Where the heck did the press come up with this stuff?

She mounted the steps, lengthened her strides, and knocked on the door.

Better make sure no one was waiting to push past her to get inside. She risked a glance and found that the reporters had edged closer, one had even started up the stairs. Questions still flew at her, but too quickly for her to distinguish them.

Not that she would've answered.

The door opened and she quickly stepped across the threshold.

"You'd think they'd be tired of hanging around by now." Paul pushed in the lock and flipped the deadbolt. "Or at least tired of being out in the heat."

Lana's smile brought a small measure of peace. "This probably won't last too long, but don't expect the phone calls to stop. Sick as it is, serial killers make for great press."

"Hey. As my friend, isn't it your job to make me feel better?"

"It's also my job to tell you the truth." The way she scrutinized him made him feel almost transparent, like she could see every little thing running through his head. "You sounded a little off earlier. Everything okay?"

Oh, life was just peachy.

He couldn't sleep, was fighting with his closest friend, had reporters living in his yard and calling his house all day, and a kid in jail.

What could possibly be wrong?

But Lana was here and she seemed like her usual self, so things were already looking up. "Tired, I guess. It's been a long couple of days."

She nodded and looked around the room. "Where is everyone?"

"Downstairs. I put on a movie for the younger kids. The older ones are playing pool. I asked them to stay inside for a while."

She leaned against the back of the sofa. "How'd you explain all this?"

"I told them I'd helped the police with something and the reporters wanted to know about it." The explanation had seemed to work okay, although he suspected that the oldest kids, the ones who'd likely heard about the murders, may have connected the dots. "How are you?"

"Fine." She arched an eyebrow. "But I'm not the one with a target on my back."

Not again. He'd hoped they were through with this conversation. "We don't know that anyone is out to get me."

"And we don't know that you're safe, either."

Time to change the subject.

"Did you come straight from work?"

"More or less. We had a big case break open yesterday so things have been really busy."

"Nice." Experience taught him not to ask about the case. As much as he'd like to know more, she wouldn't be able to talk about it anyway, so he simply nodded toward the kitchen. "We had tacos tonight and there are plenty of leftovers, if you can believe it."

"I'll pick up something on the way home later. You have enough mouths to feed."

Right. Because she ate so much. "And one more won't make a bit of difference. Come on."

Leading the way into the kitchen, he crossed to the fridge and pulled out the containers of meat and cheese he'd recently put away. "You like salsa, lettuce and tomatoes on your taco, right?"

"No tomatoes."

At least she wasn't protesting anymore. That was progress.

He plopped spoons into the meat and salsa, a fork into the cheese, and opened the tortillas and salad. After handing her a plate, he stepped out of the way. "Okay, dinner's served."

Thoughts flickered across her face.

There was that trace of stubbornness that made her want to argue – she probably already had the words on her tongue – and hints of concern, but finally, acceptance.

Hard to believe she'd let him see all that. She usually masked things so well.

Maybe she was really tired. Or maybe she finally trusted him enough to let her guard slip.

He hoped it was the latter.

"Thanks." Her voice contained a trace of fatigue that made him suspect she was more exhausted than she'd let on. "Lunch was a long time ago."

Imagine that. He'd won this round.

Probably only because she was too weary to argue, but a victory was still a victory.

"No problem. That's what friends are for."

She set the plate by the sink and washed her hands. Water dripped from her fingers as she reached for the towel folded neatly on the counter by the sink. "So. Arlington gave me an update."

"I thought you said you weren't going to work this case."

"I'm not." She glanced up briefly before adding some meat and cheese to her tortilla and placing it in the microwave. "But

I stopped by on my way here to see where they're at. Helps me assess the threat level."

Of course it did.

Well, as long as that's all she was doing, he could live with it. But Lana had a nasty habit of plunging into trouble that most people managed to avoid.

Not that there was any point in bringing that up. "Did you check out the sketch?"

"I saw it. Looks like you remembered quite a bit more than you thought."

"Not enough. It's still pretty vague."

"That's okay. Combined with the other information you gave them and the FBI's profile, it might be enough for someone to point them toward a suspect. They're plastering it all over the TV."

"Then why the heck are those reporters bothering me?"

The microwave beeped and she removed her plate. "Because it's always more interesting if they can get your take personally."

"So is there anything new?"

"Well, the FBI has created a profile. Twenty-five to forty year old male. Unassuming. You know, the type most of us wouldn't even notice."

She folded her taco and took her plate to the table. After grabbing two glasses of ice water, he pulled out the seat across from her. "That it?"

She swallowed a bite. "No. Stabbing is highly personal and the multiple wounds indicate a crime of passion. There doesn't seem to be any ritualistic elements, so they suspect he kills in kind of a blind rage. We're talking about a guy who probably doesn't interact well with women and hasn't had many serious relationships. The FBI believes something happened within the last six months to trigger the violence."

"Must've been one heck of a trigger." He waited for her to finish another bite before asking, "They have any theories as to what that might've been?"

"It's hard to say. It could be anything from his mom dying to a divorce or breakup, to being cut off in traffic or losing his job. Remember, profiles aren't hard fact. They're built on statistics and behavioral analysis, but we really don't know much about this guy, we're just guessing."

Did she realize that she was including herself among the investigators? Man, he hoped she wasn't planning to jump into this case.

"So really all they know is his victim type." Petite, twenty-something Hispanic women.

Lana nodded as she continued to eat.

Thank God Lana wasn't Hispanic. Didn't even look the part... well, unless you looked at her from the back. That view showed a petite woman with long black hair. Just like all the Ripper's victims.

There had to be thousands of women living in Jacksonville who matched that description, but Paul only cared about one. And right now, she was too close to the investigation for his liking. "I think it'd be a good idea if you steered clear of this place, well, me, for a while."

She paused with the taco halfway to her mouth. "Are you trying to get rid of me?"

A teasing tone colored the words, but he didn't feel like laughing. "Not even close. But it's safer for you if you don't come around until this guy's caught. I don't want him to see you."

"See me?" Her eyebrows drew together before understanding flashed in her eyes. A smile curved the corners of her lips. "You can't actually believe he'd go after me."

"You're his type. The right size and hair."

"That's about all I have in common with the victims." She set down the remainder of her taco, placed her hands on the table in front of her, and leaned in. "The victims are all either Cuban or Puerto Rican. I'm Greek-Italian. This man is deliberate and methodical. He does his homework on his victims or he wouldn't be able to pull off his crimes as cleanly as he has. He knows who he's choosing. He'd be an idiot to focus on a US Marshal and the man has proven that he's not an idiot. Insane maybe, but not an idiot."

The argument sounded good coming from her, but as he watched her polish off her taco, he remembered her earlier words. "You said it yourself. That profile isn't hard fact. Maybe he sees a woman and kills her. Simple as that."

"The FBI thinks it's unlikely."

"All I know is that the closer you are to me right now, the more likely that psycho is going to see you. In the papers, on the news, anywhere."

She rinsed off her plate and deposited it in the dishwasher before turning back to him. "Well then, it's already too late. The reporters saw me earlier. They probably even got pictures or footage."

Great. He hadn't thought about that.

He didn't think he could handle it if anything happened to her, especially not if it was his fault. But how could he convince her to take the necessary precautions?

She pulled out the chair next to him and placed a hand on his arm. "I appreciate the concern, but I know how to defend myself against all kinds of attacks–"

"So a guy twice your size swinging a knife would be no big deal?"

"It'd never come to that. I'd have my gun trained on him before the knife was close enough to do any harm."

Sure. That's what they all said.

Pain stabbed between his eyes. Why did this have to be so hard?

"Paul." He looked at her and she continued, "Earlier today I made the decision to leave your safety in God's hands. Not saying it was easy and that I'll never worry, but I'm choosing to trust God. You need to do the same."

Ugh. Not what he wanted to hear.

Especially not since every fiber of his being longed to keep her safe personally.

"Besides," she leaned back and shot him a grin, "Something is much more likely to happen to me as a result of my job than because you witnessed a crime, so lighten up."

Great. Now he felt *so* much better.

"Hey, Paul–" Brittany's head popped around the door frame. "Lana? I didn't know you were here."

Ah, Lana's number one fan had discovered she was in the building.

And just like that, he was forgotten. Not that he minded.

Brittany had already launched into a highly dramatized version of when a reporter tried to sneak into the backyard earlier that day. At least the topic of safety wouldn't come up again.

Not tonight, anyway.

But Lana's comment about her work settled over him like black clouds before a storm.

The man pulled the print out of the developer and hung it to dry. He didn't have to look at the picture to remember her. Every detail of her perfect face etched across his mind with an artist's clarity.

She was the one. He was certain this time.

The row of drying prints drew his eye across. If he looked quickly enough, it was kind of like those old picture flip books, the ones where it looked like the people were walking.

Sure, developing prints like this was old-fashioned. Sure, taking digital pictures and printing them off on a color printer was much easier, but he liked doing it this way. Watching the woman of his dreams materialize right in front of his eyes. Watching the colors fill in and her features take shape.

It made him feel even more connected to her than before.

This woman was a little lighter in coloring than the others

had been, but that wasn't necessarily a bad thing. Maybe it meant this one would turn out differently. Maybe those Cuban girls were just a meaner, more fickle group.

That had to be it, right? Had to be why all the other relationships had failed?

But this one wouldn't. He knew it.

The eight pictures he'd managed to get before she'd gone inside weren't enough. He needed more.

No, what he needed was to arrange a meeting. Learn her routine so he could see the places they overlapped and insert himself into her life.

Then she, too, would know that she was the one.

First he'd need to find out her name. Then her routine. He'd start with the building he'd watched her walk into so confidently and work outward from there.

It would require patience, but he could do it. And would do it.

He could tell already that she would be worth the wait.

Six

Paul rinsed off a pan and handed it to Brittany to dry. Having loaded the last of the lunch dishes in the dishwasher, Cody leaned against the counter while Paul and Brittany finished the hand washing.

"Looks good in here. Thanks, guys."

With hands stuffed deep in his pockets, Cody's shoulders lifted in a faint shrug. "We're on the schedule."

"Doesn't mean I don't appreciate the help." Paul's eyes landed briefly on the chore schedule posted next to the fridge before flicking back to Cody. "More than that, I appreciate that you help without complaining."

"I like helping out." Brittany dried her hands on the towel and tossed it on the counter. "Makes me feel like I have a real family."

Good. That meant the chore schedule was accomplishing a two-fold purpose – teaching the kids responsibility and providing a sense of home.

Not to mention lightening his workload.

"Lana wasn't at church today."

Brittany's tone was casual, but something triggered warning bells in Paul's mind nonetheless. What, he couldn't say, but this didn't sound promising.

He tried to play it off with a light tone. "Really? Hadn't noticed."

"Liar. So, if her Dad's the pastor, doesn't she basically *have* to be there?"

"Not any more than you guys have to be there. She goes because she likes it."

Church attendance was optional for all his kids. At first he and the Webbers had been the only ones going and had to alternate Sundays, but slowly more and more kids had joined him and now all of them attended on a regular basis.

"So where was she?"

Brittany wasn't going to let this go, was she? He deposited the dishcloth in the sink and turned to face her. "She had to work this weekend."

The comment snagged Cody's interest. "What was she doing?"

"I don't know. Her work is confidential so I don't ask."

Brittany crossed her arms over her chest. "So you gonna ask her out or what?"

Heat rushed through his face and he knew he rivaled a sunburned tourist in color. "I'm not... we're just friends."

"Riiight." Brittany exchanged a brief look with Cody before addressing Paul with a matter-of-fact tone. "Then you'd better stop looking at her the way you do or she's gonna figure out the truth."

How did he look at Lana?

There must be something that he wasn't hiding very well if the kids had caught on.

"You kiddin'? I bet she already knows." Confidence laced Cody's tone. "She's a cop. They always know what's goin' on before anyone else."

Paul's mouth filled with sand.

Cody was right. With Lana's skill at reading people, it was highly probably that she'd already figured it out. But wouldn't she have started treating him differently?

If she hadn't caught on yet, it was probably only a matter of time before she did.

Which meant one thing – he needed to make some serious

adjustments to prevent that from happening. He didn't think he could stand it if she suddenly put up her guard around him.

"Earth to Paul."

Cody's voice jerked him back. Mind blank, he stared at Cody, and realized he'd missed something. "Huh?"

Brittany giggled. "You've totally got it bad, huh?"

Time to put an end to all this talk. "Okay, you've had your fun. Let's drop it."

"Dude, what's the big deal? She's hot *and* nice. Just ask her already."

Excitement brimmed in Brittany's deep brown eyes. "Come on, you're cute, for an old guy. I bet she'd say yes."

"An old guy? Is that what I am?"

His mock outrage brought the desired result as grins spread across both kids' faces. Cody was the first to speak. "Well you did turn forty this year."

"Thirty-nine. And that's not what I'd consider old."

Brittany giggled. "Okay, not old, just older."

"That's more like it."

"Seriously, just do it. The worst she can do is say no, right?" Brittany's dreamy eyes reminded him that at her age, everything seemed romantic. Reality hadn't quite sunk in yet.

"That one word could change everything." He swallowed hard and tried to give the kids a stern look. "I know you guys mean well, but I need you to stay out of it. She's a good friend and I don't want to do anything to screw that up."

Brittany's smile fell. "What makes you think it would screw it up?"

A variety of answers came to mind, but he couldn't discuss them, especially not with his kids.

"One day you'll understand." Man, never thought he'd use that line. But it felt good to be able to dismiss their probing so easily. Now to keep this topic from surfacing again. "Let's say it's complicated and leave it at that. You guys have to promise me you won't say anything about this conversation to anyone, got it? Not your friends, the Webbers or anyone living here, Mr. and Mrs. Pool, and especially not Lana."

Both kids reluctantly nodded.

"We don't like to see you alone." Brittany's tone was much more subdued and the sparkle in her eyes had dimmed. "You should be happy."

He stepped between them, draped one arm across Brittany's shoulders, the other across Cody's, and gave each a small squeeze.

"Are you kidding? I'm never alone. I wouldn't trade you guys for anything." He dropped his arms and moved to face them. "Now what do you say we join everyone else and see if we can get a game of baseball going."

They brightened instantly and hurried from the room.

It still amazed him that something as simple as baseball could be so interesting to these guys, especially the older ones. Oh sure, there were a few kids who weren't into it, but the majority of his kids were always eager to play.

No matter how hard he tried to push Brittany's words from his mind, they kept replaying like some kind of scratched CD.

Where had all that come from?

Several days had passed since Lana's last visit, so it's not like she should've even been fresh in their minds.

Didn't matter.

What mattered was where he went from here. If he wanted to keep things with Lana on stable ground, he obviously needed to do a better job of hiding the way he felt.

But was that what he really wanted?

Part of him wanted to blurt out the truth and see what happened next, but the more prudent side of him knew it was best to leave things as they were. He couldn't risk having Lana withdraw from his life.

And the mistakes in his past ensured she'd have to if she ever learned the truth.

"Now only good dreams tonight, you got it?"

Maria nodded solemnly and Paul bent over to kiss her forehead. Standing, he straightened the covers and reached to turn on the nightlight next to the bed.

"Who was that man?"

His hand stilled inches from the nightlight switch.

A man? Who was she talking about?

He mentally ran through the day, but no visitors came to mind. The reporters had lost interest yesterday, Detective Arlington hadn't stopped by, no friends had come over, and no prospective parents had visited.

"What man?"

The covers moved as Maria shrunk into the bedding. "He's a stranger."

The nightlight clicked on under his fingers and he rose to full height. His eyes swept over the two other girls in the room. "Did you guys see him, too?"

The other girls shook their heads and he turned back to Maria. Maria wasn't one to lie or create stories to get extra attention. If she said she saw a man, then he believed her.

Or at least believed that she thought she had seen someone.

Could she have imagined the whole thing? She'd had another nightmare last night and had been quieter than usual all day. Hard as he'd tried, he hadn't been able to bring her around.

Either way, he needed more information. "When did you see him?"

"During baseball time. He watched the game."

He would've noticed if they'd had an observer, wouldn't he? But he didn't remember seeing anyone. Not even one of the neighbors. There were only a half dozen families who lived on this street and he knew them all.

With the rising gang problems only a few streets to the

north, they'd all formed an unofficial neighborhood watch group. No way could a stranger hang around without being noticed.

"What did he look like?"

"He was in a car."

Not the most helpful information. "What kind of car?"

"Black."

Warning bells clanged inside his head and he tried to force down a wave of panic.

The effort proved futile as one thought slammed through his brain. The killer had found him!

Lana's comment about the Ripper targeting one of his girls forced bile up the back of his throat. What if she was right? He couldn't do anything to put them in danger.

Calm down.

It was probably a reporter. The Ripper wasn't the only guy in this city with a black car.

Logical or not, the theory wouldn't stick. Shaking started in his hands and spread through his body like an epidemic.

Clenching his fists, he drew in a deep breath and tried to keep it together for the girls' sakes. "Where did you see this car?"

"By Jimmy's house."

Right across the street.

Jimmy's family had gone out of town for a few days, so there shouldn't have been anyone hanging around there. And he knew they hadn't come home early.

The driveway had been empty all day, he was sure of it.

But on the other side of the property sat a vacant lot that had become an unofficial scrap yard. Several rusted cars were a permanent part of the landscape, not to mention a pile of old tires, some burn barrels, and a refrigerator with no door.

Would he have noticed if another car had parked amidst all that junk?

Probably not.

"Maria, was it parked in the place you aren't allowed to

play?"

She nodded, eyes large, mouth somber.

Forcing a smile, he tried to sound normal. "Thank you for telling me. It was probably someone who likes baseball, but if you see that car again, can you tell me right away?"

The lines around her eyes relaxed. "Okay."

After saying goodnight to the girls, he left the room, his mind focused on what Maria had told him. Could it have been the Ripper? He should tell Lana about this.

No, not Lana. It would only give her a reason to get involved.

Maybe Detective Arlington.

But tell him what? That a six year old girl claimed to have seen a black car parked across the street? For all he knew it was another reporter. Although if that was the case, he would've expected the reporter to at least try to get an interview.

He'd have to ask the other kids about it. Maybe someone else had seen the car and would be able to give him more information about the man inside.

Maybe they would know if the man had blond hair.

Downstairs, he crossed the living room and paused to look out the window next to the door. Jimmy's family's dark house looked uninhabited, the driveway empty.

The lot next to it was buried in shadows, but looked exactly as he remembered. He didn't see any cars that fit his memory of the Ripper's car.

At least, he didn't think so. It was awfully dark out there.

Enough!

Lana's paranoia must be rubbing off on him.

He headed up the stairs that led to the boys' wing. There were days when he regretted putting up the wall in the upstairs hallway to divide the boys' wing from the girls'. His weary muscles and heavy eyes made this one of those times.

After tucking the younger boys in for the night, he went down to the basement to hang out with some of the older kids.

During the summer, house rules dictated that anyone under ten was in bed by ten. Everyone else had until midnight to turn in and most of the older kids stayed up as late as they could.

Tonight, he wished he could revoke the rule and send everyone to bed by ten.

The Webbers were early risers, so asking them to stay up with the kids didn't seem fair. Even though he felt like the walking dead.

He entered the room to find an intense game of charades in progress. Several kids called out guesses as Trevor made small swimming motions. It only took a few seconds for Brittany to correctly guess whale and end the round.

"Hey, any of you guys remember seeing a black car parked in the junkyard across the street earlier?"

The kids looked at him blankly for a second before Cody asked, "What kind of car?"

He tried to maintain a casual façade. "I don't know. Maria thought she saw a man sitting in a black car watching us play ball earlier and I wondered if anyone else saw it."

No one had and he did his best to shrug off the incident. "No biggie. It was probably just another reporter."

"When are they gonna leave us alone?" The question came from Jessi, a pale blonde girl of thirteen.

"I think they're starting to. That guy was probably a straggler."

"If all they want is an interview, why don't you talk to them so they'll get lost?" Trevor asked.

"I don't like being on camera. Besides, now it's a matter of principle." Paul lifted his shoulders in a small shrug. "Call me stubborn."

Glancing around the group, he changed the subject. "Anyone need an extra player?"

The car was definitely following her.

Lana's eyes flicked between her rearview mirror and the road every few seconds. Of all the days for something like this to happen… She didn't have the patience for this, especially not today.

Please, God, help me out here.

The prayer couldn't get any more specific than that. Truth was, she had no clue what kind of help she expected God to give her, but that was why He was God and she wasn't.

She'd first noticed the car when she left the office. It had been parked outside the employee parking garage. If it hadn't been the only car at the curb, she might not have thought anything of it.

Solid black with windows tinted darker than the legal limit, it remained a steady half block behind her. She'd changed lanes several times, turned corners at the last minute, even circled a shopping center, and the car had matched her every move.

Dang it.

In the years she'd been doing this job, she couldn't remember ever being followed before. She scrounged her memory for the training she'd received, but time had dulled the information.

Options strobed in her mind. Call for backup? Shake the tail?

Or maybe turn the tables and follow *him*.

The more she thought about it, the better the idea sounded. See how much he liked being the prey.

Now all she had to do was figure out how to do it.

Ahead of her, a single parking space opened up, the only one in sight for blocks. She whipped into it without a second thought, then waited while the black car crept by.

Okay. Now it was her turn.

She turned on her blinker and inched out, watching for

someone to let her back into traffic. A minivan stopped several feet back. She pulled out of the spot and zoomed forward, her eyes locked on the black car a block ahead.

Switching lanes, she shot by three cars, merged back into the lane directly behind the black car.

Stealth was not her goal.

She wanted the owner of the car to know how it felt to be followed.

More than that, she wanted the license plate number. No one followed her and got away with it. She grabbed her cell phone and brought up the number for Alexandra Hill.

"Hey, Lana."

"You still at work?"

"Yeah. What's going on?" The conversational tone dropped from Alex's voice and tension oozed through the phone.

No surprise that Alex had guessed something was wrong. Working closely with your best friend had some advantages.

"I need you to run a plate for me."

She heard rustling in the background. "Shoot."

The car ahead of her accelerated through a yellow light. She gritted her teeth and floored it, shooting through the intersection as the light turned red.

"Lana? You still there?" Worry highlighted Alex's words.

"Yeah, give me a minute."

The black car braked suddenly, narrowly avoiding a collision with the stalled traffic in front of him. She drew close enough to see the number once again.

"Okay, here it is." She rattled off the number as the light ahead changed and traffic started moving again.

Alex repeated the number back, then hesitated before asking, "Do I even want to know what's going on?"

"A car was following me. Now I'm following him. I want to know who it is."

The black car pulled a sharp right. She followed.

"Where are you? I'll get some police backup."

"Twenty-Third and Palm. Heading north."

An intersection loomed in front of them. The light turned yellow.

The black car accelerated. Red light.

The black car barreled forward at a deadly pace. No brake lights, no sign of stopping. Laying on the horn, the driver blazed through the intersection. A red convertible skidded to a stop, missing the car by inches.

Lana slammed on her brakes.

Tires squealed as she came to a stop with her bumper hanging into the crosswalk. Her heart battled her ribs, her breathing was rapid and shallow, and tremors shook the hand clutching the cell phone.

Up ahead, the black car turned right and disappeared from view.

"Forget it. I lost him."

"You okay?" Concern laced Alex's voice.

"Are you going to be around the office for a few minutes?"

"I can be."

Lana checked for traffic and turned right. "I'm on my way back."

"I'll be here."

Tossing her phone on the seat next to her, Lana forced deep breaths into her lungs. What had that been about? Who had been driving the car and why would they follow her?

Recent cases flipped through her mind. There was the fugitive they'd caught last week, but he was behind bars and his own girlfriend had turned him in. That seemed like an unlikely option.

She mentally discarded half a dozen cases before stopping with the highest profile case on her desk.

Raymond Bright.

A fugitive she and her team had caught a while back who'd agreed to testify against his former drug buddies. He'd be turning on some pretty powerful and unsavory people. The trial was underway. This had to be about him.

Although she had no idea why they'd come after her. It

wasn't like she had anything to do with his protection detail. Nor had she been the only one on the team who arrested him.

But she had been the one to snap on the cuffs.

Paul's description of the Ripper's car flashed into her mind.

Hmm. It kind of matched the vehicle he'd described.

No. No way.

That couldn't have been the Ripper tailing her. Because she definitely was *not* the Ripper's next target.

Was she?

Darn it, Paul! Didn't he know fear was contagious?

There had to be thousands of black cars in the greater Jacksonville area. Her sister-in-law drove a black car, for crying out loud. Besides, that car hadn't had a hood ornament; Paul had been pretty specific on that detail.

She pulled back into the secure parking area, hurried into the building and up to the fourth floor. Other than Alex, the room was empty.

The office always looked alien when it wasn't full of people and for the first time Lana could remember, it also felt kind of creepy. It was just the residual effect of having someone follow her, she knew that, but not even that knowledge could warm the chill seeping into her bones.

Weaving around the empty desks, past computer monitors that stared like the eyes of the dead, she made her way to where Alex worked.

Her friend's serious pixie features and abstract blonde hair had never been a more welcome sight. A sigh escaped from Lana's lips as she collapsed in the chair opposite Alex.

"Are you okay?" Worry shadowed Alex's ocean colored eyes.

Lana offered a weak smile. "A little shaky, but I'll live. What'd you come up with on that plate?"

Turning back to her computer, Alex scanned the screen. "It belongs to a black Crown Victoria, registered to a Harold Templing."

Lana took a moment to savor the name before slowly

shaking her head. "It doesn't sound familiar to me. You?"

"No."

"Does he have a record?" Knowing Alex, it was probably the first thing she'd looked for.

Alex shook her head. "A few speeding tickets, but that's it. Wanna go question him?"

The only thing she wanted more than interrogating him was to arrest him, but she swallowed both urges. "Not yet. I want to find out more about him so that when we do confront him, maybe we can shock the truth out of him. Do you have his DMV picture up? Maybe I'll recognize him."

Alex nodded and swiveled the computer monitor so she could see.

The man on the screen wasn't familiar, but the picture did ease her irrational concerns about him being the Ripper. Templing had short red hair, pale gray-green eyes, and thin lips that looked incapable of smiling. Judging by his face, not to mention height and weight, the man was stocky, not scrawny.

Definitely a thug, but he didn't fit Paul's description of the Ripper.

Alex studied her intently. "What aren't you telling me?"

Right. Like she would really tell Alex about her delusional friend and his virulent suspicions. "Don't worry about it."

"Lana." The tone in Alex's voice mimicked one Lana's mother used to adopt, and Lana fought the urge to obey. "You might as well tell me. We both know I won't leave you alone until you do."

True enough. When Alex latched onto something, she clung to it with the tenacity of a crocodile.

"It's nothing. Paul freaked me out a little. The other night he made a comment about being afraid the Ripper would target me. When I saw that black car following me, all I could think was that the Ripper's car was black. Pretty stupid, huh?"

Alex lifted her shoulders in a small shrug. "I don't know. I might've done the same thing. Any chance there's something to it?"

"No. From Paul's description, it doesn't sound like the same car and this guy," she jerked her head toward the computer screen, "isn't blond."

Of course, Paul had also mentioned red hair as a possibility. But he'd been pretty sold on the blond idea and that was good enough for her.

Alex turned back to the screen and studied the picture before returning her attention to Lana. "In the dark, this guy could probably be mistaken for blond. I don't know that I'd disregard it altogether. He look anything like the sketch the cops drew up?"

"Paul's description was pretty vague. That sketch isn't going to get them any closer to finding the Ripper." Not that she'd ever tell him that.

"Sounds like you need to go straight to the source then. Let me print this off."

"Don't bother."

Alex's blue eyes flicked her direction. "What do you mean, don't bother?"

"I'm not going to show it to him."

"This could blow the case wide open. You have to show it to him."

Maybe she *should* take it to Paul. If this was the Ripper, they had an opportunity to stop him before anyone else got hurt.

But if it wasn't, she'd scare Paul for no reason. "Not until we've had a chance to look into this further."

"Look into it further? What's up with you?"

"If I take this to him now, one of two things will happen. He'll either think I broke my promise to stay out of the Ripper investigation or he'll freak out because I was followed. Probably both."

A scowl lit Alex's face and Lana scrambled to come up with a reasonable argument against Templing being the Ripper. "Besides, he said the Ripper was scared of him. This guy doesn't look like he'd be scared of anyone, much less someone like Paul."

"You say that because you know Paul. But the Ripper doesn't. He looks at Paul and he sees a tall man. A tall, built man, if my memory serves me correctly. Look at this guy's stats. He's only five five. That would make Paul what, a good half foot taller than him?"

"At least."

Rubbing her forehead, Lana tried to come up with an argument, but couldn't find anything that sounded plausible. She settled for reading through the rest of Templing's statistics – thirty-three years old, a hundred and seventy pounds, corrective lenses.

Well, that was helpful.

"I'm too tired to think this through right now. All I want to do is go home and crash."

Leaning back in her chair, Alex folded her arms across her chest. "Long weekend?"

"You'd better believe it. Tracking that fugitive did not go smoothly. A six hour standoff in pouring rain, full on fistfight with pretty much his entire family, screaming baby in the background, and he still gets away. Oh, and to top it all off, the fire alarm at our hotel went off in the middle of the night and we all had to stand out on the sidewalk in our pajamas for an hour while the fire department confirmed it was a false alarm."

"So anything that could go wrong, did."

"Basically. And to make matters worse, I get on the plane this morning to find myself sandwiched between two big guys, one of whom hits on me practically the whole way home. And you know who's sitting behind me? A long-legged cowboy who pokes his knees into my seat every time he moves. Which was often, let me tell you."

The corners of Alex's mouth twitched as she tried to suppress a smile. "Poor baby. Why didn't you just find another seat?"

"The flight was full. Not even an opening in first class." She gave her head a slight shake. "Okay, enough whining. I'm going home."

"Just promise you'll be careful. This worries me a little."

Lana forced a smile. "I'm always careful."

"Oh yeah? Were you being careful when you got shot? 'Cause if that's your definition of careful–"

"Please. That's completely different."

Alex's face said she disagreed and Lana rushed to find something to reassure her. It was either that or listen to one of Alex's famous, long-winded lectures.

"In fact, I'll go talk to Barker about this right now and take a circular route home, okay?"

"Barker's gone for the night. He left about five minutes before you called."

"First thing tomorrow then."

Alex shut down her computer. "Okay. But I'm following you home. No arguments."

Every part of his body shook, from his fingers to the ends of his toes.

Never had he come so close to getting caught. If she had seen his face, it all would've been over. She would certainly recognize him, especially after the meeting he'd orchestrated only a few days ago, and then his secret would be out.

He wasn't ready to level with her, not yet.

That conversation had to wait until he could learn more about her. It was the way he always did things.

But he couldn't do that this time, could he?

She was onto him.

She would be more watchful in the future, more careful in her movements.

If he wanted this to work out, he'd have to bump up the

timeline. Approach her before she realized how often he followed her. If she knew, she'd be scared of him.

That was the last thing he wanted.

Tomorrow was the day. He'd follow her home, wait for the opportune moment, and approach her with his love.

He headed for the laundry room, camera in hand, and stepped into his makeshift darkroom. Trays full of developer fluids cluttered the counter he'd had installed on the east wall and a clothesline stretched from one end of the room to the other.

Snapping open the back of the camera, he removed the roll of film.

As he got ready to begin working, his eyes traveled the familiar space. The exposed red bulb cast a crimson hue across the pictures that hung to dry, reminding him of all the blood he'd been forced to shed in his quest for true love.

But no more.

Tomorrow, all this would be behind him.

No matter what it took, she would be his.

Seven

"You sure this is the right address?"

Lana double checked the address on the paper in front of her before turning back to Alex. "22305 Ashton Avenue."

Though the address on the paper matched the building in front of her, it seemed unlikely that anyone lived here. Undoubtedly some people spent enough time here that they may as well call it home, but certainly no one would claim it.

Except Harold Templing.

Garish shades of orange and yellow coated the walls of the old stone building in front of them. The doors and roof were trimmed in chili pepper red. Realistic looking flames licked up the sides of the building and written in flame-like letters across the wall to the right of the door the words *El Diablo* dared them to enter. Thick steel bars covered the door, making the place as inviting as the gates of hell.

"What is this place? Some kind of bar?" Alex asked, shifting the car into park.

"Certainly not a house or apartment building, that's for sure."

"So basically we wasted our time driving out here." Alex tapped her fingers against the steering wheel.

"Maybe someone inside knows our guy. It's worth a shot, anyway."

"Too bad the place isn't open. Can't ask questions when

there's no one here."

Lana reached for the door handle anyway. "I'll check the hours. We can always come back later."

Glass crunched under her shoes as she walked the ten feet between the car and the front door. She wished this dive were open now so they could question the bartender and get out of here before the regulars showed up after work. Something told her that cops weren't popular with the patrons at this particular establishment.

Depending on the crowd, her gender might make matters even more awkward. Sometimes it wasn't easy being a woman in law enforcement.

The sign next to the door listed the hours as being from four p.m. to one a.m.. Figured.

She swallowed her frustration. Whatever. It didn't really matter when she got her answers, just as long as she got them.

And she wouldn't take no for an answer.

"Tanner! What's this I hear about you being followed?" Barker's eyes narrowed in concern, his tone gruffer than usual.

Lana stepped into his office and settled in a chair. She'd known this inquisition was coming, that the meetings Barker had been in all morning offered but a brief reprieve.

Still, she wasn't sure exactly how to answer.

Should she tell him her concerns about the Ripper or simply give him the facts?

Start with the facts and leave any and all speculation for later.

She gave a thorough recap of the incident, starting with seeing the car outside the parking structure to losing it in traffic.

Barker said nothing until she'd finished. "And you're absolutely sure he was following you?"

"Definitely. I switched lanes, drove in circles, even cut through a parking lot. That car remained a steady distance behind me."

Leaning back in his chair, Barker eyed her with quiet speculation. "But you've got no idea why?"

She shrugged. "The best thing I can come up with is that it has to be connected to one of my cases. Raymond Bright was the first person to come to mind."

Barker chuckled. "He was pretty hot when you took him down."

That was putting it mildly. The man had cursed her with colorful language the entire ride in. Evidently being tackled and arrested by a woman had dealt a serious blow to his ego.

"I'm sure he'd love to return the favor."

"I don't know." Barker rubbed his neck slowly. "It doesn't make sense for him to go after you."

"Probably not him. But maybe someone trying to get to him."

"That'd require someone to actually know who you are and that you're connected to this case."

Which wouldn't be easy information to find.

"I know, it leaves a lot of questions. But it still seems like the strongest possibility." Unless you were Paul, who would no doubt blame the Ripper.

Barker leaned back in his chair. "Okay, we'll keep that option open. Any other thoughts?"

Just the Ripper, but she didn't intend to talk about that ridiculous idea.

Instead, she shook her head. "Not that I can think of. I keep coming back to Bright."

It had to be him. None of her other cases were nearly as high profile. He was set to take the stand in the next few days and his testimony would have serious implications in a major drug operation. Any number of people would want him dead.

Not to mention that the guy was a Class A jerk. There'd been times she wanted to put a few slugs in him herself.

Obviously she still had some work to do in that whole loving your enemies arena.

Still, she knew she should be praying for him, not grumbling about him.

She pushed the thoughts aside. "It has to be about him. The cartel would do anything to see him get carried away in a body bag."

"But how would they learn about you?"

That was the question. "Maybe Bright told someone."

"He's in protective custody. He's not allowed to contact anyone."

"But what if he did? It could happen." She wasn't sure exactly how, though. Protective custody ensured that someone kept a pretty close eye on him at all times.

Aside from that, she had no clue why he'd mention her specifically. She hadn't seen him in weeks. And telling people he'd been taken down by a woman half his size wouldn't do anything for his street cred.

She refocused on Barker. "Well, I have several other files on my desk, but Bright is the one with the really nasty people after him."

Barker's dark eyes drilled through her. "Either way, that still leaves us with the problem of how your name got out there. What if it's not about work?"

"I don't know what else it could be."

"Any threats in your personal life? Troubles with a neighbor or friend or someone?"

"Nope." Not unless he counted disagreeing with an overly paranoid friend who expected her to be murdered by a serial killer.

He stared at her.

Somehow, he knew. And evidently planned to stare her down until she spilled the secret she was trying to keep hidden.

"It's nothing. Just the crazy delusions of a friend."

He slowly crossed his arms over his solid chest, but didn't say a word.

"Not that my friend is delusional or anything. He's just been through a lot and…" She clenched her teeth to stop the rambling that threatened to spill out. "Really, it's nothing."

"Let me be the judge of that."

"He's got it in his head that I'll be the Ripper's next target. It's the trauma talking. Witnessing the murder really shook him up."

"Understandable."

"But not logical."

Barker agreed. "You don't fit the Ripper's victim profile."

"I told him that, but he didn't buy it. Really, I don't think it's the Ripper, but when I saw the black car and remembered Paul's description…." She rolled her shoulders in a slight shrug. "I have to admit the thought crossed my mind."

"I think it's a long shot at best. Any other reason someone would follow you?"

"Like who?"

"You tell me."

Silence dominated the air as she ran through the things she'd done lately. Work, church, pretty mundane stuff, really. No reason anyone would be interested in her.

Wait.

She'd also visited Paul. Waded right through a sea of reporters in the process.

"I suppose it could've been a reporter. There were a mess of them at Paul's place when I stopped by there the other night."

That made about as much sense as the Ripper theory. She didn't give Barker a chance to reply before shaking her head. "Scratch that. A reporter would've stopped when I started following him. Instead he ran a red light to get away from me."

A slow grin worked across Barker's face. "Maybe you're too intimidating."

Oh yeah. In all her five-foot-two inch glory, the only people she could intimidate were young kids.

"Sure. Intimidating. That's me."

Her sarcasm extracted the expected chuckle. "What about the license plate? You said you traced it?"

"It led us to a bar called *El Diablo*. I did a little research on it when we got back to the office and it has a, well, colorful reputation."

"If you call assaults, rapes, auto theft, and drug dealing colorful, then yeah."

Okay, so it was more than colorful. "Anyway, Alex and I plan to go back later this afternoon to question the bartender."

Barker's eyes narrowed and his jaw twitched. "No. I'll send someone else to check it out."

Weird. Why wouldn't he want her going?

She focused on keeping an even tone. "Alex and I can handle it."

"Tanner, if this is about one of your cases and if the guy we're looking for is a regular there, he's probably got bar buddies that would be only too happy to help him kill two deputies. Better to keep you out of it."

Much as she hated to admit it, he had a point. But so did she. "It was me this guy was following and if I'm there, maybe he'll do something stupid that he wouldn't ordinarily do."

"Forget it." Snapping his mouth shut, he appeared to reconsider. "Okay, but I'm going with you. I have a meeting at three-thirty. I'll find you when I'm done."

Eight

"Buy ya a beer?"

"Hey babe, why don't ya hang with a real man?"

"Lookin' good!"

Lana worked to tune out most of the catcalls, tossed a few well-deserved glares, and headed straight for the bar.

In spite of the comments, none of the men in the surprisingly crowded bar moved toward her. Maybe it was due in part to Barker's presence only a few steps behind. Even though he had to be pushing sixty, he hit the gym almost every day and it showed. And at a few inches over six feet tall, he likely towered over most of these idiots.

The bartender watched them approach, a lazy smile on his cheeky face. "Don't get many newcomers 'round this place."

She got the impression that he meant of the feminine persuasion. Imagine that.

"Howsabout one of my specialties?"

"How about some information instead?" Lana pulled her badge.

The smile disappeared and the bartender pulled a rag and began wiping down the counter. "Hey man, I just work here. Don't know nothin'."

Barker smacked the file he was carrying on the counter, leaned forward, and glowered at the bartender. "No one knows more in a place like this than the guy behind the bar."

The comment must've stoked the bartender's ego. He cackled. "Got me there, G-man, but I still got nothin' to say."

"Yo Mikey! Filler up." A male voice hollered from down the bar.

The bartender gave a half nod toward a man holding up an empty glass before turning back to Lana and Barker. "I got payin' customers to tend to. I'm sure you guys remember the way out."

Whistling a tuneless melody, the bartender moved away without a backward glance.

"Wonder if any of these other guys would be more forthcoming." Barker's eyes encompassed the room in a single sweep.

"I doubt it." This was their only lead. She couldn't leave without getting some answers. "Let me try."

"I guess it can't hurt."

Sitting on the closest stool, she watched the bartender fill one glass after another. That he was aware of their presence wasn't lost on her – he made a point of *not* looking their direction. At all.

She turned to find Barker scanning the room, checking for Templing, no doubt. Following his lead, she looked around the room, caught many furtive glances coming their way, but saw no sign of the man they were after.

"So this is my tax dollars at work? I oughta stop payin' 'em."

She swiveled on her stool to find Mikey a few feet away.

What approach to use? Persuasive? Charming? Disinterested?

Bartenders were usually good at reading people so she decided to play it straight. Letting out a breath, she relaxed into a smile that she hoped looked genuine. "Then you'd have the IRS hanging around. I doubt they're any better for business."

Mikey grunted, but said nothing.

"Look, Mikey, we don't want to disrupt your business any

more than we have to, but we need a little information. As soon as we have it, we'll be out of your hair, but until then, well, I guess you're stuck with us."

Studying her in silence, Mikey finally sighed. "Makin' no promises, let me say that right now."

"Fair enough." Taking the file from under Barker's large hand, she slid out a photo of Templing and pushed it across the counter.

Mikey barely glanced at the picture. "Never seen 'im."

"Look again." Barker's stern voice commanded.

A sigh burst from Mikey's lips, but he grudgingly obeyed.

A full ten seconds oozed by before Mikey dropped the photo back to the counter. "See a lotta guys in here. Can't keep 'em all straight."

Lana worked to keep her voice friendly, using a sweet tone to camouflage the persuasive undercurrents. "His name's Harold Templing, if that helps. According to his driver's license, he lives here."

"It look like anyone lives here to you? This ain't no apartment."

"Does the name sound familiar at all?"

"Can't say that it does."

He probably can't say that it doesn't either.

She forced herself to keep smiling. "Have you gotten any mail addressed to Templing?"

"You see a mailbox outside? Our mail goes to a PO Box."

"Then you should know if you've gotten any with this guy's name on it."

Mikey shrugged. "If it ain't addressed to me, I toss it."

Leaning on the counter, Barker dropped his voice. "Listen, you'd better start cooperating or you'll find this place crawling with police and Feds every day of the week. We'll haunt you until we find this guy and if we put your business six feet under in the process, it's no big deal to us."

A stony expression covered Mikey's face as he stared at Barker. "That a fact?"

"You can bank on it."

Their eyes held. The stare-down lasted several moments before Mikey blinked. "Whaddya want with this Templing clown anyway?"

"I can't discuss that–"

"He's crucial to an ongoing investigation," Lana interjected smoothly. Hopefully Barker wouldn't mind her butting in like that, but something told her that the more open she was with Mikey, the more likely he'd be to talk to them.

"And if I answer your questions, you'll leave?"

"Immediately."

"Mikey, I'm outta rum!"

Mikey looked at the man at the far end of the bar and bellowed, "Deal with it, Carlo! Can't ya see I'm talkin' to a lady?"

The response narrowed Carlo's eyes and brought a rush of color to his cheeks. "Do I gotta come back there and get it myself?"

"Don't even think it, man. You can wait five minutes." Turning back to Lana, Mikey sighed. "Look, I got a rep to maintain here. My customers like their privacy, you know? Anyone thinks I'm a snitch and my business goes straight down the toilet."

"Your name doesn't even make it in our report."

She felt herself being weighed as Mikey stared at her. Finally, he gave a barely perceptible nod. "Yeah, I seen the guy. Been a long time, though."

Barker flipped open his small spiral notebook and pulled a pen from his pocket. "How long?"

"I dunno. Two, maybe three months. Used to be a regular here; always ordered Jack Daniels, but then he stopped comin'."

Lana forced her mind back to her questions. "Any idea why?"

Mikey's eyes darted around the room like a hamster on speed before settling back on her. "Nah. Guy never talked much. Maybe he met some chick and she didn't like him comin'."

A classy place like this? What woman would have a problem with that?

The notepad in front of Barker was still blank. "Was he ever in here with anyone?"

"Guy was a loner. Never saw him talkin' to nobody. Heck, never even hooked up with one of the workin' girls who used to come here to find their johns. Used to see him eyein' one of the girls, but never approached her. Least far as I know."

Really. Now that might be a solid lead. "Do you know her name?"

He laughed. "Ain't nobody really knows their names. This one went by Cocoa and she had big..." Mikey looked between Lana and Barker. "Uh, a smokin' body. And long hair."

"Does Cocoa still come here?" Lana asked as Barker wrote down Cocoa's name and the vague description Mikey had given.

"Nah. Most of those girls don't bother with my place anymore 'cause my customers are just lookin' for handouts."

Barker glanced up at Mikey. "I need a better description of this Cocoa. As much as you can remember."

"Dark hair and skin–"

"Hispanic?" The pen stilled in Barker's hand.

"Naw, man, darker. And she was small, you know, short, and she had curly hair and, uh, she wore it up a lot. Oh, pink, she always wore somethin' pink."

"Height, weight, age, eye color...?"

Irritation narrowed Mikey's eyes and a muscle in his jaw twitched. He glanced at Lana. "Tiny bit taller 'n you, I s'pose. Didn't really notice her eyes. And I ain't stupid enough to ask a chick her weight or age."

"I don't suppose you'd know where we could find Cocoa, do you?" Lana watched Mikey's face carefully for any flicker of dishonesty, but saw none.

"I got a wife at home. And three kids. You think I'm wastin' my time on hookers?"

"What about anyone else here? Did any of them ever leave with Cocoa?"

"Couldn't say. Most nights I'm too busy pourin' booze. Kinda doubt it, though. Like I said, guys in this place are cheap."

The pen glided across Barker's paper as he filled the page with notes. "Why would Templing list your bar as his address?"

Mikey's shoulders twitched in a limp shrug. "If my job's taught me somethin', it's that people do weird things. I don't even try to figure 'em out anymore."

"Five minutes are up, man!"

"Yeah, yeah, keep your pants on." Mikey shot an irritated glance down the bar at Carlo before turning back to Lana and Barker. "That it? I've got customers."

Lana exchanged a look with Barker. "I think that covers it for now. Thanks for your time."

Without another word, Mikey turned and headed down the bar.

Lana put the picture back in the file folder while Barker stuffed his pen into his pocket.

"Man, ya sure took yer sweet time 'bout gettin' down here. Those cops?" A gruff male voice wafted down the bar.

Would Mikey tell the truth?

Most likely. These guys could probably smell a cop like she could smell the cigarette smoke that filled this room. Lying to them would only make Mikey lose their trust.

"Worse, Feds."

"So what'd they want?"

How would Mikey handle this one? Part of her wanted him to tell the truth so that maybe, just maybe, they'd get lucky enough for gruff voice to give away something about Templing – assuming he even knew who Templing was.

But the more logical side of her knew that Mikey would never reveal what they'd spoken about. He'd fudge it over somehow so that no one knew he'd cooperated with the authorities.

Mikey didn't disappoint. He even spoke loudly enough for everyone in the bar to hear him. "They were askin' some questions 'bout those hookers that used to hang out here. Told 'em those girls had moved on a long time ago."

The gruff man snickered. "Too bad 'bout that, too. They were hot."

"You ready?" Barker's voice came from behind her.

"You have no idea."

She led the way to the door, weaving through the maze of tables and chairs scattered around the room. The sooner they got out of this fleapit–

"Hey!" A crash punctuated Barker's outraged voice.

Whirling, she found a bedraggled scarecrow wringing his hands several feet from where Barker stood. Broken glass littered the floor at Barker's feet and Barker's previously white shirt now had splotches of amber.

"What–" She bit back the question. It was pretty obvious what'd happened.

The scarecrow scurried away, brushing by her. The stench of beer gagged her as he passed, whether from the spilled drink or on his breath, she couldn't say.

Barker shook liquid from his fingers.

What a mess. She glanced around the room. On the far wall, a door simply labeled "Gents" caught her attention.

No ladies room. Imagine that.

She nodded at it. "If you want to clean up, looks like there's a restroom over there."

"Guess I'll have to." He pulled a key ring from his pocket. "Why don't you head out? I'll meet you out there."

Good. She really didn't want to hang around in here.

As Barker headed for the restroom, she focused on getting to the door. Almost there. Just a few more steps.

"Hey."

A man's voice, from somewhere to her left, unfamiliar.

Ignore him.

She continued walking.

"You were asking about the hookers? I may be able to help."

Stop or keep going? She wanted to get out of this hole, but on the chance this man could tell her something...

She turned, her eyes going to a man lounging in the closest booth. Stubble covered his shaved head, camouflaging – but not hiding – a lightning bolt shaped scar above his right ear.

On his neck, a moss green skull stared at her with blood colored eyes. A busty woman in a bikini winked at her from his right arm. The thug's biceps were as thick as her neck, which he could probably snap without breaking a sweat.

After a moment's hesitation, she closed the distance between them.

The man's gaze raked her body and she fought the urge to cross her arms over her chest.

Just deal with the pig and get out.

She waited for the man to meet her eyes before speaking, her tone utterly professional. "You said you had some information?"

Straight, surprisingly white teeth flashed as he leered at her. "What, I don't get an introduction?"

Like she had the patience for this. "Do you know anything or not?"

"I know plenty. Who're you after?"

"She goes by Cocoa."

"Cocoa hangs out on the East Side o' town. Gets plenty of business on account o' her–"

"I meant anything helpful."

Should she show him the picture? Couldn't hurt.

Whipping the photo out of the folder, she showed it to the tattooed thug. "Have you ever seen this guy?"

"I look like someone who checks out dudes to you?"

"I'll take that as a no." *Thanks for wasting my time.*

"Didn't say no, did I? I remember the shrimp. Picked a fight with me once, but I put 'im in his place."

Now that was more like it.

"What was the fight about?"

"Cocoa. I was talkin' to her, bein' nice, and that guy came completely unglued. Shoved me, told me to find someone else, that she was too good for me. Couldn't have none o' that. My fist sent the shrimp runnin' for the door. Never came back."

"That's not how I remember it."

A man's smooth voice spoke up from behind her. Close behind her. She resisted the urge to glance back.

"The way I remember it, you were talking trash about Cocoa."

Tattooed Thug grinned. "That's me bein' nice."

"And I think the guy did come back after that."

Lana stiffened as someone brushed her left shoulder. Okay, serious violation of personal space here. Sliding to the right, she half-turned to face Mr. Smooth Voice, who stood right behind the spot she'd occupied only seconds before.

The lanky man had a good ten inches on her. Dark eyes peered out from under shaggy dishwater blonde hair, eyes that were clear and focused.

Not drunk.

Which, in her mind, made his intentions even less honorable than the guys who couldn't walk a straight line.

God, I might need some help here. Please send Barker soon.

The smile that curled his lips contradicted what she read on the rest of his face. Firm set to the jaw, tension in the muscles, ice in the gaze. His eyes traveled her body, but unlike the rest of these clowns, she didn't think he was simply imagining what he couldn't see. The lingering on her shoulder, her hip, her ankle told her he was checking for weapons.

There was no reason for him to see if she was armed. Unless he was looking for trouble.

Her every instinct screamed to run away. Fast.

And where the heck was Barker? Shouldn't have taken him

this long to get cleaned up.

"Let me see the picture." The man's request sounded more like a demand.

She pulled out the photo. Taking it from her hand, Smooth Voice studied it for a second before offering it back. "He came back a few more times, but when Cocoa stopped coming, so did he."

Good enough. Time to get out of here.

"Well, thanks for the information." She turned to go.

A hand clamped onto her left arm just below the elbow. "Hold up. Don't you need to ask me questions, too?"

Not particularly.

Eyes narrowed, she looked pointedly at his hand before meeting his eyes. The man didn't budge. Didn't release her arm, didn't apologize.

"I don't believe you're really a Fed." The challenge in the man's voice burned her.

"I can slap the cuffs on you and haul you in to prove it. And if you don't release me right now, I'll charge you with battery of a Federal officer."

The threat didn't appear to bother Smooth Voice.

From behind him, Tattooed Thug snorted. "Howsabout me? I've been a bad boy."

No doubt that was true.

She ignored him, kept her attention focused on the man in front of her. "Now."

Several seconds ticked by before his fingers loosened and he released her arm. "Lemme buy you a drink so we can get to know each other. We'd have a lotta fun, you and me."

Without another word, she strode for the entrance, back so stiff it ached, head level, eyes moving.

"You know where to find me when you change your mind," Smooth Voice called after her, eliciting chuckles from the men sober enough to notice.

She threw the door open and stepped outside, almost plowing into several dirt-covered construction workers twice her size. A slight tremor shook her hands and she clenched her fists.

How dare they treat her like she was nothing more than a piece of flesh!

To objectify her like that, bully her. She'd treated them with respect, was it too much to ask to be offered the same in return?

Evidently.

She hit the unlock button on the electronic key fob as she approached the car. Collapsing in the passenger seat, she punched the lock button and slumped against the fabric.

Calm down.

A rap on the driver's side made her jump. She glanced over before hitting the unlock button so Barker could get in.

"You okay?"

Part of her wanted to tell him what had happened, but it would do no good. They couldn't arrest people for being juvenile and stupid.

Unfortunately.

Managing a tight smile, she nodded. "Fine. But you were right. Bringing Alex with me would've been a mistake."

Not that he'd actually said as much, but now that she'd been here, it was pretty obvious.

The key scraped into the ignition and the engine quietly turned over.

Barker glanced at her as he put the car in gear. "I've heard things about this place over the years, none of them good. The daughter of one of my friends was attacked here. That was a few years back. My friend's been trying to get the place shut down ever since."

The tension leaked from her muscles and Lana eased her hands open. "Too bad he didn't succeed."

"Give him time. He works for the county. If the owner of this dump makes just one mistake – forgets to renew his liquor license or fails a health inspection – he can kiss his business goodbye." Barker fell silent as he pulled into traffic.

"What was your friend's daughter doing at a place like this? I wouldn't even think about going near it unless I was packing heat."

He hesitated. "Missy's too trusting. At least she used to be. It was hard to see. She and my daughter Sharice grew up together. Missy was the one who believed the best about people and would chat with strangers about anything, but Sharice, well, I guess she followed my lead."

For several moments, the only sound in the car was the hum of the tires on the pavement and the steady throb from the engine.

Barker's voice was softer when he finally spoke. "Actually, you've always reminded me of Sharice."

Really? Maybe that explained part of the reason he seemed so protective.

Barker had great rapport with all the deputies working under him, but she'd always felt that he treated her like family. "How so?"

"Oh, she's stubborn, strong-willed, jumps into things without thought–"

"I don't do that!"

He glanced at her with raised eyebrows. "Do I have to remind you of the time you jumped in front of a bullet?"

First Alex, now Barker. They really needed to leave that incident in the past. "Hey, I thought that through, but I couldn't let my friend die."

"A friend who turned out to be an assassin's accomplice."

How had they gotten on this conversation?

"I still couldn't let him die. Besides, you have to admit he gave us some useful information." The box containing Stevens' files, the ones detailing his hits and who hired him, had shown up on her doorstep two years ago. Hand delivered with a letter from Nate stating Stevens had been killed. "The FBI arrested what, thirty people, all because of evidence he provided us with."

"Actually, last I heard the number was pushing fifty, but

that still doesn't change the fact you almost died. And for what? Some hit man's lackey?"

"There's a good guy hidden deep inside. Look, I know it sounds hokey, but I saw the man he could be. And before you ask, no, he hasn't contacted me."

It seemed like every few months someone would ask her if she'd heard anything from him. Her answer was always the same. Not only had she not heard from him, she never expected to.

You'd think after five years, people would leave it alone.

"But you'd tell me if he had, wouldn't you?" The warning note in his voice said there was only one right answer.

"Definitely. There's no gray area with me, you know that. Right is right and wrong is wrong. I wouldn't like it, but I'd do it anyway."

"That's what I thought. Just checking."

Silence filled the car for the rest of the ride. As he pulled into the parking structure, Barker glanced her way. "I know a cop working narcotics that might be able to help track down Cocoa. I'll give him a call tomorrow."

"Sounds good. I'd like to talk to her."

He pulled up next to her car and shifted into park. "I don't like the idea of someone following my deputies. Go ahead and do some digging, but don't even think about going out to question people without me."

Turning to face him, she arched an eyebrow. "What about my current cases?"

"Obviously those take top priority, but I think you can manage both."

"Of course." She stepped into the muggy garage. "Well, have a good evening."

"I'll follow you out, make sure no one's waiting."

Given that his stubborn streak was almost as big as her own, arguing would be pointless. "Thanks. I'll see you in the morning."

She got in her car and headed for the exit, Barker keeping

pace two car lengths behind. On the street, she saw no sign of anyone waiting for her, much less someone in a black car. It looked like she was in the clear.

Barker followed her for a few blocks before turning off.

Finally. She hated it when people fussed over her.

A glance at the clock showed it was almost seven. So much for her plans to see Paul and the kids. That visit to *El Diablo* had taken longer than she'd expected.

While she could still stop by and see how things were going, it wouldn't be a short visit. It never was.

Right now, all she really wanted was to get home, change, and go for a three mile run to burn off some steam.

And shower. Thanks to *El Diablo*, she smelled like a chain smoker.

She turned the car toward home. Tomorrow, she could visit Paul and the kids tomorrow.

Nine

A shiver tickled between his shoulder blades. But not from cold. No, the dampness of his armpits confirmed that.

It was time.

His attention locked on the blue-trimmed house across the street. Flower beds in the front yard. Two wicker chairs and a small table on the covered porch.

It even looked like her. Cute. Charming. Welcoming.

Lights glowed from the windows, but thankfully she hadn't left the porch light on.

He clipped the knife's sheath to his belt and grabbed the rope. Surely he wouldn't need them, not with her, but it was best to be prepared for all scenarios. In case she required a little convincing.

Now for the bait.

He twisted around and grabbed the shallow cardboard box from the backseat. The life-sized baby doll inside didn't look real, not upon close inspection, but from a distance it could fool anyone. Especially if all that could be seen was the hair and one of the little hands. He adjusted the pink blanket around the doll to hide the plastic face and cloth body.

Slipping out of the car, he eased the door shut and glanced around.

Deserted. Just what he liked to see.

Of course, it was almost ten on a weeknight. Most people

were probably getting ready for bed.

His tennis shoes were silent as he mounted the porch steps.

After arranging the box in the middle of the porch, he stepped back and took a look. Good.

A board creaked under his weight as he turned.

He froze. Had she heard that? Had anyone else?

No. No, it was too faint. He was sure.

Still, probably best not to linger. He crossed to the front door and rang the bell, then stepped into the deep shadows on the corner of the porch.

He closed his eyes and allowed her to invade his mind. Her athletic build. Silky dark hair. Delicate features.

She was perfect. And soon she would be his.

Footsteps inside. Approaching.

His breathing shallowed, his hands quivered. He opened his eyes, squinting as the porch light on the other side of the door blinked on.

The deadbolt scraped and the door cracked open. A chain rattled.

Not yet. Not until she unfastened the chain and stepped out. Forcing his muscles not to move, he remained still.

She'd never be able to see him without putting her head outside.

"Hello?" Her voice, so sweet, drifted through the cracked door. A gasp. "What…?"

The door quickly closed only to reopen a moment later. She stepped onto the porch, her gaze locked on the baby.

He came up behind her.

Slapping a hand over her mouth, he kicked the box into the house as he pulled her against his body and backed inside.

A scream filtered through his fingers, but not loudly enough for anyone else to hear.

He pushed the door closed with his shoe.

Lavender teased his senses and for a few seconds, all he could do was breathe in the scent of her. She had known he would come for her. Why else would she make herself smell so good?

She twisted in his arms.

The movement snapped him out of his thoughts.

Yes, of course. He'd have the rest of his life to enjoy her scent. For now, there were some details which needed his attention.

"Lock the door, sweetheart."

She tensed at the sound of his voice. Made no movement to obey.

Weird.

Well, he didn't dare let her go as long as the door was unlocked. Not until he was assured of her intentions. He'd been burned too many times before to completely trust her yet.

"Do it." His voice was harsher that time. "Now."

A tremor shook her body.

If she'd only obey, she wouldn't have anything to fear.

Pain shot through his hand. A curse flew from his lips as he jerked his hand away.

Blood puckered from a small cut by his finger.

She'd bit him?

His foot! His groin! Agony ripped through his body and his vision darkened.

A scream shredded the silence in the room. She thrashed, pulled, tried to jerk from his arms.

Focus! He couldn't lose her now. He clung to her as pain pulsed.

"Let me go!" Her voice now sounded more like a banshee's cry. "Someone help!"

His legs buckled and he fell forward, landing on top on her. She twisted and thrashed, squirming her way out from under him.

Slipping from his grasp, she pushed to her feet.

No! He was losing her.

Had to stop her. He snagged her ankle as she started running. The momentum jerked his arm, sent pain spiking from his shoulder down, but he didn't let go.

She flailed.

A small scream split the air as she crashed to the ground. Her head bounced off the hardwood floor.

The scream died and her body went still.

Ragged breathing, coming from his own mouth, was the only sound in the suddenly silent room.

Pain still ravaged his body from her brutal attacks.

What had just happened? How could she do this to him?

He had to get out of here. The noise she'd made might've been heard by one of the neighbors. Sound travelled well, especially at night.

A groan broke free as he pushed himself to his knees.

She still hadn't moved.

Had he killed her? It would serve her right if he had.

He crawled to her and rolled her over. A knot was already forming on her forehead, but the steady rise and fall of her chest told him she was alive.

Now what? He could take her with him. In her condition, it would be easy.

But after all this, was it worth the risk?

He stared at her face, traced a finger down her cheek. Yes. It was worth it. She was worth it.

After all, she hadn't gotten a good look at him to see who it was who held her, right? That was his own fault. She'd probably thought she was being attacked by some psycho.

If he took her to his place, they'd have time to talk this out and once they did, then everything would be perfect. Just like her.

Grabbing the rope, he bound her hands and feet. He pulled the baby blanket from the box and wrapped it around her mouth, just in case she should wake up before they reached his place.

Okay, now to get her out of here.

He couldn't carry her out the front door. If one of the neighbors saw him, they'd call the police.

What other option did he have?

Wait. This was an older neighborhood. The kind that might have a garage or alley out back.

He jogged through the living room and spotless lemon-scented kitchen and peeked into the back yard.

Yes! There was an alley back there.

And the area was dark enough that he likely wouldn't be seen as he carried her to his car.

He unlocked the door, but didn't turn on the light, then hurried back through the house.

The minutes it took him to bring his car around to the alley seemed to drag, but he had yet to hear sirens or see any of the neighbors peeking through their curtains.

So far, so good.

She hadn't moved from where he'd left her.

Sliding his arms beneath her shoulders and knees, he tried to pick her up, but couldn't get her more than a few inches off the floor.

What the heck? She was tiny! It shouldn't be hard to carry her.

He tried again. No luck.

Dang it! How was he going to get her out of here?

He could wake her. But if he did, she'd likely fight him all over again.

He pulled her upper body to a sitting position and put her bound arms around his neck, then slowly straightened.

Finally. Guess that's what they meant by the term dead weight.

Ducking out of her arms, he put his shoulder into her stomach and hefted her up.

The extra weight threw him off balance, but he managed to remain standing.

He staggered toward the back door. Sweat dripped down his forehead and stung his eyes.

Only a few more feet.

He opened the passenger door and dumped her inside,

stuffing her legs and arms in before closing the door as softly as he could.

A siren pulsed in the distance.

They were coming for him!

He ran around the car, climbed into the driver's side, and slammed the door. The engine purred to life and he stomped the accelerator.

It wasn't until he'd put a few miles between him and her house and the sirens had disappeared that he was able to breath normally. Still, it would be wise to stick to the back roads as much as possible.

He glanced over at her profile, so still in the darkness.

She was a fighter, all right. Much more so than any of the other girls.

Which made her better than all of them. She was strong, spunky. Attributes that would make her a better companion and lover than any of the others could've hoped to be.

Of course, the skirmish in the house might set them back a bit, but he was a patient man. He could wait for her.

Besides, surely she'd realize none of that had been his fault.

She'd made him do it. By attacking him.

A muffled moan made him jump. He shot a look her direction to see her stirring.

Not good. She was supposed to stay out until he could get her safely tucked away at home.

Okay. So he'd have to revamp his plan.

The business district a few blocks to the north might be his best bet. At this time of night, everything would be closed. There were no restaurants or houses nearby. They should be able to talk without fear of interruption.

He adjusted his course, eyes scanning the landscape for the perfect place to pull off.

He passed some office buildings, doctor's offices, lawyers, a bank. None of them were quite right.

There! He turned left into the lot of a shipping company and pulled to the back of the large parking lot. Turning off the engine, he twisted so he could watch her.

Although she was writhing, her eyes remained closed.

Even in the dark, with her forehead creased in pain, she was so beautiful. And the perfect size to fit in his arms.

He ran his fingers through her hair. Like satin, just as he'd imagined.

He traced her chin, let his hand slide down her neck.

Her eyes shot open, lit with panic. The blanket in her mouth muffled her cry.

"Shh, shh." He dropped his hand. "I know we had a rough start, but it's okay now. I'm not going to hurt you."

She swallowed hard and stared at him, liquid shimmering in her dark eyes.

Holding her gaze, he spoke slowly. "We need to talk. There's no one around to hear you, but I really don't like screaming. I'll take the gag off if you promise to be quiet, okay?"

A halting nod responded.

Good. That was progress, anyway.

He eased the blanket out of her mouth and let it settle around her neck.

Tongue flicking over her full lips, she stared at him, unblinking.

"That's better."

"Why are you doing this?"

What was she talking about? His smile slipped but he forced it back in place. "Isn't it obvious?"

"No." A sob broke from her. "What do you want?"

What kind of stupid question was that? "You. I know things went poorly–"

"You attacked me!"

This wasn't his fault, it was hers. "No. You attacked me and got hurt in the process."

Tears flowed down her cheeks and she slowly shook her head.

She probably had a headache and while it served her right,

he couldn't help feeling sorry for her. Sorry that she had to suffer because of her own actions.

He ran his fingers through her hair. "Are you hurt?"

"Don't touch me!" Her voice reverberated off the windshield. Several seconds passed before he saw recognition light her eyes.

"You. The guy from the coffee shop."

"I knew you'd recognize me once you calmed down. The way we connected–"

"I just said 'hi'!"

He shook his head. "With words maybe. But you said so much more than that."

"No. No, I didn't."

He started to reach for her again, but stopped himself. It was too soon, obviously. But she'd come around. "Honey, don't fight it. A connection like ours is rare."

"There is no connection! I don't even know you."

What was she doing? Trying to pay him back for what happened earlier? Punish him?

"I-it's you. The Ripper. Y-you killed them."

Uh-oh. He had to make her understand.

"No, honey."

"Stay away from me! Help!" Hysteria seeped into her voice. "Someone help!"

"You can't believe everything you hear on TV." He raised his voice to be heard over her screaming. "They've got it all wrong."

If she heard him, she gave no indication. Her shrill voice seared his ears. "HELP!"

Clamping his hand over her mouth, he waited until he had her full attention to speak again. "Remember what I said about noise."

Wide eyes held his as she nodded.

He dropped his hand before she decided to bite it again.

"What do you want from me?"

Really? She hadn't struck him as stupid, but what kind of

question was that? "Companionship. Friendship. Love."

A slow nod responded. "Okay. I had to make sure we were on the same page."

Same page? She was the one, wasn't she? A grin stole across his face.

Months of searching, several false attempts, and countless hours of heartache had led to this. And it was wonderful. "I've been looking for you for a long time."

She shifted in the seat a little, but didn't come any closer. Not that he could fault her for that. After all, she hardly knew him.

But she would. It wouldn't take long for them to get acquainted, not really.

And then they'd have the rest of their lives ahead of them.

"And I've-" Her voice was scratchy and she cleared her throat before continuing, "I've been waiting for you to find me."

This couldn't have gone more perfectly if he'd planned it. Finally, after all this time, things were going to work out.

"My arms really hurt. Can you untie me?"

"Of course." He picked up the knife and removed it from the sheath.

The thought that she might try to get away flashed into his mind, but he stamped it down. No, they'd already cleared the biggest hurdles. And on the off chance she did try to leave – not that she would – he still had the knife.

Besides, her feet would still be bound.

She held out her hands and he cut through the rope.

The smoothness of her hands felt so good in his that he never wanted to let go.

But he forced himself to release her. The knife would remind her of everything she'd heard about him; he wanted to get it back in the sheath.

"Thank you." The words were whispered as she massaged her wrists.

A coconut-sized lump lodged in his throat. How long had

he waited for someone to say that to him? He couldn't remember the last time he'd been this happy–

A fist crashed into his throat.

The blow came at him so fast he barely saw it.

The dome light blinked on as she used her other hand to push open the passenger door.

Crushing pain consumed his thoughts as his hand went to his throat. His vision darkened and his breath came in rattling gasps.

"Help me!" Her voice filtered through his pain, soft, distant.

She was getting away!

Fog clouded his vision, but he swam through it, forced his eyes into focus. Fingers tightening around the knife, he threw open the door and stepped into the night air.

His head cleared in time for him to see her round a corner. How had she untied her legs without him seeing?

Gripping the knife, he sprinted across the lot.

The little witch.

She'd deceived him. The worst kind of tease, that's all she was. He probably wasn't the first one she'd done this to, but he would be the last.

He rounded the corner. There! Half a block away.

Legs pumping, he closed the gap, drew closer, closer, could almost touch her. He pounced.

The tackle caught her around the hips and took her to the ground.

"Get off me, you monster!"

She thought he was the monster? She'd ripped his heart into pieces. If either of them was a monster, it was her.

He rolled her onto her back.

Eyes wild, she twisted, punched, and kicked as she fought to get away. Several blows landed against his chest, her fist struck the side of his head, her nails gouged his neck.

Scrambling forward until he straddled her stomach, he pulled the knife from its sheath.

Her screams rose in intensity as she caught sight of the blade, the high tones nipping at his ears.

"You brought this on yourself, Ana."

"I'm not–"

Gripping the handle of the knife, he brought it down.

Each plunge of the blade restored part of the dignity she'd stolen from him. Each wound mirrored the ones she'd inflicted on his heart.

Wide, vacant eyes stared at him from her frozen face. Was she–

A shrill wail sliced the night. Sirens!

He jerked and glanced around. No sign of them yet, but it sounded like they were close.

Time to go.

He picked up a clump of her hair and wrenched it out. Pushing up from her body, he sprinted toward the lot where he'd left his car.

The sirens grew louder and he tried to run faster, but his feet were already moving as fast as they could.

Down the road, around a corner, almost there.

He jumped in the car.

The engine roared to life and the tires spun as he slammed the pedal to the floor. He shot across the lot, reached the entrance, and barely slowed before hanging a tight left.

The speed limit.

He glanced down at his speedometer, eased off the accelerator.

The last thing he needed was to be pulled over for speeding. The cops would take one look at the blood on his hands, the rope on the console, and the knife on the floor before slapping him in cuffs.

As he drove further from her body, the sirens faded, leaving only burning questions.

How had the cops known where to find him? Someone had to have called it in. Was there now another witness?

A few blocks back, lying in a pool of her own blood, the woman's eyes slid shut. A soft moan slipped from her lips and her head rolled toward her right shoulder.

"Not...Ana..."

Wait. Did she hear sirens?

She opened her eyes, saw no movement or flashing lights, couldn't find the strength to turn her head to check behind her. "Help, please, help..."

Ten

Paul glanced at his cell phone one last time before setting it aside. No missed calls.

She wouldn't call him this late, anyway, so he might as well stop watching the phone. Hours had passed since he'd left that message on Lana's voicemail and she still hadn't called him back. It wasn't like her, not at all.

She was probably caught up with work. Hadn't she said things had been busy lately?

And it seemed like he remembered her saying someone had been out sick. That would mean more work for her, like she didn't have enough on her plate already.

Seriously. Did he really think she was working after ten at night?

Maybe she'd worked late, had her phone on silent so she wouldn't be interrupted, then forgot to check it. It could happen.

No matter the arguments he came up with, none of them made him feel any better. In the year that he'd known her, he couldn't remember a time she had worked past seven or eight.

And she always returned his calls.

Maybe her phone was dead. He should've called her home number, just in case.

He glanced at the clock. 10:30. It was a little late now. She was probably already asleep and he refused to wake her up just to soothe his paranoia.

Then again, she had told him to call any time. Day or night. Maybe it wouldn't be so bad if he took her up on that.

And say what? That she didn't call him back?

Right. He'd sound completely needy and possessive.

Or he could tell her what was really bothering him. That he was obsessed with the idea that the Ripper had gotten to her. Oh yeah, he could hear how that conversation would go right now.

Yeah, Lana, just wanted to make sure you hadn't been attacked by some knife-wielding psycho. Sleep tight.

Right.

He knew his anxiety stemmed from the nightmare that had kept him up a good portion of the previous night. Somehow knowing that truth didn't change the way he felt. Couple that with not hearing from her in several days and he'd almost convinced himself that her body was on a slab at the morgue.

Seriously. Who thought like that? What was wrong with him anyway?

So she hadn't stopped by for a few days. Or called to talk. She had a life of her own, one that didn't revolve around him and the kids.

Punching the pillow helped vent a little of his frustration, but he still lay in the dark, his eyes staring at the glowing red numbers on the clock. A sure-fire way to ensure he stayed awake all night.

He rolled over, closed his eyes, and tried to pray.

Sleep eluded him. The glowing red numbers next to his bed clicked past 11:30, then midnight. Finally, at a little after 1:00 a.m., his eyes refused to stay open. He surrendered to the waiting exhaustion.

The phone shrilled.

Paul jerked, the pen in his hand drawing a bold black line to the bottom of the form he was attempting to fill out.

Stupid piece of junk. Why'd he think turning the ringer back on was a good idea?

Because no reporters had called or stopped by yesterday, that's why. Life was finally returning to normal. Whatever normal was, anyway.

He snatched up the receiver on the third ring.

"Is this Paul Van Horn?"

An unfamiliar woman's voice. Alarms blared in his head. "Yeah. Who's this?"

She fired off a name, followed by words he'd thought he was through hearing. "I'm a reporter with the Jacksonville News. Another woman was murdered last night. Are you still helping the police? Can you tell me anything about the Ripper that my readers–"

"I'm sorry. No comment."

The scrambled eggs he'd eaten for breakfast bounced in his stomach as he hung up the phone. His thoughts flashed like slides on a projector.

The Ripper had struck again.

Another woman was dead.

Lana had never called.

He grabbed his cell and brought up her number. It rang six times before going to voice mail.

This was her cell phone. She always had it on her. Why wasn't she answering?

He could think of one very solid reason, but it wasn't one he wanted to consider.

"Lana, it's Paul. Call me. It's important."

He texted her next. Just in case she was in a meeting or something and couldn't answer the phone.

Now all he could do was wait.

His office phone rang, taunting him, but he didn't answer. Lana would call his cell phone; that call was likely to be another reporter.

How long would it take her to call him back? Even a minute was too long.

Maybe if he called her home number he could reach her.

He glanced at the time. Unlikely as it was that she'd still be there, he had to try.

The other end rang six times before being answered by a mechanical, bland voice requesting that he leave a message after the beep.

Not good.

He had to reach her, had to hear her voice, had to know she hadn't been murdered last night.

Five minutes had passed since he'd texted her.

A faint buzzing filled his head. The room seemed to shrink around him and he thought he was going to be sick.

What if something had happened to her? How would he find out about it?

Work. He could call her there.

He'd never done it before, but she had given him her business card. And this was an emergency.

Now where was that card?

He pawed through his desk drawer. It had to be here somewhere!

Why had he never taken the time to organize this drawer? He grabbed a small stack of cards and dumped them on the desk, pushing through them until he found the right one.

Fingers shaking, he punched in the number.

This was stupid. All this worry wouldn't amount to anything.

Lana was fine. Like she'd said, she could handle the Ripper. If that killer ever did set his sights on her, she wouldn't let him get close enough to do what he did best.

But what if she never saw him coming?

He tried to halt the tirade, but it came anyway. What if the Ripper had gone after her, what if it was his fault, what if she needed his help?

Stop! There were too many "what if"s in life.

The line rang and rang. Once again, leave a message after the beep.

He wanted to slam the receiver down, but forced himself to wait for the tone. By the time he hung up, his hand shook like Maria after a nightmare.

Only he was living this nightmare.

Calm down.

He forced a deep breath. The chances of it actually being Lana...

Images of the dead woman flashed through his mind: the empty, staring eyes, the slack mouth, the blood. And then it was no longer the dead woman, it was Lana. Just like in his nightmare.

Pinpricks of light burst behind his eyes, his lungs felt crushed, and his limbs wouldn't stop trembling. No way could he sit here and do nothing while he waited for a call back.

The police!

Arlington would know the identity of the woman murdered last night. Paul wasn't sure how privacy issues might play into things, but surely Arlington could at least confirm that Lana wasn't the victim.

Now to find Arlington's card.

He rummaged through the heap on his desk, searching beneath piles of government documents that needed to be filed, bills that needed to be paid, and debit purchases that needed to be reconciled with his records. With everything that had happened the last week, he'd gotten behind on tasks he normally had no trouble completing.

It wasn't here. Where else could he have put it?

Maybe he'd put it in a different drawer.

He opened the top drawer, dug through the pens, pencils, paper clips, and sticky pads that seemed to have multiplied overnight. There it was, standing up behind a box of rubber bands.

He snagged the card, punched in Arlington's number, and waited for the line to connect. The other end rang.

Once, twice, three times. With every ring, he felt his hopes deflate a little more. When the voice mail kicked in, he wanted to swear.

He settled for leaving another message.

The mountain of paperwork in front of him forgotten, he stared at his closed office door but barely saw it. He could call the morgue, find out the name of the victim.

Or maybe the hospital could give him a name.

No. Neither of those places would release the name to him, no matter how strong a reason he might have for needing to know it.

What about the church?

Lana's Dad was the pastor after all. The church should know if she was okay.

Not a good plan. If she was fine – and more than likely she was – he'd freak them out for nothing.

Besides, what would he say? *Yeah, just wondering if Lana was murdered last night.*

No, not a good plan at all. But there had to be some way–

His cell phone rang and he snatched it up. The callback number was almost as familiar as his own.

"Lana?"

"What's wrong?" The words were tight, abrupt. Not angry, just concerned.

His hand shook so violently he nearly dropped the phone. She was alive. But of course she was.

In his head, he'd known the truth, but he'd let his fears get away from him.

For crying out loud, she'd survived encounters with two hit men and who knew how many fugitives; like she'd let some two-bit serial killer get the better of her. What had he been thinking?

"Paul?"

The concern in her tone snapped him from his thoughts.

What had she asked him? Clearing his throat, he tried to formulate an answer. "Uh, yeah, things are fine now."

She let out a long breath. "Don't do that, okay? You scared me half to death."

He'd scared *her*? She had no idea what he'd just gone through.

And she'd never find out, not if he could help it.

"Sorry. I, uh, I…"

What could he say? After all that, she deserved some sort of explanation, but he didn't want her to know how crazy the whole thing had made him. If she knew, she'd probably remove him from her friends list and file him under "psycho stalker" or "to be avoided at all costs".

"Are you sure everything's okay?"

The truth. Honesty was always the best choice. Besides, it was what Lana expected from him.

Not that she always got it.

He smothered the troubling thought. "Yeah. A reporter called asking me to comment on the latest murder–"

"There's been another one?"

She didn't know? Then again, why would she? Not her case, not her problem.

"Uh, yeah. Last night, I guess."

She was quiet for a moment. "Sorry, go ahead and finish."

"Well, when you didn't return my message last night and then I couldn't reach you this morning… I guess I'm still a little edgy."

"Don't worry about it. If it makes you feel any better, this is perfectly normal. The paranoia can last for months, but it should get better soon. It might help if you talked to a counselor."

The only person he wanted to talk to about this was her. "Just knowing it wasn't you is enough."

"You seriously thought it was me?"

It sounded so ridiculous. He felt heat blaze across the back of his neck. At least she wasn't here to see his head turn into a tomato. "I know, I know, crazy, huh."

She was too nice to agree with him.

"Did the reporter say anything else? Where the murder happened or when?"

"No, just that it was last night."

"Well, I'm sorry I didn't call you back. I accidentally left my phone on my desk last night so I didn't get the message until this morning. Things have been a little hectic here and I've been so busy that I haven't had a chance to return any calls."

"Don't worry about it. I overreacted."

A muffled voice said something in the background and Lana agreed before returning her attention to him. "Look, I need to get back to work, but I was thinking maybe I'd stop by tonight."

That would be the bright spot in what was already shaping up to be a challenging day. "See you then."

"How's the hunt going?"

Lana turned to face Alex. "Slowly. I found more information on Harold Templing than I expected, but nothing that leads me to where he is right now."

Reaching for a file on the corner of her desk, she flipped it open. "Let's see, born in Miami, appears to have moved around a lot when he was in his twenties, married two years ago, divorced two months ago, no kids."

"I wouldn't mind talking to the former Mrs. Templing."

"I was thinking the same thing." Lana referenced her notes. "Her name's Sally. Maiden name was Green and I'm betting she went back to it."

"I would've if I'd been married to Senor Creepy."

"I'll try to track her down. Maybe she can point us to Templing's current address."

Alex nodded slowly. "You know, in spite of the arguments against it, I'm still wondering if Templing is the Ripper. I wouldn't mind knowing what Sally Green looks like."

"Sally Green doesn't exactly sound Hispanic." But you never knew. Anything was possible.

The idea that her shadow and the Ripper were one and the same still struck Lana as absurd. "I guess we'll have to wait and see. If nothing else, maybe she can tell us something that will confirm Templing isn't the Ripper so we can put that idea to rest."

And maybe if she started right now, she'd find Sally before she had to meet with the VICE detective from Jacksonville PD. It was worth a shot.

Eleven

"That's Cocoa." Detective Jose Ramos nodded at a petite woman wearing a pink mini skirt and pink and white striped tank top.

Even without Detective Ramos at her side, Lana would have recognized Cocoa. The bartender's description had been dead on.

Cocoa was only a little over five feet tall, African American, with a wave of black curly hair. Her generous curves, large eyes, and quick smile probably earned her a good deal of money.

The smile faded as Cocoa watched them approach.

"Look Detective Ramos, how many times I gotta tell ya, I'm clean." Cocoa held out her arms, showing him the inside of her elbows. "See, no tracks."

"Not why I'm here."

Lana stepped forward, pulling out her badge. "I'm hoping you might remember a certain man."

A rich laugh bubbled from Cocoa. "You gotta be kidding, right? Hon, you got any idea how many men I meet?"

"Tons, I'm sure, but I think you'd remember this one. You would've met him at *El Diablo*–"

"Huh uh." Cocoa's smile flipped into a scowl. "No way. None of us hangs out there. It ain't safe for us, ya know?"

Like anything about their profession was safe?

Lana didn't point out the obvious. "Believe me, I know. But I'm told you used to."

"Hon, lemme tell ya. Me and summa the girls tried to find work there, but those drunks were lookin' for freebies, ya know what I mean?"

Pulling the picture of Templing from her file, she handed it to Cocoa. "His name's Harold Templing. I was told he watched you."

Cocoa looked at the picture for a few seconds before recognition lit her eyes. "Yeah, I remember him. Guy creeped me out. Men like him was one of the reasons we stopped chillin' there."

"Did he ever approach you?"

"Picked a fight with another guy over me once, but never threw money my way."

Strange.

"Did he ever talk to any of the other women?"

"No. Just sat there at his little table in the corner and stared. I went up to him once ta see if he was interested in some black sugar," Cocoa gestured down her body with a little flourish, "but he told me he just liked lookin'. Now honey, I don't mind lookin' but there was somethin' in that guy's face that didn't sit right. I told my girls and we all booked it outta there."

"And you haven't seen him since? He hasn't come out here looking for you?"

Cocoa lifted her shoulders in a small shrug. "Not that I know 'bout. Like I said, the guys in that joint didn't wanna pay for nothin'."

Another dead end. Lana put the photo away and pulled a card from her pocket. "Well, thanks for your time. If you see him, could you let me know?"

"No sweat. Whatcha want with him anyway?"

"He's just a person of interest in something I'm working on."

Cocoa laughed again. "You lookin' for that, you got the wrong man, 'cause believe me, honey, he ain't no person of interest."

Where was Maria? Paul glanced around the back yard, but didn't see her. It had been a while since he last saw her and it wasn't like her to not be with the rest of the group. While not the most talkative or extroverted child, she hated being alone.

He walked over to a hefty red-headed girl who was one of Maria's roommates. "Jackie, have you seen Maria?"

"She was lookin' out the window."

"In your room?"

Jackie nodded, climbing up the ladder for the slide. "She's been lookin' outside a lot."

Strange.

Thanking Jackie, he headed for the stairs and took them two at a time. The door to Maria's room was open but he still tapped on the door as he entered. "Hey, kiddo. What's going on?"

Maria didn't even look his way.

"The man's back." Her voice was so soft that he almost didn't hear her.

Almost.

But those three small words drove a stake of fear through him.

"The stranger?" Stepping behind her, he looked out the window over her head.

Parked under a massive tree, trying to blend in with the abandoned cars in the overgrown field, was a black car he'd never noticed before.

He focused on the car. Dang. The driver's seat looked occupied. "Has he been out there for a while?"

"A long time. It's Uncle Richie."

"Naw. Uncle Richie knows better than to come here." He

ruffled her soft black hair. "It's probably just another one of those pesky reporters."

Yeah, sure. That seemed likely.

Maybe it was another reporter. Or maybe it was the Ripper, staking out the house to find the best way to break in and kill the only witness to his crimes. He tried to determine if the car was the same one the Ripper had driven, but he was too far away.

Only one way to find out for sure.

But could he really walk out there and confront the person in the car? Part of him wished Lana were here so he could borrow her gun.

Right. Like she'd even give it to him.

More likely he'd get a lecture about the dangers of a gun in untrained hands.

Besides, if she were here, she'd do something really dangerous – like confront the man herself. No, it was better if he handled this his way.

"Well, he's out there and we're in here. Let's go downstairs and not let this guy spoil our day, all right?"

Maria let him take her hand and lead her out of the room. When they reached the back door, he knelt. "Why don't you head outside and play with everyone else. I'll be there soon."

Rising, he turned to go but she wouldn't release his hand. "Where're you going?"

"To see what that guy wants."

She tugged his arm. "I don't want you to."

The look on her face just about killed his desire to confront the stranger, but it had to be done. Whoever that man was, he couldn't hang around the house and scare the kids. Paul wouldn't allow it.

Maybe he should call the cops.

But if it was another reporter, he'd look stupid. Really stupid.

And it probably was a reporter.

The chances of it being the Ripper rated up there with

being struck by lightning.

Kneeling back down, he pulled Maria into a hug. "Hey, it'll be okay. I just want to make him go away."

The arms squeezing his neck contained a surprising amount of strength for such a small child.

He leaned back and nodded at the door. "Now go on. You're missing all the fun."

She reluctantly released him, but made no move to join the other kids.

No point in pressing the issue. Paul left her in the hallway and strode for the front door.

Maria's dark eyes held his mind.

Most of his kids wouldn't get so freaked out by something like this, but the past abuse held Maria captive.

It didn't matter who the man in the black car was, how dare he come here and scare his kids! This was a place where society's throwaways were supposed to feel safe and that man had the nerve to intimidate? He ought to go out there and slam his fist into the jerk's face, teach him a thing or two about minding his own business–

Calm down.

He wasn't going to beat the man senseless, or probably even use any of the harsh words running through his mind right now. No, he would force himself to be firm and in control, and would ask the man to get lost.

Eyes focused on the black car, he stepped off the sidewalk and onto the street.

Still too far away to make out the car's model, but it appeared to be a Chevy. Dust created a film over the vehicle and the front license plate had been removed.

Which was illegal. He faltered.

There was no good reason for someone to remove their license plates. But there were plenty of bad ones.

An engine fired up and the car shot forward, jumped off the curb, and raced toward him.

He dove, his shoulder smacking the pavement.

The car zipped by him doing at least thirty, passing close enough that a wave of heat slapped him.

Gravel flung from the car's tires, smacking against his face and arms. Dust billowed in the air, making him cough, but he kept his gaze on the fleeing vehicle.

The smoked windows prevented him from getting a clear view of the driver. All he saw was a dark colored baseball cap pulled low over the driver's face.

Figured.

He watched the car until it rounded the corner. Had that been the Ripper?

Part of him wanted to say yes, but it seemed like the Ripper would've done more to try to kill him.

If that was an attempt to get rid of him, it'd been a pretty pathetic one. The car hadn't swerved toward him or anything.

It couldn't have been the Ripper. The Ripper wouldn't have run away so quickly.

But who else? A reporter would've stuck around for a story, especially since he'd made it so easy by walking straight for the car.

Brushing the dust from his torso made him cough some more.

Forget it. He needed to head inside and get cleaned up. He crossed the lawn and started up the steps.

Only then did he realize how his hands and legs shook.

What had he been thinking? He'd almost confronted someone who had possibly murdered multiple women in cold blood! Had he seriously thought that just because he wasn't a petite woman the man wouldn't attack him?

Sometimes he had more guts than brains.

Activity blurred the lobby of the police station as Lana

stepped inside. People came, went, filled out forms, and raised their voices. There had to be at least a dozen people sitting in the hard plastic chairs, waiting.

She crossed to the security door, showed her badge, and went through as the door buzzed open. The hallway beyond the door was significantly calmer.

According to the officer at the front, the last office on the left belonged to Arlington. She headed for it, nodding at the various officers she passed along the way. Voices filtered out of some of the offices on her left and the hum of myriad conversations drifted from the bullpen to her right.

Hopefully Arlington was in. Stopping had been a last minute decision and she hadn't called ahead.

"I don't care what you have to tell people, no one hears she's alive, got it?"

Arlington's voice came from the room ahead of her, his tone slowing her step.

Maybe she should've called ahead after all. He sounded like he was in one horrible mood.

But of course he was. A serial killer was on the loose, the bodies were piling up, and the only witness hadn't seen enough to lead to an arrest.

"Yeah, tell everyone she was in a car accident. You can say the stab wounds were caused by glass or metal or something. I don't want anyone knowing she's connected to this. And you make sure those EMT's don't go around flapping their lips either or there's gonna be trouble."

The phone wasn't exactly slammed down, but it wasn't replaced gently either.

Yikes. Hopefully she wasn't walking right into the line of fire.

"Detective Arlington?"

"WHAT?" He looked up at her and noticeably worked to calm down. "Look, I'm not tryin' to be rude, but I've got a lot goin' on right now."

"If I can take a few minutes of your time..."

His gusty sigh said he'd really rather not, but he glanced at his watch. "Five minutes. I'm timing you."

Taking the closest chair, she met Arlington's eyes. "I hear the Ripper struck again."

"Yeah. Sure wish your guy had caught a license plate number or something. Maybe we'd already have this butcher in custody."

"But his latest victim survived?"

An unidentifiable twinge flickered across Arlington's face. "The Ripper doesn't leave survivors."

"Nice try. I heard part of your conversation–"

Some of his earlier fury bubbled to the surface. "You eavesdropping on me?"

"Absolutely not. People three doors down from you heard the exact same thing I did."

He studied her, his expression stony, his eyes narrow. "What's your interest in all this anyway?"

"I told you before, it concerns a friend of mine, so it concerns me. It's as simple as that." She checked her watch. "My five minutes are almost up. Are you going to give me a straight answer or should I go check the hospital myself?"

"You're a royal pain in the neck, anyone ever tell you that?"

"I've heard it a few times, normally from my older brother." Leaning back, she settled in to wait.

"Fine, but this doesn't leave this office, got it? Don't care who it is, you don't tell no one." He waited for her to nod before continuing, "The Ripper went after another girl last night. Stabbed her 'bout a dozen times, but somehow missed all major arteries. Don't get me wrong, she's in pretty bad shape, but she's gonna pull through."

"And you're trying to keep her alive by letting the media and the Ripper think she's dead."

"Yeah. We released a press statement saying there'd been another victim, that her name was being withheld until we could notify next of kin. I'm hoping we can keep the media in the dark."

He didn't have to tell her that if the Ripper found out his victim had survived, he would stop at nothing to finish what he'd started. "So she's at the hospital, probably in ICU to control access to her, with a plainclothes officer guarding her at all times. How am I doing so far?"

The corners of Arlington's lips curled in a hint of a smile. "Not bad. You forgot that we're rotating guard detail between three officers and that they're all pretending to be family members."

"Of course they are. Has she been able to tell you anything?"

"Not so far. She's spent a lot of today in surgery or recovery. I'm hoping to get a statement tomorrow when she might be more lucid." Arlington laced his fingers behind his head and leaned back in his chair.

"Was there any new evidence at this scene?" Stupid question. Every crime scene had new evidence. "Something that might help ID this guy, I mean."

"Got quite a bit of skin from under her fingernails. Looks like she scratched him up pretty good. Maybe we'll get lucky and find a hit in CODIS."

Somehow she doubted it.

The Combined DNA Index System had provided suspects in numerous cases, but the suspect had to have his or her DNA on file for it to work. Her instincts told her that wouldn't be the case this time.

Maybe she was wrong. She hoped and prayed she was wrong.

"Well, now." Arlington made a point of looking at his watch. "Time's up. I've got work to do."

She stood. "Would it be all right if I went with you to question the victim? After what she's been through, she might be more comfortable opening up to another woman."

Arlington looked like he wanted to refuse, but held whatever arguments he had inside. Finally he nodded. "As long as we're clear about one thing: this is my case. I ask the questions, I lead the interview."

"I wouldn't expect anything less." Lana pulled her card out of her pocket and jotted her cell number on it. "This is the best way to reach me. If you want to call me before you head down there, I could meet you outside the ICU."

He stuffed the card in his pocket. "We're looking at first thing in the morning."

"See you then."

Twelve

"What happened?"

No matter how much Paul wished he could dodge Lana's perceptive eye, he had known such a wish was unlikely to happen. Two small cuts, one on his cheek and one on his forehead, beckoned like search lights and the scrape going down his arm looked worse than it actually was.

He offered a small shrug. "I hit the ground pretty hard earlier. No biggie."

Shapely black eyebrows lowered over serious dark eyes. "That sounds like an evasive half-answer."

"You hungry? I just pulled hot dogs off the grill."

"And now you're deflecting. Stop dodging the question and give me a straight answer. I'm not moving until you do." She crossed her arms over her chest. "What happened to you? Specifically?"

He sighed. "I was almost hit by a car."

"What do you mean, you were almost hit by a car?"

Where was Brittany when he needed her?

Not that any of the kids could get him out of this one. At best, they might buy him a brief reprieve, but no way would she let the matter drop.

"Maria saw an unfamiliar car parked across the street. It scared her. I went to confront the driver, but he took off in a hurry."

Tension boiled off her like steam off hot water. "And you thought the best plan was to do this yourself? What if it had been the Ripper?"

"What was I supposed to do? Call the police and ask them to check out what might be nothing?"

"Yes! That's part of their job." She hauled in a long breath. "Did it look like the Ripper's car?"

He wanted to say no, but couldn't bring himself to do it. "Maybe."

"I can't believe you'd be so reckless. What if it was him? He could've killed you."

"He was scaring the kids."

"And you being murdered right across the street wouldn't?"

"I couldn't just let it go."

"He got rid of the bad man." Maria's quiet voice sounded seconds before her small arms wrapped around his leg.

"Hi, Maria." Lana knelt at Maria's level, but didn't approach.

Maria turned her head, giving Lana that shy smile that was reserved for people who were working their way onto Maria's good list. It took a long time for any adult to earn Maria's trust, but Lana seemed to be getting close.

"You mentioned the bad man. Do you know who he is, Maria?"

Several seconds of silence passed before Maria finally answered, her voice so low he wondered if Lana could even hear it. "Maybe Uncle Richie. He was there for a long time and wouldn't leave."

"Have you seen that man before?"

Maria bit her lip and slowly nodded.

"When?"

"A few days ago. He was in a car."

The smile Lana gave Maria looked forced, but he doubted Maria would notice. "Thank you. Mmm, is that hot dogs I smell?"

That finally brought Maria around. "I'm hungry."

"Well, you'd better go get some dinner then." Paul watched her run off and wished he could go after her.

The hot dogs had been Lana's version of a distraction. Too bad it worked.

"When were you going to tell me that a black car was hanging around your place?"

The irritation in her tone cautioned him to step carefully. "Uh..."

"Unbelievable." She shook her head. "You weren't going to tell me, were you?"

"Honestly?"

"This isn't just about you! Other people could get caught in the crossfire."

"I know, I know. But that was the first time I saw the car. Maria told me a few nights ago she'd seen a man in a car, but I wasn't sure how seriously to take her."

"Fine. But you still should've known better than to try to confront him on your own. You knew I was coming. You should've waited."

His own anger surged to the surface. "And throw you into the middle of this? No way. You promised to stay out of it and I'm not going to do anything to make you break that promise. What's with the third degree, anyway?"

The irritation drained from her face and she let out a slow breath. "Sorry. It's been a stressful couple of days at work and then I come here and step into all this."

"Yeah? Well, you're not the only one who's stressed."

"Maria mentioned an Uncle... was it Ricky?"

"Richie. I haven't told you about him?"

"No. Any chance it was him?"

"I doubt it. There's no reason why he would be hanging around here. The state was pretty final when they removed Maria from her family's care."

"Next time, call the police. Let Arlington do his job."

"I wasn't thinking clearly, okay? All I wanted was to get

that guy away from here."

She still didn't look pleased. What had happened at work to put her in such a bad mood?

"Look, if he comes back, I promise I'll call the police immediately and stay indoors where it's safe."

"And away from all the windows."

"Far away. Trust me, I'm not trying to get myself killed."

Maybe it was his placating tone or maybe she caught something on his face, but her eyes slid shut for a moment. When she opened them, they were markedly softer. "I'm sorry. Like I said, it's been a rough couple of days, but that doesn't mean I should take it out on you."

"No biggie. You probably needed to let it out, anyway."

"So. Other than having me show up and yell at you, is everything okay here?"

"Yeah. It's been weird not having Austin around, but I think the kids did a better job of accepting it than I have. I hate to say it, but things are a whole lot smoother without him here."

"He'd been giving you trouble?"

She was beginning to sound more like the Lana he'd always known.

Good thing, too – he didn't know how to handle the stressed out, bite-your-head-off Lana that had walked through his door tonight.

"He didn't mean to, but when you have a kid that frequently breaks the rules, it affects everyone. Not to mention that I was afraid his buddies would try to jump some of my other kids into their gang. I'm really glad to not have the bangers hanging around any longer."

"Have you gotten to talk to him at all?"

"Not much. I visited with him once and was at his arraignment, but with all that's been going on I haven't made it back down there." But he really needed to make a point to do it. The poor kid had to be scared. The least Paul could do was let Austin know he loved him and that he wasn't going to go through this alone.

"How'd the arraignment go?"

"As expected. He's gonna be tried as an adult and the public defender's already angling for a plea deal." Enough about Austin. He paused for only a second before asking a question to which he didn't expect much of an answer. "So why're you so stressed?"

The hesitation on her face said it all. There were so many things she couldn't talk about that it was a small wonder he knew anything about her at all.

Still, she tried, he had to give her that.

"I–It's mostly my workload. There are a few cases that are really pushing my buttons. There's also this..." She pinched her lips shut for a second before continuing, "Yeah, that's about it. Sorry. You know I can't really talk about it, but thanks for asking."

She was holding something back. Whether she couldn't talk about it or simply *wouldn't*, he didn't know, but clearly her guard was up about something.

Caring about a US Marshal wasn't easy.

Loving one was even harder.

He forced a light tone. "Hey, no problem. Long as you know I'm here if you need me."

A small smile touched her lips. "And sometimes knowing that is enough."

His rumbling stomach reminded him that he'd been on the way to eat dinner when she'd arrived. "Let's grab a few hot dogs. We can talk more after we eat."

"'Bout time you got here." Arlington stopped pacing and speared her with his eyes.

Arching an eyebrow, Lana glanced at her watch. "You only

called me twenty minutes ago. Really, I made excellent time."

His scowl softened. "I guess I've only been here about five minutes myself. I'm just not sure how long she'll be up with all those drugs in her system."

Probably not long. "Well, let's get in there."

A nod at the nurse inside got them buzzed through the security door. Lana waited until the door closed behind her to ask, "Is she in ICU because she needs to be or just because it's the most controlled wing in the building?"

"Little of both. She was in bad shape when they brought her in. She's doing better, but I told 'em to keep her here. Easier to protect that way."

"Smart move." No matter how hard Arlington tried, eventually news of this magnitude would leak and the media would be all over it.

And once the press knew, everyone would know. Including the Ripper.

He stopped outside the third door on the right and turned to her, examining her face for a moment. "I'm thinkin' you oughtta take the lead on this. After what she's been through, she might respond better to you."

A smile threatened, but she forced herself to remain stoic. His words mimicked what she'd said last night.

But of course now, he passed the idea off as his own.

She didn't mind, not really. It felt good to be included in this case, especially since she had no jurisdiction.

Yet.

This victim would likely be going into protective custody until they caught the Ripper, which meant the Marshals would be getting involved very soon.

Lana led the way into the room.

A man sitting inside the door rose as they entered, a small Ruger cradled in his hand. He visibly relaxed as Arlington stepped in behind her and nodded at them before returning to his seat.

Arlington closed the door behind them.

Moving further into the room, Lana approached the lone bed, which swallowed the petite woman on it. Dark brown hair framed a colorless face and fear haunted the woman's large hazel eyes.

The television ran softly in the background, the volume too low for her to discern what was on.

In spite of what he'd said, Arlington spoke first.

"Ms. Bishop, I'm Detective Arlington and this is Deputy Tanner." Soothing as a hot bath, his tone surprised her.

Who knew he had that in him? It sounded unlike anything she'd heard from him before.

Bishop stared at them, eyes unblinking, unregistering. A large scrape marred her left cheek and a plum-like bruise colored her forehead.

Movements slow, Lana gently touched Bishop's hand. "How are you doing?"

The mask crumbled.

"H-how do you think I'm doing?" Tears spilled from Bishop's eyes, cutting wet arcs down her cheeks. She cried for several minutes, unable to form words, before fighting the tide to gain control. "I–I'm sorry. I know you n–need–"

"Take your time." Arlington rounded the bed and sat in the chair in the corner.

Taking the tissue Lana handed her, Bishop blew her nose and rested her head back against the pillow.

"I'll help any way I can." Bishop's soft voice shook and testified to the exhaustion clearly visible on her face.

While Arlington got out a recorder, notepad, and pen, Lana pulled a chair close to the bed. Using her gentlest tone, she tried to coax the story out of the injured woman. "Ms. Bishop, why don't you tell us what happened. Take all the time you need."

Fresh tears glimmered in Bishop's eyes and she swallowed hard. "Felicity. My name's Felicity."

"Okay, Felicity, how about if you start from when you first saw him."

"It–it was at the coffee shop. I get a triple shot every morning and last week, the guy behind me started talking."

Arlington glanced up from his notes. "What did he say?"

"I–I don't remember. It was just small talk."

"He didn't tell you his name?"

Felicity's hair brushed her cheeks as she gave her head a small shake.

"Was that the first time you'd seen this man?" Lana asked.

"I think so. And I didn't see him again until last night. It took–" Felicity's voice broke on a sob and she swiped at her cheeks. "I didn't know who he was at first. But then I realized it was the guy from the coffee shop. I don't know why he–"

The battle for control ended. Tears poured from her eyes, drenching her cheeks.

Lana handed her another tissue and adopted a soothing murmur. "It's okay. There's no way he can get you in here. You're safe."

"He said we had a co-connection. That we clicked." Swiping the tissue across her cheeks, she focused drenched eyes on Lana. "Ana, he called me Ana."

Ana?

Lana stared at Felicity for a few seconds. Why had the Ripper called her Ana?

Something told her this was significant, but what did it mean?

Felicity's tears subsided. Her face slackened and her eyes took on a slightly glazed look.

"Does the name Ana mean anything to you? Your middle name or anything?"

"No."

"Did he say anything else that was weird?"

If Felicity heard Lana's question, she ignored it. Eyes focused on the wall straight ahead of her, Felicity's voice took on a detached tone. "There was a box on my porch. It looked like a baby. I went to check and he forced his way in. He–he had his hand over my mouth. I bit him and he got really mad.

I don't remember anything else until I woke up in the car."

The almost mechanical way Felicity spoke concerned Lana, but she recognized it as a coping mechanism. As long as Felicity didn't shut down altogether, this might work. "Do you remember anything about the car? Anything that might help us identify it?"

"The windows were dark. There was a rip in my seat."

Not exactly the concrete details she'd hoped to hear, but that wasn't surprising. "You're doing great. Can you tell us anything else?"

"I pretended to be dead. I remember pain, but then nothing. It was weird. I could hear him breathing, hear the knife-" A few stray tears slipped out and Felicity released a shuddery breath. "Sirens, I remember sirens. And he pulled out my hair."

Standing, Lana followed the hand Felicity lifted limply. In spite of the surrounding hair covering it, she had no trouble seeing the bald patch above Felicity's left ear.

Definitely the Ripper.

If she'd had any doubt - which she hadn't - the missing clump of hair would've banished it.

All that remained was to get a description. Lana didn't want to ask the question; it would force Felicity to focus on her memories of the attack.

Like Felicity needed any help doing that. The attack likely consumed all her thoughts.

But no matter how much she dreaded doing it, Lana had to ask. "Can you describe this man?"

Felicity's eyes reddened and she blinked rapidly. Four times. "I-I…"

Placing her hand over Felicity's, Lana tried to stem the coming tide. "It's okay. You're safe."

Tears flowed anyway. A choked sob ripped from Felicity's throat. The pitiful sound filled the room, drowned out the TV, and Lana's heart cramped at the pain and fear contained in the tears.

There must be something she could do to help. Some way to offer comfort.

She'd never been very good at the touchy-feely stuff.

Too bad Alex wasn't here.

Lana closed her eyes and breathed a silent prayer, then looked at the suffering woman in front of her.

Hesitating briefly, she stood, gently reached for her and offered an awkward hug. It must've hurt like crazy, but Felicity straightened, wrapped her arms around Lana, and cried with body-shaking sobs.

Tears burned like acid behind Lana's eyes, but she couldn't let them out. If she started crying, they'd both be lost.

Instead she forced her anger to the surface.

The Ripper may not have killed Felicity, but he'd destroyed her life. How long until Felicity would be able to be alone without fear? How long until she could even go back to her own home?

The Ripper had to be stopped, no matter what, and if Lana could do something to prevent this from happening to another woman, she would.

The anger dissipated and a prayer for Felicity bubbled to the surface. Followed by another. As Lana stroked Felicity's dirty, matted hair, she closed her eyes and prayed.

For safety. For solace. For peace.

Most of all, that somehow, some way, God would use this situation, horrible as it was, to bring Felicity to Himself. That she would find her security and shelter in the One who had given His life out of love for her.

How long they stayed like that before Felicity's tears lessened and she released her stranglehold was beyond Lana, but finally the other woman sat back, face red and blotchy, eyes bloodshot, but once again in control. Lana eased into her chair.

Felicity shook her head. "I'm sorry. I'm such a mess–"

"Don't be so hard on yourself. After what you've been through, you're allowed to be upset."

"Yeah," Arlington chimed in. "You were attacked by the Ripper. It's a miracle you're not dead."

What the heck? Where was the gentle tone from earlier?

Arlington must've skipped the sensitivity training.

The glare she shot him made him quickly look away. Lana took a deep breath and masked her anger before turning back to Felicity.

How could a *detective* be so stupid? It's not like the guy was a rookie.

Until now, no one had mentioned the Ripper.

The idea might've crossed Felicity's mind, but even if it had, she'd probably convinced herself that she was jumping to conclusions.

Felicity's eyes were dinner plates on her face, which held the ghostly hue of fine china. "I thought it was him. I asked him. He said not to believe everything I'd heard."

Arlington leaned forward, but didn't move closer. "Did he say anything else?"

"He said they had it all wrong. The police or media or something."

The tears started again, different from before. They trickled out of unblinking eyes one at a time, leaving fat wet trails on her face. Felicity didn't make a sound, didn't reach to dry her face, didn't move.

Several moments passed before she blinked three times in rapid succession.

Felicity's voice was little more than a whisper. "He's done this to other women. How many others are there like me?"

Drawing a breath, Lana hesitated. "You're the first to survive."

"So I guess I'm the lucky one." A harsh sound escaped Felicity's lips that could have been half laugh, half cry. Felicity sniffled and wiped a few more tears. "I'll do whatever I can to help."

"Can you describe him?" Lana asked again.

Hopefully Felicity would be able to answer the question

this time.

A shaky breath slipped out. "He was a little taller than me, but not by much. And skinny. Very skinny."

"How tall are you?"

"Five-four."

"You said he was a little taller. One inch, two, more?"

Felicity leaned her head back against the pillow, her dazed eyes fixed on Lana. "I dunno. Maybe four inches? I'm not really good at this sort of thing."

"That's okay. You're doing great."

Arlington's pen scrawled across the notepad. "What about facial features? Hair, eyes, that kind of thing."

"Um, I... I don't know. It was dark. He wore a baseball cap and I didn't see his eyes or hair or anything."

"I'd like to send in a sketch artist. See if you can give us a picture of the guy." Gentleness laced Arlington's tone once again.

Biting her lower lip, Felicity nodded.

Tears glistened in her cherry-red eyes, but none made their way down her cheeks.

"Do you remember anything else? Anything between the first time you met him and now that seems odd?" Lana hated to ask, but there might be something that Felicity hadn't mentioned, maybe hadn't even thought was important.

"Well, there was this one time when I thought I was being followed. But I sometimes have an overactive imagination."

Followed?

Lana exchanged a look with Arlington before focusing on Felicity once again. "When was this exactly?"

"Last Friday. After work. It was a black car and made every move I did. I got nervous, pulled into a mall parking lot, and it followed me. But when I got out of my car and looked at it, it went on by."

Arlington scribbled on the notepad concealed in his large hand. "Was that guy driving?"

"It went by too fast. I didn't see the driver."

The door opened behind Lana and she turned to find a nurse approaching. "I'm going to have to ask you folks to leave now. Felicity needs her rest."

"We were done anyway." A curt nod accompanied Arlington's words.

Lana pulled a card from her pocket.

Jotting her cell number on the back, she handed it to Felicity. "If you need to talk, you call me, okay? Any time, day or night, even if you just want to hear someone's voice, don't hesitate to call."

Lips mouthing "thank you," Felicity took the card and set it on the table next to the bed.

Lana turned, following Arlington into the hall. The plainclothes police officer nodded at them from his post next to the door as they passed, but she barely noticed.

A part of Felicity had died last night, the part that believed in safety, the part that trusted people.

The Ripper had taken another life, although this time he'd trapped his victim in a living hell.

Thirteen

The security door opened easily from this side and Lana stepped through, Arlington right behind her.

"Where's her family? Doesn't she have anyone who can help her deal with this?"

Arlington shook his head. "Nah. Folks died several years back. She's got a brother out west somewhere, but I guess they don't really talk much. I left him a message yesterday but so far he hasn't called me back."

"Close friends, coworkers, boyfriend, anyone we can call? She really shouldn't be alone right now."

"She's not alone. She's got one of my best plainclothes–"

"Yeah, you're right. She has a plainclothes officer in her room, a man doing his job for what, six hours, when he's replaced by another plainclothes officer who's doing his job. It's not the same." A measured breath eased through her lips. "You didn't have any sisters, did you?"

Studying her face for a second, Arlington pulled out his phone and made a call. "Smitty, do me a favor, okay? Ask her if there's anyone she'd like us to call and call me back." He listened for a minute. "Fine, as soon as you get the chance."

He ended the call and focused his sharp eyes on her. "Soon as the nurse is done looking her over, Smitty'll check on that and get back to me."

The tone was one he might use to placate a petulant child,

but she'd take it. "Thank you."

Stuffing his hands in his pockets, Arlington leaned against the wall. "What're your thoughts on all this?"

Lana arched an eyebrow. "What, you're interested in collaborating all of a sudden?"

A wry grin twisted his lips. "With a Fed? You kiddin' me?"

"Just making sure you weren't going soft."

"At this point, I'm willing to accept all the help I can get. I wanna catch this guy before he does that–" He jerked his head toward the ICU, "–to anyone else."

"I hear you."

"'Sides, you ain't too bad for a Fed. And you did good work back there."

Anything else Lana might've said caught in her throat as an older couple walked by carrying a large vase of daffodils.

What was she thinking? They couldn't discuss the case here, out in the open where anyone and everyone could overhear. A glance at Arlington told her the same thought had gone through his mind.

"Let's grab some coffee," he suggested, his tone as casual as if they were discussing the weather rather than a serial killer.

They took the elevator down to the first floor and headed for the cafeteria, which was surprisingly empty. The coffee looked like liquid asphalt and Lana opted for a bottle of peach mango juice instead.

She followed Arlington to a table in the far corner of the room and pulled out the chair across from him.

He nodded at her juice. "Not a coffee drinker, huh?"

"Not when it looks like road sludge." She eyed his cup suspiciously. "I make it a point to avoid cafeteria coffee." Or anything made by Alex.

"It's not normally too bad." To prove his point, he took a swig of the black liquid. A grimace that he wasn't completely able to hide crossed his face. "Although this might be enough to change my mind."

He pushed the cup away and rested his elbows on the

table. "Hopefully we'll get an updated sketch circulating by the end of the day."

The case loomed in her mind as she shifted into work mode. "He's changed his MO. Felicity's lighter. Brown hair, not black. White, not Hispanic.

"You caught that too, huh?"

Lana nodded. "She remembered hearing the sirens. Who called it in? Another witness?"

"Nah. The sirens were headed to a DV call a few blocks away. The officers at the scene called in backup and the responding officers almost ran over her on their way there."

Which still left Paul as their only other witness.

Dwelling on that thought was much too troubling. "It also sounds like the Ripper thinks he's developed some sort of relationship with these women–"

"And kills them when they reject him," Arlington finished for her.

"So what's next?"

"Guess I'll have to throw this to the Feds and see what they do with that profile. Gotta tell you, I hated bringing them on board, but it wasn't my call. I think that profile stuff is a load of–" He caught himself. "Uh, a poor substitute for real police work."

"I'd think you'd be game for anything at this point. Besides, profiles can help narrow the suspect pool."

"S'pose you're right. Guess I'm old school."

Lana took a drink of juice and set the bottle down to find Arlington looking at her, his cop mask in place.

The bland expression concealed a man whose thoughts moved faster than light. But what was he thinking? And why hide it from her when they were having such a frank discussion?

No point in asking what was on his mind – he wouldn't tell her, not if he was anything like her or any of the other members of law enforcement she knew. Aside from that, this wasn't her case, a fact she needed to keep at the front of her mind.

That knowledge didn't stop her from voicing her thoughts. "What we need is a way to draw him out. Trap him."

He didn't move, just stared at her with those unblinking blue eyes that sliced right through her. "What we really need is live bait."

"That only works if you know where to find him."

"I'm thinking we leak that his last victim survived. Our guy shows up at her house, finds a woman there that looks like her, and figures it is her. Course it'll be one of our people instead, but he won't know that."

"And when he goes after her, your people move in. Now the only problem is finding someone who looks like Felicity."

Arlington tapped his fingers on the table. "Got that one covered. There's an officer working white collar that I think could stand in for her. Her hair looks different but that's no biggie."

"She'll have to be convincing. Something tells me the Ripper knows his victims pretty well."

"Won't let the guy get that close. We'll nail him before he can see it's the wrong lady." He leaned back in his chair. "If you got a better plan, I'm open. Waiting for him to choose his next victim ain't an option."

Arlington was right. Time to take a proactive approach to the investigation.

Speaking of time... Lana checked her watch. "I need to get going. I have a job of my own to do."

"I was beginning to think you Feds were only good at pokin' your noses into police business." Serious tone, but a twitch at the corner of his mouth gave him away.

"Depends on the badge." She sobered. "Thanks for letting me come along. I'd like to see that sketch once you have it."

"I suppose I could give you a call. I'll need to show it to your guy anyway." He downed the last of his coffee and stood.

Arlington's phone rang as they stepped out of the cafeteria.

After several short phrases, he terminated the call. "That was my guy upstairs. Felicity wants us to call some friend from work. Thought you'd wanna know."

At least Felicity wouldn't have to go through all this alone. Lana nodded. "Thanks. She needs a friendly face right now."

Lana headed for her car, her mind full of what the Ripper had done. Slides flashed through her brain, images of the women the Ripper had attacked.

Bloody.

Terrified.

Dead.

This plan had to work. He had to be stopped before he claimed another victim.

"Any luck on Templing's ex-wife?"

Lana looked up as Alex perched on the corner of the desk. "Do you have any idea how many Sally Greens there are in this city? And what if she moved out of town? That opens up a whole new list to work through."

"Sounds like I got the better end of the bargain. I found out that Templing reported about seventy-five thousand last year, with his occupation filed under private security."

Security?

If he was the Ripper, that could be how he found his victims. Security guards were paid to notice people without drawing attention to themselves. That could also explain why no one seemed to have noticed him.

Wait, did Alex say seventy-five thousand?

"That's a lot of money for a security job. He's not just watching monitors at the local mall."

A shrug lifted Alex's shoulders. "I'm guessing he works for a paranoid person who has entirely too much money. Or maybe some crime boss. Could even be a hit man for the mafia."

"None of which helps us find him." Lana opened a new window on her computer screen. "Which brings us back to his ex. I think I'll double check public records. Maybe the divorce record will include her middle name or some other identifier."

"That's a good place to start."

A glance at her watch revealed it was later than she'd thought. "It'll have to be a good place to start later. I'm meeting with Bright before he takes the stand."

Alex stuck out her tongue. "Sure glad I didn't get stuck with that loser, but I'm sorry it had to be you."

"I just keep reminding myself that I'm almost done with him. By this time next week, he'll no longer be my problem."

Paul glanced at the flashing readout on his answering machine as it changed from nine to ten.

The press was relentless. The way they constantly hounded him for an interview made him want to disconnect his phone just to make it stop.

It's not like he'd been anywhere near the murder last night, but no other witnesses had come forward. Looked like the press would continue to make his life miserable until someone better popped up.

A rap on his office door brought his eyes up. "Come in."

The door opened and Jason Pool poked his head in. "Got a minute?"

"Sure, come on in."

Jason pushed the door open and let Stefani precede him into the room. Serious expressions covered both their faces and Paul's breath thickened.

Had they finally chosen a child? They'd long since fulfilled all the requirements.

In addition to all the government regulations, Paul also insisted that any prospective parents volunteered in his home at least three times before they could officially adopt one of his kids.

While the unorthodox method had turned a few people away, most embraced the idea. It not only gave the parents a chance to get to know the children before adopting one, it gave him a chance to get a feel for what the parents were like. All his kids were special to him; he had to know that they were going to a home where they would be well cared for and, most importantly, loved.

It had been almost two months since the Pools had first approached him and they still hadn't adopted a child. They continued to volunteer, coming over several times a week, stopping by his office to discuss specific children at least once a week.

Leaning back in his chair, Paul crossed his ankle over his knee. "Made a decision?"

Jason exchanged a look with Stefani before returning his attention to Paul. "We can't choose."

"We never thought this'd be so hard," Stefani explained. "We've even talked about adopting several. I mean, we have two extra rooms in our house–"

"And could turn my study into a third if we wanted–"

"–but how do we tell the others that we don't want them?" Stefani's voice choked off and she touched her fingers to her lips as she struggled for composure. "I can't do that."

Paul leaned forward and rested his elbows on his desk. "Don't think about the other kids. If you could choose without any of the kids knowing, who would you pick?"

They exchanged another glance before Jason answered. "We have it narrowed down to two and honestly, we'd probably adopt them both. Andy and Maria."

"Maria?"

The question slipped out before Paul could stop it. Andy

was a talkative kid with big dimples so that choice didn't surprise him, but he'd never expected Maria's name to come up. A part of him had believed she'd be with him forever. Well, until she grew up, got a job, and moved out, anyway.

Stefani nodded, blinking tears from her eyes. "She's the most precious little thing I've ever seen. And when she told me about Uncle Richie-"

"Wait, she told you about that?"

Hesitation appeared on Stefani's face and she took her time answering. "Well, yeah. I, uh, I mean... wasn't she supposed to?"

Way to go.

Now they'd know Maria wasn't just an abandoned child. Now he'd have to tell them the truth. Now he'd probably ruined Maria's chances of having a normal family life with parents who loved her.

He sighed. "I'm surprised, that's all. She hardly talks about him to anyone but me."

"She's really scared of him. She thinks he's been hanging around and is going to take her away."

Part of him hurt to no longer be Maria's only confidant, but he forced the jealousy aside to focus on more important issues. "I know. I've tried telling her that Richie's long gone, but he really left his mark. She'll probably be afraid of him her entire life."

"Who was he?" Jason asked, abstractly tapping his fingers on his knees.

"Someone Maria lived with before she came here. From everything I've heard, he was very abusive."

How much should he tell them?

He didn't want to wreck Maria's chances of being spoiled by these two loving, wealthy people, but he also couldn't let them adopt her without knowing the truth.

Swallowing hard, he pushed through what he had to say. "Out of all my kids, she carries the most baggage. She was shuffled around between family members and it seems like each house was worse than the one before.

"You should've seen her when she first came here. She didn't talk to anyone, wouldn't let any of the adults touch her, cried if we turned the lights out. She's come a long way since then, but there's still a lot of damage."

Stefani and Jason exchanged an uneasy look and Paul cut it short. "Look, I'm not trying to talk you out of picking Maria, although the selfish side of me doesn't want to give her up. But I can't let you adopt her without knowing exactly what you're getting yourself into. It wouldn't be fair to you or to her. The fact that she told you about Uncle Richie tells me that she trusts you. With Maria, that's huge. It took her almost three months to open up to me."

"What happened to her parents?" Stefani's eyes glittered with tears.

"A car accident. From what I hear, they were good people, nothing like the rest of the family. She was only two when they died and doesn't really remember them."

What she did remember was the many homes she lived in after that. He knew little about that time in her life. A few of the details he did know had come from Maria, but most came from CPS. None of them were good.

Focus. The past was gone, but the future remained.

Paul forced his attention to the Pools as Jason began to speak.

"What can you tell us about her family?"

"They're a bunch of..." He pressed his lips together and inhaled deeply before continuing, "She bounced around a lot. Sounds like most of them were involved in criminal activities of some sort. Drug dealing, prostitution, and I don't even know what else. I do know that when CPS removed her from the home, she'd been sleeping on the floor in a closet."

Lips parted, Stefani stared at him. "And there wasn't anyone decent in her family who could take care of her?"

"I guess not." Paul folded his hands on the desk in front of him. "But she's a great kid and with a lot of love she'll be fine.

She's just going to be a little higher maintenance than any of the others."

"I-I think we need more time." Stefani's face was a shade paler than it had been a minute ago.

"I understand."

Jason cleared his throat. "Thank you for being so candid. We didn't know-"

"It doesn't mean we won't choose her, but it's good to know about her past. Is there anything we should know about Andy?" Apprehension colored Stefani's eyes as though she didn't want to hear the answer.

"No. His mother died during childbirth and his father was arrested six months ago for drug trafficking. No history of abuse that I know of." Not to mention that Andy didn't act abused, which was always the surest sign.

"I'm sorry it's taking us so long." A shaky smile crossed Stefani's lips. "I want to take them all home."

"You do that and I'm out of a job."

"That, uh, that's actually something else we wanted to talk to you about."

Paul blinked at Jason's words.

"Stef and I have also talked about doing something like this-" Jason gestured to the room around them, "-ourselves. Helping you here has been great and as much trouble as we've had deciding, we've wondered if maybe God wasn't calling us to open a home of our own. We've actually already completed the required classes to become foster parents."

Wow. He hadn't seen that coming.

Paul searched for words, but Jason wasn't finished.

"We'd sell our house and get a bigger one. I could do a lot of my work from home so I'd be around to help."

"Uh, that's great. You guys would be awesome at something like this, but just really think it through. Do your research first."

"We have been. And we were also thinking that if you ever needed to get away, maybe we could step in for you. You know, give it a trial run to see how we liked the responsibilities twenty-four seven."

Stefani's words practically ran over her husband's. "Like if you wanted a vacation or if you and Lana…" She snapped her lips shut.

The answer probably wasn't one he wanted to hear, but he had to ask. "What about me and Lana?"

Cheeks the color of a rose in bloom, Stefani focused on her hands. "Oh, you know, if you guys…" Her eyes wandered the room before focusing directly on him. "If you ever got married."

"It's not like that with us."

A slow smile spread on Jason's face. "Whatever you say, man."

For crying out loud, did the whole world know?

"Well, thanks for offering, but I don't think you guys'll have to worry about filling in for me anytime soon."

"There's also this whole…" Jason hesitated.

Uh-oh. This didn't sound good either. "What?"

"Ripper thing." Jason leaned forward, an intense expression covering his face. "If you had to go into witness protection or something, we want you to know we're here for the kids."

For several long seconds, Paul had no idea what to say.

It was amazing, mind blowing. Never had he imagined someone would offer to step in for him if he ever needed it.

But with the amazement came a sense of dread.

He hadn't been a Christian long, but he could tell this was God's doing. Was God trying to prepare him for something?

Like losing his kids. Or maybe even his life.

Who said it had to be a bad thing? Maybe this was God's way of opening the door to more with Lana. God knew how much he wanted that.

Not likely. Lana deserved someone whose past wasn't so tarnished.

Or maybe this was a subtle push for him to tell the truth.

Maybe it was time to bring his past out in the open.

No, he couldn't.

God wouldn't ask him to do that.

It would destroy everything. Lana's trust in him, the relationship he shared with his kids; everything he held dear would be ruined because of sins that would be better off left buried.

Which brought him back to losing his kids or his life.

The idea paralyzed him. Dying he could handle, but he didn't know what he'd do if anything happened to one of his kids.

Who of you by worrying can add a day to his life?

Man, that verse got him every time. And God had a habit of bringing it to mind exactly when he needed it.

Stefani's voice snapped him back. "Not that we're trying to get rid of you or anything."

"Yeah. We just thought it'd take a load off your mind to know you have options," Jason added.

"Thanks. You guys have no idea how much that means to me."

Jason stood to go. "I'm sure you've got work to do. Is it okay if we come by tomorrow afternoon?"

"It's not like we'll have decided, but we want to spend time with the kids." Stefani's words were a heater to his heart. It was good to know that someone besides him and the Webbers wanted to invest in these kids.

"You guys are welcome any time. The kids all think you're great."

He watched Jason and Stefani leave, already dreading the day when they'd walk through that door for the last time. But sooner or later they'd decide and would take at least one of his kids with them.

Over the last year, he'd said goodbye to several kids and it never got any easier. But if they took Maria, well, that would hit him harder than anyone else.

A noise at the door drew his attention.

Maria peeked into the office, her face pressed against the doorjamb. It didn't take a degree in child psychology to see something was wrong. Wide eyes stared at him, her lower lip quivered, and her small hand formed a fist at her side.

He set his pen down and forced a light tone. "Hey, kiddo. What's up?"

The dark eyes and troubled face gave no indication she'd heard him. She stared at him silently for several seconds before stepping into the room. "Uncle Richie. He's back."

"Uncle Richie's gone. He's not going to get you, ever." At least not as long as Paul was around.

"I saw him. Across the street. In the car."

Air caught in his throat and for a second he forgot how to breathe.

The car was back.

"Now?" He barely waited for the small nod before pushing away from his desk. "Can you show me?"

Reaching the doorway, he took her offered hand and let himself be led down the hall, up the stairs, and to Maria's room. She stopped in front of the window and surveyed the street below in silence.

The lifeless lot across the street contained the same junk it always had. No sign of the black car.

For that matter, there wasn't a black car within sight, not anywhere on the street. Could Maria have made it up? Why would she?

"I don't see him. Is he still there?"

Silence ensued for a moment before she shook her head. "I think he's hiding now."

Okay, time to put an end to this Uncle Richie nonsense.

"Maria." He knelt beside her and waited for her to look at him. "I know Uncle Richie's a bad man, but he's also a coward. He won't come here."

"B–but what if he does?"

The tears pooled in her eyes made him want to hunt Uncle Richie down and torture him. Slowly.

He locked his emotions away before she could see them and concentrated on reassuring her. "He won't hurt you anymore. I won't let him."

"What if he hurts you?"

"He won't."

Richie didn't scare him in the least. He'd found that many people who abused small children were cowards who would never consider challenging an adult, not that Maria could understand that at her age.

Maybe he could put it in a way she would understand. He'd never seen Richie, but he was guessing that Richie was a smaller man, probably someone who'd been bullied himself over the years. "I'm bigger than Uncle Richie, aren't I?"

She wiped at her tears. "Yeah."

"So he wouldn't try to hurt me because I can hurt him back. He'd be scared of me."

He watched Maria's face closely. It looked like she believed him.

"Besides, I don't think it was Uncle Richie in that car. Remember, I went out to talk to him? It didn't look like Uncle Richie to me."

Any of his older kids would've pointed out that he wouldn't know Uncle Richie if he ran over him, but Maria was young enough that such a thought would probably never occur to her. The tension leaked from her body.

"Then who was that man?"

He gave her the same answer as before. "I think it's another reporter. They sure are pests, aren't they?"

"Pests," she repeated, her tone as solemn as ever.

It seared his heart to see a child so somber, so full of fear and sadness.

Would this poor girl ever get to feel like a kid? Her six-year-old eyes already held a lifetime's worth of sorrow. Laughter was a rarity. The smiles, while more frequent than they used to be, contained a knowledge children were never meant to have.

Much as he'd miss her, he hoped the Pools would adopt Maria. Maybe settled in a real home, with parents who loved her, she could finally start acting like other kids her age.

If he could, he'd adopt her, but it wouldn't work out, not as long as he ran this home. Besides, as much as Maria loved him, he wasn't enough. Not on his own. She needed parents – plural – not just a father.

Given the way he felt about Lana, well, he wouldn't be getting married anytime soon. He wasn't interested in anyone but her and he couldn't tell her how he felt.

Not now. And probably not ever.

The man rubbed his damp forehead with a shaking hand. Fries sat in the fast food bag on the passenger seat and a half eaten hamburger cooled on the center console but he couldn't take another bite.

He'd just heard the news. The impossible, unbelievable, horrible news.

The woman had survived.

How?

He didn't know how many times he'd stabbed her, but it had been a lot. More than enough to kill her. Yet somehow she'd lived. And was going home tomorrow.

Maybe the cops were lying.

Yeah, that had to be it. Probably a lame attempt to draw him out.

This was a trick to get him to screw up so they could ruin his life. Well, he wasn't falling for it.

But what if she had lived? She'd describe him to the police and he'd spend the rest of his life alone.

Then again, that witness had described him and the sketch looked nothing like him.

So let her talk.

She didn't know his name or anything else that might help the police track him down.

And if the police thought he'd return to her house to finish her off, they were wrong. Only an idiot would fall for a ploy like that.

He started the car, shifted into drive, and pulled into traffic.

The woman consumed his thoughts no matter how hard he tried to block her out. Part of him did want to track her down. Rub her nose in what she was missing. She'd had her chance with him and she blew it. Her loss. There were other women out there, ones who would appreciate his attention.

He'd find someone to fill the gaping hole Ana had left in his life. Or die trying.

Fourteen

Come on. Pick up.

Lana tapped her fingers on the desk with one hand, held the phone to her ear with the other.

"Hello?" The soft, cultured voice conjured up an image of a classic southern belle.

"Hi, is this Sally?"

"It is."

"Sally Templing?"

"Who is this?"

The sudden ice in the woman's tone chilled Lana through the phone. "Deputy Milana Tanner. I'm with the US Marshal's office."

The silence on the phone was so absolute that for a moment, Lana thought the woman had hung up. Until the heavy sigh drifted through the receiver. "Look, I haven't talked to Harold in months, so I don't know anything about whatever he's done."

So she did have the right Sally.

Lana allowed herself a moment of relief before pushing forward. "How did you know this was about Harold?"

"It's always about Hal. That man was the worst mistake I ever made and just when I think I'm rid of him, something drags him back into my life. I can't seem to get away."

Interesting.

If all Sally wanted was some peace, she might be willing to help them catch Templing.

"Well, I'm sorry to bring him back up, but I'm hoping you can give me some information about him."

"Are you going to arrest him? Because if you are, I'll tell you whatever you want to know, just so I can put him behind me once and for all. What did he do anyway?"

Aside from following me and giving me the creeps? He might be a serial killer.

But of course she'd never tell Sally that.

She went for the vague answer. "I can't really discuss it, but let's say he's gotten this office's attention. How long were you two together?"

"It would have been five years this Christmas. But we were only married for two of them."

Lana hesitated. How personal could she get before Sally would stop talking to her? There was only one way to find out. Besides, Sally *had* opened herself up to personal questions.

Sort of.

"Do you mind if I ask what happened?"

"Lots of things, but basically, I got sick of all the cloak and dagger stuff. When we first got together, it was kind of fun. But it got old. I guess I thought things would get better if we were married, but if anything it was only worse."

"What do you mean exactly?"

The sigh Sally expelled spoke louder than words.

"Oh you know. Can't tell you how work went 'cause I might have to kill you. Can't tell you who I work for 'cause I might have to kill you. Can't tell you where I'm goin' this weekend 'cause I might have to kill you." Sally's voice took on a gruff tone, no doubt mimicking the one she'd heard Templing use many times. "He tried to play it off like it was a big joke, but never would tell me what he was doing. Like I said, it was kind of fun at first. I was sure I was dating a spy and that seemed so exciting and romantic. I guess I watched one too many spy movies or something, but after hearing it over and over again, it really got on my nerves. Momma told me not to waste my time on him. Figures she'd have to be right."

Sounded like Sally wouldn't know as much about Templing as Lana had expected. All the hopes she'd hung on this phone call deflated around her.

None of her disappointment showed in her voice as she continued her questioning. "Do you know what kind of work he did? Anything about his employer?"

"Not much. He said he was doing security and the way he talked, I got the feeling he wasn't working for the government or a store or something. Honestly, I don't think everything he did was totally legal."

"Why do you say that?"

"It was a lot of little things. Nothing I can prove. The way he talked about cops, for one thing. The people I'd see him with on the rare occasion that I saw anyone connected to his work. He was suspicious of practically everyone. Even me, sometimes. Oh, and he had this huge gun collection with rifles and handguns and uh, what do you call those? Um... silencers, that's it. Had a silencer for almost every handgun in the safe."

Silencers? Gee, that was *slightly* illegal.

Definitely not a cop. She didn't know any law enforcement officer who would have their own stash of silencers, let alone be stupid enough to store them in the first place anyone would look.

She focused back on the conversation as Sally continued to talk.

"To be honest, I think he worked for a millionaire. Hal made good money. Of course, with the amount of time he was gone, he better have made good money, that's all I have to say. It cost him his marriage."

"He worked long hours?"

"You better believe it. I could've handled that, but

sometimes he didn't even come home. Normally he at least called to let me know, but never said he was sorry, just that he had to work late and he'd see me tomorrow or the next day. You know, I even wondered if he was having an affair, but I couldn't see anyone else putting up with his trash."

An affair? Maybe this was a good time to bring up the name Felicity said the Ripper had called her. "Does the name Ana mean anything to you?"

"Ana?" Sally fell silent for a few seconds. "No, I don't think so. Why? Was Hal having an affair? With her?"

"Not necessarily. It's just a name that's come up in connection with our investigation. So he never mentioned it to you?"

"Not that I remember."

Scratch that one. Then again, if Templing was involved with another woman, his wife would likely be the last person to know the other woman's name.

Lana refocused on Templing's job. "And you never saw his paychecks or anything to indicate who he was working for?"

"No. He deposited the checks himself and if there was a pay stub, I never saw it. Knowing him, he burned it."

"Paranoid?"

"To put it mildly. We couldn't talk about anything out in public because someone might overhear. I couldn't even mention what street we lived on. When we talked about anything at home, all the windows had to be shut with the curtains drawn and the blinds pulled down. That's another reason why I decided it was time to trade up."

All very informative, but not terribly relevant.

Lots of people were overly paranoid – it didn't make them killers.

Although dying to know what Sally looked like, she wasn't about to ask. Besides, now that she knew where Sally lived, it should be simple to get a DMV photo. "What about coworkers? Did you ever meet anyone your hus… Harold worked with?"

Sally was silent for a few seconds. "Well, there was this one time he invited a couple over for dinner. We barbecued hamburgers and the other lady brought this nasty potato salad. Hal never said as much, but I got the impression he and the other guy worked together."

"Why's that?"

"Hal was always good at talking a lot without really saying anything. This guy did the same thing. And when his wife helped me clear the table, I asked her what he did and she gave a vague answer. Kind of like I always did when someone asked me about Hal."

Not concrete proof, but it was worth following up on. "Do you happen to remember their names?"

"Uh, it was over a year ago. Let's see, his name was Bob, Bill, Brian… no, Brad. Yeah, that was it. His wife was Callie."

"And their last name?"

"I don't think I ever knew it."

So much for talking to Brad or Callie. Lana eased a breath through her barely parted lips. "What else can you tell me about Harold?"

"He had a bad temper. I guess that's not surprising since he's a redhead. He expected the house to be perfect when he came home. You know, everything spotless and nothing out of place. Never mind that I had a full-time job, too, the house had to be immaculate. He controlled our finances. I had to tell him any time I needed to go grocery shopping or buy shampoo, if you can imagine."

"Did he abuse you?"

A bitter laugh drifted through the phone. "Never touched me, but he was good at making me feel stupid."

"I don't suppose you know where Harold lives now."

"It was a clean split. We don't exactly exchange Christmas cards."

"A phone number or email address or anything?"

"Sorry. I knew I never wanted to talk to him again, so I didn't bother with any of that. You could try his lawyer I guess, the one who handled our divorce. Nick Allman."

Like an attorney would tell her anything. Lana knew better than to waste her time on that one. "Well, I think that covers it. Thanks so much for your time, Sally."

"Don't mention it. Whatever Hal has coming, he's earned it in my mind. I gave him the best I had and he treated me like a goldfish."

"A goldfish?"

"You know, you feed it, look at it sometimes, but you never touch it and never do anything fun with it. You just keep it in a fishbowl and watch it swim around. That's kind of how I felt."

Lana felt a smile pull at the corners of her mouth. "I see what you mean. So if I have more questions, is it okay if I call you?"

"I guess." Sally's voice softened. "Look, don't get me wrong, Hal wasn't all bad, but he was real detached. Here I was giving him all I am and half the time he didn't even see me."

After thanking Sally again, Lana hung up. It took her less than ten minutes to acquire a picture of Sally Green, aka Sally Templing.

Well, if Templing was the Ripper, he wasn't subconsciously killing Sally with each victim.

About the only thing Sally Green had in common with the victims was her height – a diminutive five-foot-one.

Sally's picture matched her voice – delicate features, rich, dark eyes, honey blonde hair haloing her head in large rings, and skin so pale she probably had trouble finding makeup that matched.

Could Templing have been having an affair?

Maybe when Sally left him, the other woman found out he was married and dumped him, too. Maybe he blamed her for the divorce. Maybe it was the other woman who had pushed Templing over the edge and maybe she was Cuban or Latin American.

Or maybe Templing hadn't been having an affair. He could've met someone after his divorce. Maybe that relationship soured quickly and caused a psychotic break.

Or, more likely, Templing wasn't the Ripper after all. Which meant he'd followed her for some other reason.

At this point, it didn't matter. She didn't know where Templing was or how to find him.

Not yet anyway.

She couldn't believe Templing had gotten away with listing the bar's address as his own. Unless...

Who owned that bar? The bartender had led them to believe the bar was his, but it could've been a lie. He could've also lied when he said he didn't know Templing. In fact, he most certainly would've lied if Templing was his boss.

But there was still the issue of Cocoa.

No matter how much she tried to make it fit, she couldn't see the owner of that place acting like a patron and silently lusting after some hooker. Cocoa didn't fit the Ripper's profile and both the bartender and Cocoa said Templing had shown interest in her.

Unless they were both lying. Maybe Templing had dozens of people willing to lie for him.

Slow down.

In spite of the questionable nature of her occupation, Cocoa had seemed honest enough. Lana was usually pretty good at reading people and her instincts told her Cocoa was on the level.

The bartender not so much, but maybe she wasn't giving him enough credit. He had been honest about Cocoa after all.

"So you found her?"

Blinking, Lana found Alex standing a few feet away. "I didn't hear you come up."

"I figured. It looked like your mind went on vacation and left your body behind."

"I guess that's one way of putting it." With a small shake of her head, Lana swiveled her monitor for Alex to see.

"Anyway, yes, I found Sally Green."

Alex sat on the corner of the desk and studied the picture on the screen. "So Templing's not our guy."

"Not necessarily. I mean, the things Sally told me about him line up with our suspicions about the Ripper–"

"You do know we don't want Templing to be the Ripper, right? 'Cause if he is, that means he's after you now." Alex crossed her arms over her chest and pinned Lana with a look that dared her to argue.

It was a dare she willingly took. "Not necessarily. I saw him before this last victim was attacked. If he were fixated on me, *I* would be the one he went after. That kind of lets me off the hook, don't you think?"

"Because the Ripper couldn't possibly fixate on two women at the same time?"

"It's unlikely. Especially now that we know that he feels like he has a connection with them."

"The guy's unstable. I don't know that I'd look for a lot of logic in what he does. Anyway, what did Sally tell you?"

"Templing's a dominating control freak. Paranoid, works long hours, has a collection of silencers–"

Alex held up one of her hands. "Whoa. Silencers? Plural? As in more than one?"

"According to Sally, Templing had one for almost every gun in his collection."

Alex sifted her fingers through her short blonde hair. "You've gotta tell Barker."

"I will, when I give him my next update. Right now, there's too much that doesn't add up."

"Yeah? Like what?" Alex's tone was skeptical.

"Like something else Sally said." She relayed Sally's comment about living in a fishbowl. "Everything we know about the Ripper suggests he's obsessive and needy, but Templing doesn't fit that."

"Not when he was with Sally, but he might now. The Ripper's escalating. Is it unrealistic to think his personality isn't changing, too? Maybe the idea of being left by another woman is more than he can handle."

Hmmm, she hadn't considered that.

"Talk to Barker." Eyes narrowed intensely, Alex leaned forward. "Now, Lana. Get up, march into his office, and tell him now."

The worry in Alex's tone kicked Lana's own concerns into overdrive. The silencers proved Templing was a very bad man.

And that alarmed her.

While she could take care of herself, a lot of the people around her wouldn't know the first thing about defending themselves against someone like Templing.

What if he followed her and attacked her parents? Or Reilly and Des? Or Paul? Or one of the kids?

Templing had his pick of weapons, and with a silencer, he could kill someone most anywhere without attracting much attention. If Templing was the Ripper, he would want Paul out of the way and now they knew he had the means to make it happen.

Calm down.

She swallowed hard, blinked, and focused on Alex's face. "I think we're getting a little too worked up about this–"

"No. We're not. What kind of people have silencers? Killers. Templing has silencers. Follow the logic."

"Still–"

Alex smacked her fist down on the desk. "Darn it, Lana. Do *not* ask me to sit by while a killer follows you around! He could pick you off in the middle of a busy street and no one would even notice what was going on until it was too late."

Leave it to Alex to get worked up about something without thinking it all the way through first. If Templing wanted to kill her, wouldn't he have already done it?

"He had the opportunity, but he didn't take it. That tells me there must be something else he wants from me."

"Yeah. To be up close and personal when he pulls the

trigger." Alex didn't even try to mute her mutterings.

No way would she win this battle.

Besides, Alex was right. Regardless of Templing's intentions, Barker needed to know what she'd learned.

"Fine. I'm going."

She was being followed. Again.

Not the black car from the other night, but she had no doubt it was the same person. Lana's glance flicked to her rearview mirror.

Behind her, a dark blue convertible followed at an unsafe distance, but that car didn't interest her. The mid-sized silver SUV behind the convertible commanded her full attention.

The SUV's driver probably thought putting a car between them would keep her from noticing, but she was onto him. It was kind of hard not to notice since the vehicle had intentionally kept a car between them since she'd left work.

Call Alex.

She reached for her phone, hesitated with her hand over it.

What if she was wrong? She'd raise an alarm, have police descend on some poor little old lady on her way to buy milk.

No, better to test it first.

Something told her it was Templing, but she wanted to be sure. She had to play it cool or Templing would get away – just like last time.

Approaching a stop light, she turned on her signal and got into the left turn lane. The convertible stayed put, but the SUV followed. Traffic crossed in front of her as she waited for the red arrow to change to green.

The driver of the SUV stopped too close for her to see the plate number. The bold Jeep emblem above the chrome grill identified the make of the SUV and she was pretty sure the model was a Grand Cherokee. She wasn't an expert on Jeeps, not by a long shot, but the vehicle in her mirror appeared to be about the right size.

Eyes focused on the rearview mirror, she studied the driver. Light haired, maybe red, maybe not, with skin as pale as a corpse and aviator sunglasses that hid half his face.

Definitely not a little old lady, but was it Templing? Possibly.

The light changed and she turned the corner. The Jeep allowed several yards between them, but never fell out sight. She switched lanes, sped up, slowed down, took a sudden right; the Jeep kept pace with her through each maneuver.

Time to call for backup.

Fifteen

The phone rang twice before Alex picked up. "Hey, Lana."

"He's back."

Tension split Alex's voice like shrapnel. "Templing? Right now?"

"I don't know for sure it's him. It's not the same car, but it's tailed me since I left work."

"I'll call the police. Think you can string him along?"

"I hope so." Lana slowed for a pedestrian. "Call Detective Arlington. Sixth precinct."

"Okay. Where are you?"

"Grove Street." Lana's gaze flicked to the street sign as she breezed through an intersection. "I just passed twenty-ninth. Tell him I'm headed his way."

"Got it. Your doors locked?"

Stupid question. They were always locked and Alex knew it.

Still, Lana pushed the automatic door lock button for good measure. "Yes. Tell him to hurry. I don't know how long it'll take this guy to figure out I'm onto him."

That he might already know wasn't lost on her. The way she'd driven to test her theory lacked subtlety.

Lana terminated the call and dropped the phone into the cup holder.

The busy streets thinned out, the well-groomed restaurants

and boutiques gave way to graffiti covered warehouses, and the cars passing her changed from new and shiny to old and rusty.

Yes sir, she was almost to the sixth precinct all right.

She hoped Alex had been able to reach Arlington, that Arlington had already dispatched some men.

Her phone rang and she snatched it up.

Arlington's no-nonsense voice greeted her with "Where are you?"

A glance out the driver's window showed the Tropical Sun juice factory. "A few blocks from the station."

"I'm sending units right now. Go three blocks past the station and turn right. We'll pen him in."

"Got it." Lana ended the call and set the phone aside.

Forcing her muscles to relax, she eased her grip on the steering wheel. It helped to know she wasn't facing this guy alone, that a plan existed, that she'd soon learn the truth.

More than all that, that they'd have Templing in custody by the end of the night.

The station was ahead of her. She passed the building without so much as a glance. Three blocks seemed like three miles when she wanted this thing to be over now.

She slowed and turned onto a narrow two lane street.

No cars were parked along the side of the road, police cruisers or otherwise. There were no people walking on the sidewalks, no birds swooping through the sky, no alley cats rummaging through the garbage.

No life at all, in fact. Just her and the silver Jeep.

Had she gotten the wrong street? Arlington had said three blocks, hadn't he?

She drove through one intersection. Then another.

Still no sign of backup.

How the heck were they going to pen him in if she was on her own?

The limit on the road was thirty-five, and she forced herself to go at least thirty. She didn't want to put any extra distance between her location and the police station, but she couldn't make the Jeep's driver suspicious either.

No matter what speed she went, the Jeep stayed at least half a block behind her.

Sirens cut the silence. Lana's gaze flew to the rearview mirror as a police cruiser appeared behind the SUV.

About time. She let up on the accelerator.

The Jeep bore down on her, filled her rearview mirror.

Wait, what was he doing?

A loud crunch scorched her ears.

The windshield rushed toward her. The seat belt cut into her shoulder and chest, jerked her back into the seat, but not before her head bounced off the steering wheel.

She slammed her foot on the brake. The tires screamed across the pavement as the Jeep pushed her several feet. Her car stopped, the noise replaced by a silence that seemed even louder.

Pain pulsated through her abdomen and across her chest. Her neck felt like overcooked spaghetti and just holding her head up required unusual effort.

Had they caught him?

She turned her head as another ear-shattering screech split the air. Her car rotated a few degrees.

The Jeep raced by her window, a cruiser only a second behind. Another cruiser skidded to a stop beside her.

Two cops inside. The passenger lowered his window.

"Are you okay?" The officer's shouted words filtered through her window.

She lowered her window. "Fine. Just don't let him get away."

The officer nodded even as the driver pulled away.

Watching the chase felt surreal. How many times had she seen something like this on TV?

She blinked. But this wasn't TV, this was reality.

And Arlington had sent two cars as backup. Two! Both from the same direction, no less!

What was he thinking? Had he not taken her serious–

Several police cars shot out of a cross street in front of the Jeep, lights swirling and sirens blaring. Angled across the road, they blocked both lanes and trapped the Jeep between them and the cruiser behind it.

The Jeep skidded to a halt. Officers swarmed the vehicle from all sides, guns aimed and ready.

Even from two blocks away, she could hear them yelling for the driver to get out of the vehicle. Slowly.

She could make out movement inside the Jeep, but not clearly enough to see if the driver was complying.

Officers descended on the Jeep.

One jerked the door open, another pulled the man out, another snapped on handcuffs. Several others stood a few feet back, weapons ready.

She should go down there. See what was going on.

She eased off the brake.

Reality crashed in. She couldn't drive down there. Her car was a crime scene.

She shifted into park and turned the engine off.

Amid the fray, Arlington appeared and wasted no time taking charge. The distance prevented her from hearing his words, but his gesturing arms evidenced the orders he was no doubt giving.

She really wanted to know what was going on.

And look her pseudo-stalker in the eye.

She unbuckled her seat belt and pushed it aside.

Pain ricocheted through her body. Needles pricked her neck and moved up into her head, where it felt like a marching band had taken up residence.

Ooh, she hadn't hurt this much since being shot.

She closed her eyes against the tears that threatened and focused on breathing. In and out. In and out.

Funny how she no longer cared about Templing. All she wanted now was to go home and soak in a nice hot bath. And pop three or four painkillers to take the edge off.

A slap sounded on the roof above her head. She jumped.

Bolts of fire shot up her neck as she turned toward the driver's window to find Arlington there, bent over to look at her.

"We got 'im."

No duh.

She opened the door and stepped out. The sweltering evening seized her in its embrace.

The world around her darkened and her vision narrowed. She locked her knees to keep from going down and leaned her back against the hot metal of her car.

Okay, scratch that. This hurt worse than being shot.

At least her body had shut down after that trauma, but this time she felt every single ache.

Come on, toughen up. She could fall apart later, when no one was around to see.

She wouldn't let the police view her as a victim.

"Tanner, you okay?"

She forced her lips to curl up as she faced Arlington. The late afternoon sun reflected off the sweat coating his forehead. Serious eyes studied her and she wondered if he had any clue how much pain she was in.

"You sure you should be moving around?" The concern in his voice almost did her in.

She released a shuddery breath. "I'm fine."

Not very convincing, even to her own ears.

Arlington put one of his damp paws gently under her elbow and gestured to someone further up the road. A few seconds later, an unmarked sedan pulled up, stopping several feet away.

Releasing her, Arlington opened the passenger door. "Sit. I'm gonna get an ambulance out here."

"Don't worry about it. I'll live."

But maybe sitting down would help. Her head pounded and every second spent on her feet took energy she didn't have. She moved toward the car, aware of Arlington's eyes watching her slow progress.

"Murphy, radio for an ambulance, will ya." Arlington's tone said it was an order, not a request.

"Don't both–"

Arlington's eyes narrowed on her. "Murphy. The ambulance."

The officer barely glanced at her before moving to obey.

Maybe an ambulance wasn't such a bad idea after all.

She hated the idea of everyone fussing over her, but if she had a concussion and slipped into a coma, she'd never hear the end of it. Her family would chew her out and – coma or no coma – she bet she'd hear every word. Better to deal with it now than risk her family's wrath.

She lowered herself into the seat and tried not to feel completely worthless.

Seeing the man with his hands cuffed behind his back brought a small measure of satisfaction, but the pain pulsing through her body dampened her mood. What the heck had he been thinking anyway? Had he seriously thought he could outrun the police?

An officer led the man toward a waiting patrol car.

Even now, the man's eyes locked on her in a squinty glare.

One of the officers walked over, appraising her before giving Arlington his full attention. "Guy's name is Harold Templing."

No surprise there. Now all they had to do was figure out if Templing was the Ripper.

And if he wasn't, why he'd followed her.

In spite of the pain, she couldn't help smiling.

No more looking over her shoulder. No more wondering if Templing were close by. No more imagining herself gutted in some desolate alley.

Templing was going to prison.

After this fiasco, it should be easy enough for the prosecutor's office to convince a judge to hold Templing without bail. She hoped.

Arlington's voice brought her back. "So you think that's our guy, huh?"

"I don't know. I think it's suspicious that he's followed me on at least two different occasions."

"Even more suspicious since he tried to run."

"I spoke to his ex-wife earlier and the things she told me line up with the profile. Mostly." The pain ravaging her body muddied her thoughts. "I don't know."

Arlington watched as the cruiser carrying Templing crept by them. "Kinda matches the description we have. But his car's not black. Heck, it's not even a car."

"He was in a black car the first time he followed me. I think he switched vehicles to try to throw me off."

"Could be."

She relaxed back against the seat, her head angled up to look at Arlington. "You don't have to babysit me. I know you have things to do over there."

With hands stuffed deep in his pockets, he lifted his shoulders in a small shrug. "My officers can handle it. 'Sides, like it or not, you're a victim now."

And his job wasn't just about the perps, it was also about the witnesses and victims. She hated that she fell into any of those categories.

Arlington glanced at the rear of her car. "Looks like he hit you pretty solid."

She followed his gaze.

The trunk had crumpled into the back seat. Plastic from the light covers and broken glass from her rear windshield littered the pavement like confetti. Tire skids showed the point where she'd slammed on the brakes and the distance the SUV had pushed her.

Man, he'd had some momentum going when he hit her. It was amazing the SUV had even been able to get that kind of speed in such a short distance.

Arlington was still speaking. "Can't believe your airbag didn't deploy."

The pounding in her head grew louder with each second. "I had it disabled."

"Why'd you do that? You know those things are supposed to keep you from gettin' too friendly with the windshield, right?"

She glanced up at him. Tall people never thought about details like this. "I'm short enough it could do more harm than good."

He looked at her as though seeing her for the first time. "Yeah, guess so. Never really thought about it before."

Where was that ambulance?

Her head felt like it could explode any second. Closing her eyes, she slumped back against the seat.

"Hey, Tanner, you okay? Can I get you anything?" Arlington's voice filtered through the cloud surrounding her.

Could he get her anything? Not unless he had some serious painkillers in his car.

Wait, didn't she have some aspirin in her purse? It might not help much, but at this point she'd take whatever she could get.

"My purse?"

"Yeah, hold on."

She heard him move away, forced her eyes open when his footsteps returned. Murmuring a thank you, she took the bag from his hands and dug through it. Her wallet, cell phone, badge… where was that pill case?

Her desk.

A frustrated breath seeped through her lips. She'd taken some aspirin the other day and forgot to put the case back in her purse.

"Can I help?"

She blinked Arlington's face into focus. "You don't happen to have any painkillers, do you?"

"Back at the station. Honestly though, I wouldn't give 'em to you even if I did. Not until the EMTs say it's okay."

At this point, she couldn't care less what the EMT's wanted.

But she understood Arlington's position and knew if their roles were reversed, she'd say the same thing.

"Anyone you want me to call?"

Paul sprang to mind. As did her parents, Reilly, Des, and Alex.

She rejected each one. "No. I'm okay."

Dealing with Arlington's concern was bad enough; she didn't have the energy for anyone else's well-meaning meddling.

But it was nice to know maybe Arlington had learned a thing or two from their conversation regarding Felicity that morning.

Had it really only been that morning that they'd visited her at the hospital?

"Look, we both know you're not drivin' that car anywhere tonight. You're gonna need a ride. 'Sides, you're the one that told me no one should go through hard stuff alone."

The shrill scream of sirens sliced through the night, reverberating in her head as they drew closer and saving her from having to reply. The noise choked off with a short blip and the ambulance rounded a corner, swirling lights adding to the crimson glow that cloaked the street. It coasted toward her car, stopping several yards behind her mangled bumper.

Okay. Now all she had to do was find the strength to walk over there. Piece of cake.

She braced herself against the door and rose. Her muscles were stiff, uncooperative. Every inch of her felt damaged and she didn't think it would take much for her to shatter like the glass on the pavement around her.

Arlington stepped in front of her, his bulk filling her view. "Huh uh. They can come to you. Sit back down."

Pride insisted she argue, but she swallowed the urge.

It'd be even more embarrassing if her body gave out on her way to the ambulance. Her legs shook as she lowered herself to the seat.

It took less than a minute for the EMTs to reach her, even

less time for them to start fussing over her. Light in her eyes, hands probing her neck, and the incessant "where does it hurt" questions.

Man, did she hate being injured.

Then there were the words she'd dreaded hearing most. "We need to take you in. Let a doc look you over."

She gave the EMT what she hoped was a firm look. "I'll go in tomorrow. Just give me something for this headache and we're good to go."

"You need to have x-rays done–"

"They can wait twelve hours." She glanced at Arlington, who hovered in the background. "I want to be there when you question him."

Arlington seemed to consider it before shaking his head. "I can fill you in later."

No way. She couldn't gauge his reaction if she wasn't there. "Look, whether or not this guy's the Ripper, he was after me. I have a right to know why."

"And I'll tell you. But there're things more important than that."

The EMT kneeling in front of her drew her attention. "Listen to the man. He knows what he's talking about."

She couldn't win this argument with all of them ganging up on her. Not in her current condition and murky state of mind. Besides, Arlington's lowered eyebrows and firmly set jaw convinced her that he'd personally handcuff her to the gurney if she wouldn't go willingly.

But she also couldn't give up without a fight. "I might be able to help. This guy followed *me*. Maybe if I question him, or if I'm in the room, he'll slip up."

Arlington opened his mouth to argue, only to snap it shut a second later. Surveying her, he finally nodded. "We could let the guy sit in a holding cell and sweat it out for a while. That way you can get patched up before coming to the station. If you feel like it."

Oh she'd feel like it all right.

She glanced between the EMTs. "Then let's get this over with. I want to get back down here as soon as possible."

Sixteen

The phone rang as Paul loaded the last of the dinner dishes into the dishwasher.

Reaching for his phone, he nodded at the kids who'd been on dish duty that night. "Thanks, guys. Looks good in here."

The two kids grinned before scampering off.

The number on his phone wasn't familiar, but it was his cell, so at least it shouldn't be the press. He accepted the call.

"Van Horn, that you?"

"Yeah." The man's voice was vaguely familiar, but he couldn't place it. "Who's this?"

"Detective Arlington here."

Paul's breathing quickened. "Did you catch him?"

"Well, maybe. I was gonna ask you to come down and look at a lineup."

He'd drive all the way to California if that's what it took to get life back to normal. "I'll be right there."

"Well, hey, hold up a sec. That wasn't the main reason why I called."

Not why he called? What else could it be?

He struggled for air like an asthmatic without an inhaler. A call from the police was never a good thing.

At least all his kids were accounted for this time.

Arlington cleared his throat. "Look, the uh, reason I called…"

Just spit it out already. Paul bit the inside of his lip to keep his mouth shut.

"Tanner was in an accident tonight. You might swing by Jacksonville General on your way here."

Lana. Accident. Jacksonville General.

The thoughts strobed through his head, followed by a flurry of questions. Was Lana okay? How did Arlington know? What did it have to do with catching the Ripper? Why hadn't Lana called him herself?

He quieted all but the most crucial question. "Is she okay?"

"Stubborn as ever. She tried to refuse the ride to the hospital."

Well, if she was arguing and fighting help, that was a good sign. But it still didn't answer the question. "So she's not hurt?"

"Not too bad. Little whiplash, some bruises, maybe a concussion. Now her car's another story."

He couldn't care less about her car. "What happ... you know what, never mind. Jacksonville General, you said?"

"Yeah. She's likely to be mad as a hornet 'cause she didn't want me callin' anyone, but I figured you'd wanna know."

That sounded like Lana.

"Thanks for the heads-up. I'll pick her up and take her home, then come right down to see about that lineup."

"Fine by me, but she was talkin' about coming here when she was done at the hospital. I'll let you two battle that one out."

Oh they'd battle it out all right. No way was he going to take her anywhere but home.

He said a hasty good-bye, slid his phone into his pocket as he turned, and almost ran into Brittany, who was standing so close she probably could've heard Arlington's end of the conversation.

"Who's at Jacksonville General?"

Calm. No point in getting Brittany as riled up as he was. "Lana. She was in a little car accident tonight, but the police said she'll be okay. I'm just gonna go pick her up and take her home."

"You should bring her back here." Brittany offered a cheeky grin. "You could tell her you love her and nurse her back to health and convince her to never leave."

"I thought we agreed to leave this issue alone."

She tossed her curly black hair over her shoulder. "I know you said it's complicated, but come on, how hard–"

"Enough!" Paul slashed his hand through the air. "We are done talking about this, do you hear me?"

A gasp slipped out and Brittany stared at him, moisture rimming her chocolate eyes. Whirling, she ran from the room. Pounding footsteps on the stairs told him she was going to her room.

Dang it. Why'd he have to take his frustration out on her?

Especially since he was really frustrated with Lana. She should've been the one to call him, not Arlington. After all, he called her when any little thing went wrong, but would she ever let him return the favor?

Heaven forbid she show any vulnerability.

She wanted everyone to think she was some kind of superhero. Invincible and strong.

He jogged upstairs and retrieved his keys and wallet from his bedroom, touched base with the Webbers so they'd know he was headed out, then strode to the front door. With his hand on the doorknob, he froze.

He should really make peace with Brittany before he left. No telling what time he'd be back and he wasn't one to withhold an apology, especially from one of his kids.

Crossing the room, he headed up the stairs to the girls' wing.

The door to the room Brittany shared with another girl was closed. He tapped on it lightly. "Britt?"

"Go away." A sniffle told him her state of mind.

"Come on, open the door. I'm sorry."

Movement came from inside and the door swung open. "I

was just tryin' to help! Lana's good for you. And she needs someone to watch out for her, too."

He leaned against the doorjamb. "I agree with you there, but good luck telling her that."

"Maybe if she knew…"

"We've been over this." He kept his tone gentle. "It's better if we're just friends, nothing more."

Brittany crossed her arms over her chest and frowned. "I don't know why."

"Just drop it, okay?"

A fat tear trailed down her cheek. She shuddered out a sigh and slowly nodded.

"Thanks. And I'm sorry again for snapping at you. I was frustrated about what happened to Lana and took it out on you."

"It's cool. I'm worried about her, too." She stepped forward and wrapped her arms around his chest.

He hugged her in return, then stepped back. "I better get going."

"Yeah. But you should put on some cologne or something. You smell like chicken."

The painkillers were finally kicking in. About time.

Unfortunately, she could tell they were dulling her thinking, too.

Lana rubbed the back of her neck, massaging the muscles that had already begun to stiffen. Man, was she ever going to feel this in the morning.

A trauma case had come in a while ago and she'd been bumped down the list. While it was understandable, she hated sitting here, knowing that Arlington had Templing at the precinct right now. Maybe already questioning him.

Ugh. She had to get out of here.

What would happen if she just got up and left?

She sat up, the plastic under the sheets on the exam table crackling with her movements, and swung her legs over the edge of the table. The world spun. She closed her eyes until the ringing in her ears stopped.

Okay. Slow movements.

A tap on the door. She looked up as a nurse walked in, a large vase of brightly colored flowers in her hands.

"A cute guy asked me to bring these back."

Cute guy? "You sure they're for me?"

"Absolutely. He specifically said Milana Tanner."

What? Who knew she was here? Arlington must've called someone after all.

"Thanks." She plucked the card from the vase and flipped it open.

The message was short and to the point: *Can I come back? Paul.*

So. Arlington had called Paul, even though she'd asked him not to.

Part of her wanted to deny him access for the sole reason that Arlington had defied her wishes, but that wasn't Paul's fault.

The nurse was almost out the door. Had to make a decision now.

"Excuse me."

The nurse turned.

"Would you be able to bring him back here?"

The nurse smiled. "Of course."

The door clicked shut behind her, leaving Lana a few minutes of peace before Paul arrived.

Okay, so this day hadn't gone as she'd hoped. Not even close, actually. Paul showing up at the hospital was just one more hiccup in a day that couldn't end soon enough.

At least the flowers were pretty. She fingered the petals of a lavender tulip.

A knock sounded at the door.

She turned as the nurse pushed the door open and let Paul in. The door clicked shut as the nurse disappeared back into the hallway.

The color drained from his cheeks and she heard his breath catch in the silent room.

"That bad, huh?" She hadn't yet looked in a mirror, and judging by his reaction, maybe she didn't want to.

"No, no. I'm just… are you okay?" Worry laced the words and crinkled his forehead as he crossed the room to stand in front of her.

Just peachy.

She bit back the sarcasm. This was one of her closest friends, someone who'd dropped whatever he'd been doing to check on her at the hospital. He deserved openness and honesty.

"I've had better days, but I don't think anything's broken."

He dragged the room's sole chair over to sit across from her. "What happened?"

No point in trying to sugarcoat anything. Paul could clearly see the evidence by looking at her. Besides, the man responsible was in custody, so telling him the full truth shouldn't make him worry.

She relayed the story, beginning with being followed the other night and ending with Templing in handcuffs.

As she spoke, Paul's eyes narrowed slightly and a frown twisted his mouth. "So this has been ongoing for several days and you didn't tell me?"

"You have enough to worry about right now without taking my troubles."

"That's what friends do."

She scooted back on the exam table to lean against the wall behind her. "Besides, I knew if I told you, you'd jump to the Ripper conclusion again."

"Yeah, and maybe I was right, wasn't I?"

"I guess we'll see."

Silence descended for several seconds. "Have they examined you yet?"

"Briefly, but then a trauma case came in. I'm tempted to just leave."

"Not a chance."

She smiled at his adamant tone. "Oh yeah? You think you can stop me?"

Crossing his arms over his chest, he leaned against the back of the chair. "A shrimp like you? No problem. Besides, I'm your ride outta here, so we don't leave until I say so."

She chuckled. Stabbing pain attacked her ribs, stealing her breath.

Ouch; lesson learned. Laughing was a very bad idea right now.

"Lana? You okay?"

"I'm good." Her breath had a raspy quality. "But laughter is *not* always the best medicine."

"Are you headed to the precinct?" Lana's voice was softer than usual, but Paul had anticipated the question.

Paul shortened his steps to match Lana's unusually slow pace and looked over at her. Red-webbed eyes, swollen and discolored face, and stiff movements; she shouldn't be going anywhere but home. "I'm taking you home. Then I'm headed to the precinct."

The hospital doors swooshed open and they stepped into a sticky breeze.

"I'll go with you."

"Nope, don't think so."

She stopped and stared at him with eyebrows drawn together and a firm set to her lips. "You can't stop me from going to the precinct."

Plunging his hands into his pockets, he planted his feet. "I don't see your car around here, which means you're at my mercy."

"Fine. If you won't take me, I'll call a cab."

"Your statement can wait until tomorrow."

"It's not about my statement. It's about Templing's interrogation."

Of course. He should've known. "You can't be in there anyway, can you?"

"Beside the point. I want to hear what he has to say. In person."

"What, you don't think Arlington will share the details?"

"That's not it. I can't read Templing if I'm not there. And if this is related to my work somehow, I might think of questions Arlington wouldn't."

One arm was wrapped around her stomach, the other hanging limp by her side. Her normally bright eyes looked dull.

Even her arguments lacked their usual fire.

She had no clue how fragile she looked right now, or how desperately he wanted to take her in his arms and just hold her. He kept his hands in his pockets. "Lana. Look at yourself. You've been through a lot. Please let me take you home."

"Can't do it. I need to know why this happened. Why he was following me."

"Come on. Be reasonable–"

"Please." A quiver shook her voice. "I'm doing this with or without you. I could use your help."

God, what should I do?

No divine voice thundered. All he heard was the soft whistling of the wind in the trees.

She swayed. The wind wasn't that strong, which meant that it was her own lack of strength that threatened to topple her.

Standing here arguing was doing more harm than good.

"Fine." The word came out half-spoken, half-sighed. "But if you start looking too drained, I'm taking you home. No arguments. And we're stopping to pick up something for you to eat on the way. Deal?"

A hint of a smile touched her lips. "Deal."

The public parking lot at the sixth precinct had exactly two cars in it. Although the food they'd picked up seemed to have revived Lana's energy some, Paul parked as close as possible. Energy levels aside, she had to still be hurting.

He hurried around to the passenger side, but she'd already gotten out and shut the door by the time he arrived.

Big surprise. Sometimes she was too independent for her own good.

Matching her stride, he remained within arm's reach. Just in case she needed a little help. Not that he expected her to.

They walked through the double glass doors and into the lobby of the police station.

Lana had called Arlington as they'd left the hospital so he could get the lineup ready. Hopefully this wouldn't take too long; Lana needed her rest.

The plastic chairs lining the wall looked anything but comfortable, but they were better than nothing. He nodded toward them. "If you want to have a seat, I'll let them know we're here."

"No need." She pulled her badge from her pocket. "I've got our all access pass right here."

She approached the bullet-proof glass and handed her badge to the officer sitting on the other side. "Deputy Tanner and Paul Van Horn, here to see Detective Arlington. We're expected."

The officer made a brief call before buzzing them through and directing them to meet Arlington at his office. The door crashed behind them, the noise bouncing down the hallway.

Was Lana slowing down even more?

Paul watched her closely as they headed down the hall but couldn't tell. She was good at hiding her emotions, too good.

As they approached the end of the hall, Arlington stepped out of his office and closed the door.

"Took you guys long enough to get here." Arlington shifted his attention to Lana. "How are you?"

"I'll be better once we get some answers."

"Girl after my own heart." Arlington grinned and turned to Paul. "Ready for that lineup?"

"Let's do it."

Arlington led them to a dim observation room. A large glass window dominated one wall, revealing a brightly lit room on the other side. Snagging a chair, he settled it behind Lana. "Take a load off. I'll go get 'em."

Lana crumpled into the chair. Silence descended.

"How're you really doing?"

"I'm tired." The words were so soft that any other noise would've completely drowned her out. "And hurt pretty much everywhere."

"Let me take you home. I'll ID this guy, then we'll get outta here."

"And miss the interrogation? No way."

Part of him wanted to lecture her. But most of him wanted to take care of her, starting with getting her out of this place and away from the slime responsible for her pain.

He did neither. "Well, if you change your mind, just say so."

A small nod was the only indication she heard or agreed with what he'd said. He'd never seen her like this before and never wanted to see her this way again. It scared him worse than the gangs that roamed the neighborhood. "You sure you shouldn't be spending the night at the hospital?"

"I'm sure. I know I look a little worse for wear, but seriously, I was given a clean bill of health."

Of course she was. Would she really tell him if she hadn't

been? Usually he'd never question her honesty, but she had a tendency to downplay things.

Especially if it made her appear weak.

"Okay. Here we go."

He turned as Arlington's voice came from behind him. A glance toward the glass showed a line of men filing by on the other side.

Paul stepped up to the glass. There were half a dozen men, ranging in height from five and a half feet to nearly six foot, all with short cropped hair in various shades of blonde, red, or light brown.

His first glance confirmed that the Ripper wasn't among them. "He's not here."

"Look more closely and hold off until we're done. I'll have each man step forward so you can get a good look, okay?"

Paul nodded, even though he already knew it was an exercise in futility.

Joining him at the glass, Arlington pushed a button by a speaker in the wall and spoke into it. "Number one, please step forward."

The blonde man at the left end of the line took a step forward. "Not him."

Arlington pushed the button again. "Step back. Number two, step forward."

The next four men followed the same pattern. When he'd said no to the last man, Paul turned to Arlington. "He's not there. I thought you said–"

"I said maybe." Frustration darkened Arlington's eyes. "You're sure our guy isn't in there?"

"Definitely. The Ripper is scrawnier than those guys. Think of a scarecrow and you've got the right idea."

He glanced at Lana.

The disappointment on her face gutted him. All she'd been through tonight and they were no closer to the Ripper than before.

"Which of those..." He caught his tongue before he said

something he knew Lana wouldn't want to hear. "Who hit you?"

"Number four."

He turned his attention to the stocky redhead toward the center of the line. A smirk covered the man's face.

That scum was actually pleased with the damage he'd caused tonight!

Paul wanted to break through the glass and do some damage of his own.

A sure-fire way to ensure he spent the night locked inside these walls instead of escorting Lana home.

He forced his attention to Arlington. "So what now?"

"Well, we got him for vehicular assault, fleeing the scene, and eluding. This guy isn't goin' anywhere."

Good. After what he'd done to Lana, Paul hoped they locked that jerk up until every last red hair had either fallen out or turned gray. He looked at Lana. "Why'd he go after you?"

"No clue. That's why I have to be here for the interrogation." Her eyes shifted to Arlington. "Have you talked to him yet?"

"Nope. Waiting for you. Sit tight while I get 'im in interrogation and you can observe."

As Arlington left the room, Paul studied Lana. The knot on her forehead looked like it had grown larger and the left side of her face had darkened into what would likely be an ugly bruise. "You sure I can't take you home now?"

"I'm fine."

Terseness lined the words, but he didn't take it personally. Not after the day she'd had. "Can I get you anything? Something to drink? Or an ice pack?"

"Actually, something sweet sounds really good, but I don't know where you'll find that."

"I remember seeing some vending machines. Be right back."

He found the vending machines just where he remembered

them and returned with a can of pop and some chips for himself and peanut butter cups, a dark chocolate bar, a package of cookies, and a bottle of water for Lana.

"Wow. That's a lot of sweet."

He shrugged. "Didn't know what you were most in the mood for, so I got you a variety."

"Thanks. And thanks for being here. I know it's not exactly how you wanted to spend tonight."

Wrong. Spending time with her was precisely how he wanted to spend tonight – and every night. Maybe not ideal circumstances, but they were together, alive, and safe; that was what counted the most.

"Okay, guys." Arlington's voice came from behind Paul. "Follow me."

Seventeen

Lana stared through the glass at Templing, who sat in an unpadded chair in front of a stainless steel table that was bolted to the floor. With his arms folded across his chest, he leaned back casually in the chair. A small smirk curled his mouth as he stared directly at her.

Not that he could see her, of course. He was on the wrong side of the one-way glass.

Still, somehow he knew she was out there. And had correctly guessed her approximate location.

She moved the chair Arlington had brought into the room half a dozen feet to her left.

Arlington nodded at Templing. "He's been in there since we brought him in. The only time he left was for the lineup."

"And no one's talked to him yet?"

Arlington shook his head. "Nope. Guy's been like that since we first put him in there. Just sits there, staring. Blinks sometimes, but not much. Cool as can be."

Not the actions of an amateur criminal.

Templing had seen the inside of interrogation rooms before, definitely on more than one occasion.

And yet he'd never been charged. Interesting.

Lana glanced at Templing once more before giving Arlington her full attention. "Are you ready to get started?"

"Born ready. You might as well get comfortable. Somethin'

tells me he's not gonna break easily."

"I think you're right." Unfortunately.

The drugs the doctor gave her had taken the edge off the pain, but it still lingered in her joints, pounded dully in her head. She'd hoped Templing would break easily, but that hope was dashed in the face of his cocky demeanor.

Lana glanced back at Templing, keeping her eyes glued to his face as the door opened and Arlington strode in.

The chair across from Templing slid out with a loud scrape and Arlington settled his tall frame into it. Aside from looking away from the mirror to watch Arlington, Templing barely moved as Arlington leaned forward and folded his hands on the table in front of him.

"You got no right to keep me here." Templing's voice was casual, unconcerned.

Arlington ignored him. "You're in a heap of trouble, you know that?"

"It was a fender bender. Write me a ticket and I'll be on my way."

Templing's gaze strayed from Arlington, returning to the mirror once again. The vacant look in his eyes, so cold and void of emotion, lifted the hair on her arms.

"A fender bender? That what you call purposely ramming another vehicle?" Arlington's tone was flat.

A slight lift to his shoulders was the only indication Templing gave that he even heard the statement.

Arlington slammed his palm onto the table. "You better look at me when I'm talkin' to you. I've got enough right now to charge you with malicious mischief, assault on a federal officer, and fleeing the scene of an accident."

Face still blank, Templing returned his attention to Arlington. "I don't know what you're talking about."

"Find that hard to believe."

Resting his elbows on the table, Templing laced his fingers together and kept his eyes fixed on Arlington. "I freaked, okay? I hit her car, saw the lights and heard the sirens, and accidentally pressed the accelerator instead of the brake. Could've happened to anyone."

"Accidentally pressed the accelerator? For almost two blocks? Don't think so." It was Arlington's turn to lean back and cross his arms. "I think you were angry she called for backup and rammed her on purpose."

"Why would I do that?"

"Why would you follow her halfway across town?"

"I didn't." Templing fell silent for several seconds. "Look, this is all just a big mistake."

That did it. She didn't have the patience to sit here all night while the two of them went in circles. Hands clenching by her sides, she pushed up from the chair and almost smacked into Paul.

"Where are you going?"

He wouldn't like the answer. Stepping around him, she stalked from the room, her muscles protesting every step.

That stupid idiot. What did he think he'd accomplish by denying everything?

She brushed by the officer standing guard and flung the door open. It crashed against the wall and bounced back toward her, stopped from hitting her only by her outstretched arm.

Templing jolted and whipped his head around. With a flick of her wrist, the door thumped closed behind her.

"Was it a mistake the last time I caught you tailing me? When I found you waiting for me outside of my office? I've seen you following me on at least two different occasions and you want me to believe it's a *coincidence*?"

Templing's cool veneer momentarily cracked as a hint of panic lit his eyes.

A second later, the calm mask slipped back in place. His tone was casual when he spoke. "I've never seen you before in my life."

"Except when you followed my car earlier and when you waited outside my office on Monday–"

Arlington held up his hand and she snapped her mouth shut. She needed to rein it in. It wasn't like her to get so worked up about something like this.

She could probably thank the mixture of pain medication and sugar for that one.

She stepped to the right of the one way glass and leaned against the wall. It was best if she stayed out of this until she cooled down. For now, she'd watch while Arlington did the interrogating.

Lord, I need some control here. I've got nothing left.

Arlington broke the silence. "Wanna know what I think?"

"No, but I bet you're gonna tell me anyway." Templing's voice oozed sarcasm.

"I think you've been stalking and killing women and that you chose this woman–" Arlington's finger flung her way "–to be your next target. I think you were going to follow her, abduct her from her home, stab her over and over, and leave her for dead–"

"Hold up." Templing's eyebrows lowered. The carefully constructed indifference evaporated. "You can't... you think I'm the Ripper?"

No. They knew he wasn't the Ripper, but he didn't know that.

A slow and deliberate nod moved Arlington's head. "And I think you made the mistake of picking a Fed for your latest victim."

"No way. Look, I hit her car, all right? But that's it. I didn't kill no one and I wasn't gonna kill her."

"And I'm supposed to just take your word on that."

Templing nodded emphatically. "Hey, I got an alibi for at least one of the murders. I was outta town."

"I want the city you went to, the name of the hotel you stayed at, and the names of everyone who went with you or might be able to vouch for your whereabouts during that time." Arlington pushed a notepad and pen across the table.

"No sweat." Templing wrote for a few minutes before

pushing the notepad and pen back to Arlington. "You check into that and you'll see I'm tellin' the truth. 'Sides, I don't even know that chick's name."

Templing nodded her way, but kept his eyes on Arlington's face.

"I doubt that." Lana didn't move from her perch by the wall. "You were waiting outside my work Monday night. Waiting. For. Me."

Sweat glistened like an oil slick on Templing's forehead. "He described you! That's all-"

"He who?"

Templing swallowed hard and clenched his jaw. "No one."

"If someone put you up to this, you better speak up now." Arlington's menacing stare was met by a blank one.

"I've got nothin' to say."

Lana pushed off the wall and stepped closer. "Does it have something to do with Ana?"

"Who?" Confusion traced the word as it slipped from Templing's mouth. "Don't know any Ana."

"Look, we'll even drop some of the charges. Just give us a name." Glancing at the clock on the wall, Arlington rested his elbows on the table. "Offer expires in-"

"You can talk to my lawyer about it."

Arlington stood, his chair clattering to the hard floor. "That's the way you want it, fine. Sit tight."

"Like I've got a choice."

And just like that, they were done.

Arlington rapped on the door and the officer opened it. The sweeping motion of Arlington's arm indicated that she should precede him into the hall.

Pushing the door closed, Arlington turned to her. "Took him longer than I expected to lawyer up."

Which didn't make it any less frustrating.

Paul met her at the door to the observation room. He didn't say anything - although she had no doubt there were many things going through his mind - but instead pulled her into a hug.

Tears pierced her eyes. Ugh. She would not cry. She hated crying.

The warmth and strength of his arms felt good, but would be her undoing if she stayed here long. So she returned the hug, then stepped into the room to observe Templing, who hadn't moved.

At least the cocky expression was gone, replaced with a blank look that told her nothing. Was he nervous, scared, worried?

"What do you think?"

She turned to find Arlington leaning against the wall. "I think he was telling the truth about someone putting him up to following me. I don't think he meant to say it, either."

"Agreed."

Too bad he hadn't clammed up after letting that person's name slip. While they had Templing in custody, whoever had organized this whole thing was still out there.

What if they tried again?

Lana looked a few heartbeats away from collapsing.

Well, the interrogation was over, so maybe now she'd finally be reasonable about leaving. "Let's get out of here."

"Sounds good to me."

Stiff movements told him that her muscles had tightened up. No doubt that trip into the interrogation room hadn't helped matters. Moving slower than his kids doing their chores, she headed down the hallway.

He hovered close by in case she was weaker than she looked.

The last thing she needed in her condition was to hit the floor. Being ready to catch her if her legs gave out didn't seem like much, but he didn't know what else he could do to help.

Or if she'd even let him.

Muffled voices came from somewhere behind them and a phone rang in the bullpen off to their left, but the hallway was deserted. After stepping through the security door, they crossed the lobby and inhaled the muggy evening air.

Lana finally broke the silence when he started the car. "I'll call a cab from your place."

"No need. I'll take you home."

"It's too far out of your way."

He shot a look her direction. "That's not what you'd say if our positions were reversed. I'm taking you home."

"Thanks." She seemed too tired to protest further. Reclining the seat a few notches, she slumped into the worn cushions with a sigh.

"I take it your car's totaled."

"I'd guess so. The back end was pretty mangled."

Better the back end than the front or driver's side. "Why'd he do it? Why not just try to get away?"

"I think he figured out we'd set a trap and was trying to get even. His ex-wife says he's got a bad temper."

"You've spoken to his ex?"

"After he followed me the first time. Alex ran his plates, learned his name, and we started digging."

The conversation played like a recording in his head, snagging on one word. Trap. That almost made it sound like... she couldn't really mean... had she volunteered herself as bait? Had she and Arlington created some crazy scheme to draw the Ripper out with Lana as the target?

Careful.

He drew a deep breath. If she had set herself up that way, this was some dangerous ground he was about to tread on.

But he had to go there. The questions had to be asked.

Not taking his eyes from the road, he concentrated on keeping a neutral tone. "What do you mean you set a trap?"

"When I saw the car following me earlier, I had Alex call

Arlington." Her jaw creaked as she yawned. "Arlington and I formed a plan to trap the guy. I'd hoped it would close the case."

So she hadn't chased after trouble, it had found her.

Like it always seemed to.

It hadn't taken him long to learn that Lana attracted trouble like a shooting star attracted wishes. She was clearly good at her job, but what he wouldn't give for her to have a safe job.

Salesclerk or teacher perhaps.

Heck, even being a pilot or racecar driver would be a step up. Sure she might crash, but at least she wouldn't have psychos with guns and knives and bombs chasing after her.

He made sure to keep his thoughts hidden. "You got any ideas about why he was following you?"

Silence.

A glance over showed her eyes closed, her breathing slow. Several strands of hair hung over her face. Capturing them, he tucked them behind her shoulder. She didn't even stir.

Wow, she must've been zapped.

A variety of questions still haunted his mind, but no way would he wake her up to ask them. He could question her another time. For now, it was more important that she got some much needed rest.

He transferred his gaze back to the road, but couldn't stop his eyes from straying to her time and time again. A small frown curled her lips, and the dark circles ringing her eyes made them appear sunken.

She looked so small. Young. Vulnerable.

Definitely not like a capable, brave, grown woman who juggled a dangerous and demanding career, personal life, and small home on her own.

Wait. What was he thinking?

He turned toward his house. Someone had tried to kill her tonight. No way was he going to leave her by herself.

There was an empty bed in the girls' wing and the kids would love having her there.

No doubt Lana would fight him, but maybe exhaustion would overrule her stubborn streak.

He hoped she'd be too tired to fight him.

Especially since all he wanted to do was protect her. But no matter how much he wanted to, tonight had proven that there wasn't a thing he could do to shield her from danger.

"Ripper's latest victim released from hospital."

The headline taunted him, pointed out his failure, threw the woman back in his face. He crumpled the newspaper and hurled it across the room.

Barely a column long, he'd read the article so many times he could recite it from memory. Of course the victim's name had been withheld, not that he needed it. He knew exactly who she was and where to find her.

But he couldn't go to her. Couldn't finish the job and end her miserable existence.

The police thought they were being clever. Releasing just enough information to bait him, hoping he would make the world's oldest mistake and return to silence the woman.

Too bad for them he was smarter than that.

But what if that woman could lead the police to him? He didn't think he'd done anything to give away his identity, but she *had* seen him. What if she ran into him somewhere and identified him?

And the police would surely do up another sketch. Nothing about his appearance made him stand out in a crowd, but all it would take was the wrong person seeing the police sketch and he'd be sunk.

No. That wouldn't happen.

It couldn't.

He couldn't go through life alone. Especially not in prison.

Besides, the police already had a sketch and no one had connected it to him. The other witness was next to useless; why should she be any different?

Maybe because she'd gotten a closer look at him.

He pushed out of the recliner. It might not be a bad idea to change his appearance. He could dye his hair, maybe buy some of those non-prescription glasses.

And his sudden change in appearance could send up red flags to all the people who knew him. Nothing like calling a little extra attention to himself to make others suspicious.

No, he'd continue just as he was.

The witness couldn't identify him, this woman wouldn't be able to either. He'd be free to go about his business, find the woman of his dreams, and live a life that would make everyone around him jealous.

But it would be prudent to keep an eye on both the woman and the witness. Just in case. Killing wasn't his goal, but he'd do what was necessary.

And if that required shedding more blood, then more blood would be shed.

Eighteen

"I thought I ordered you to stay home."

Lana glanced up from the statement on her desk to find Barker glowering at her. While his look would've sent rookies running for the door, she knew he wasn't angry. Worried maybe, but not angry.

"I'm fine. Like I said earlier, I'm not even taking prescription pain meds."

The doctor last night had wanted to write up a prescription, but she'd turned it down, something she briefly regretted when she'd first climbed out of bed that morning.

Over the counter painkillers made the pain manageable, though. Popping four ibuprofen every few hours was a cruddy way to get by, but it worked. And most importantly, allowed her to function normally.

"So you aren't on drugs. That give you the right to disobey a direct order?"

"No, sir, but I figured you'd forgive me for wanting to do my job." She tapped a file on the corner of her desk. "Besides, Bright's supposed to take the stand this afternoon. I'm just killing time until we have to pick him up."

Barker studied her face. "So you're really feeling okay? Because you look awful."

A grin played with her mouth. "Boy, you sure know how to give a compliment."

No matter the amount of makeup she'd caked on, there'd been no disguising the plum-like knot on her forehead.

And then there was the bruise on her cheekbone. The location caused most of the color to rest under her eye, making her look like the loser in a fistfight.

It took only one glance to see that Barker still waited for an answer – an honest one – and she smothered a small sigh. "There's a little pain, but it would hurt no matter where I am. I figured I might as well be working."

If she were being one hundred percent honest, she'd have to admit there was more than a little pain. Much more. Her face throbbed and she didn't even want to think about how much it would hurt when she scrubbed off her makeup tonight.

The rest of her body wasn't doing much better. The ibuprofen took the edge off, but her muscles still protested with almost every movement.

Her answer apparently satisfied Barker, because he didn't try to push her into going home.

"So what happened to your face? I heard you were rear ended."

"I was. You're looking at the handiwork of a steering wheel against a hard head."

Her forehead had taken the brunt of the hit, striking against the top of the wheel, but the crossbeams in the center of her steering wheel were to thank for the bruise on her cheek. She was pretty sure her car's emblem was still visible on one side of her nose.

"But the guy who did this never talked?"

"Actually, he did." Picking up several sheets of paper, she handed them across the desk. "His lawyer showed up this morning and convinced him to work with us. With Arlington threatening to charge him with attempted murder for last night's episode, Templing decided to talk. That's his statement there."

Barker skimmed it for a few seconds before returning his

attention to her. "I take it you've read all the way through this."

"I was finishing it up when you walked over."

The file landed on the desk in front of her. "Why don't you tell me what it says. In a nutshell."

Nutshell, huh? The statement covered a range of topics.

Once Templing had started ratting people out, there'd been no stopping him.

But Barker was probably only interested in last night. "Templing was trying to find our safe house. He'd been hired to track down Bright."

"So Templing's a hit man."

"Not according to him. Supposedly he was hired to find the location, which he would pass off to his boss who would give it to someone else to handle after that." Not that Templing was likely to own up to being a hit man. The conversation with Sally Green played through her mind. "Then again, if the man has as many silencers as his ex-wife says, I don't know if I buy that."

"We still like him for the Ripper?"

She shook her head. "I think we've pretty much ruled that one out. Arlington had the last victim view a photo lineup and she didn't pick him out. Neither did Paul. And during at least one of the murders, Templing did have an alibi. Several dozen people saw him in a bar and his credit card shows a charge there just after the murder."

"How'd he learn you were involved with the Bright case?"

Good question. They had yet to hear a good answer. "He said his boss told him but he doesn't know how his boss found out."

Barker rubbed the back of his neck. "Has Bright made any phone calls? The guy's got a big mouth. It'd be just like him to flap his jaws about being in protection and the people assigned to his case."

The same thought had crossed her mind. "I plan to look into it."

"Well, at least we know why he was tailing you." Barker pushed himself out of the chair, spearing her with a stern look. "If you start feeling worse, I want you to go home. Have Alex drive you or something, but you are *not* to stay here if you're in a lot of pain, got it?"

"Yes, sir." She tried to hide a smile.

The narrowing of Barker's eyes told her she'd failed.

"Don't you give me that smile. I mean it." Tossing the words over his shoulder, he headed for his office.

Sure, he meant it. But Barker wasn't as tough as he wanted everyone to think.

Okay, now to poke into Bright's business. But first...

Lana pulled Arlington's card from the top drawer of her desk and punched in his number. He answered on the third ring.

"Arlington."

"It's Tanner. Thanks for sending the statement over."

Papers rustled in the background. "No sweat. I was really hoping he'd be our guy."

"Wouldn't that have been nice."

"Upside though, we got a new sketch. I sent a sketch artist to see Felicity and she helped with a composite. Got a little more detail than your friend was able to give us. We're gonna run it on the news tonight, maybe release part of the profile the Feds created."

Good. Someone out there had to know who this guy was.

And maybe that someone would be watching and would recognize the picture or the profile and would phone in the tip that'd break this case wide open.

On the other hand, they'd get a lot of fake tips, wasting valuable man hours as they followed up on ones that seemed credible but weren't. "I take it the FBI's added more agents to this case."

Arlington snorted. "I'm beginning to feel like there are more Feds here than cops, but it's a small price tag if it helps us nail this guy."

"Well, the way he's escalating, extra help isn't a bad thing."

There had been three weeks between the first and second murders, then two weeks, then eight days. Felicity had been attacked on day seven.

While there was no telling who'd be next, it seemed reasonable to believe it would happen very soon. The clock was already ticking on someone's life and they had no clue where to begin searching.

As if reading her thoughts, Arlington said, "The Feds expect another body in the next forty-eight to seventy-two hours. Commissioner's increased patrols in that part of town, but it probably won't do no good."

"Especially with Hurricane Gino just off the coast. Once that hits, you and I both know the city will be shut down."

"Eh, maybe we'll get lucky and it'll skip us. Hey, hold on a sec."

Maybe Gino would skip them. It wouldn't be the first time. Jacksonville usually experienced the residual effects from a hurricane rather than a direct hit.

But experts were saying this one would be different.

Voices mumbled in the background before Arlington came back on the line. "Gotta go. But hey, you might give Van Horn a heads-up on this. Since the media can't get to Felicity, they're sure to go after him instead."

"I'll let him know."

It was nothing short of a miracle that Felicity's name had remained a secret, although with each new person brought in to help on the case, her identity stood a greater risk of being revealed.

Lana glanced down the block before proceeding up the path to the unassuming house. The drive to the safe house had been smooth and she'd seen no trace of a tail, but a witness's life was at stake. Extra caution wasn't just a good idea, it was a requirement.

She crossed the lawn, but didn't go to the front door. It looked real enough, but a brick wall had been erected behind it. The only way in or out of the house was through the back door.

Short of wiring the door with explosives, anyway. But she'd left her C4 at home.

A six-foot privacy fence surrounded the back yard. The gate blended in with the rest of the fence, but she knew where to look. She released the latch, pushed the gate forward and slid it open on the track hidden amidst the too-tall grass.

The opening of the gate had already sounded an alarm inside and the team would be tracking her progress from the cameras hidden in the house's eaves.

She approached the back door and rang the bell. The heavy steel-core door prevented her from hearing the doorbell echo inside. She glanced at the camera mounted to the overhang above her head and gave a small wave.

The door swung open to reveal Johnson, one of the deputies on duty. He glanced around the yard before slowly lowering his weapon. "You're early."

She gave a small shrug. "Had a few questions for our favorite witness."

Johnson grunted in reply. Stepping back, he let her inside before closing the door and reengaging all the locks. "He's in the living room."

God, give me wisdom.

Although she probably should've prayed for restraint so she wouldn't lay him flat on his back. Attacking the witness was frowned upon in her line of work.

Lana headed through the kitchen, down a short hallway, and into a living room that contained a sofa and two chairs covered in a retro orange and lime green flower print. The furniture was still in surprisingly good condition given their age, although she suspected they'd need to be re-upholstered soon.

The television blared, the sound harsh in the tiny room. A remote sat on the end table closest to her and she picked it up, clicking off the TV.

"Hey!" Bright turned and glared at her. "I was watchin' that."

"And now you're not. You'll have to get ready to leave pretty soon anyway."

A smirk contorted his lips as his gaze swept across her face. "Didn't know the battered look was in. You pull it off pretty good."

She clenched her teeth, but refused to acknowledge his sarcasm. "How'd you get access to a phone?"

"What're you talkin' 'bout?"

Crossing her arms over her chest, she pulled out her fiercest stare. "I know you called someone and I know you gave them information about me. Now *I* want to know who you talked to, how you got a phone, and what else you told them."

"But Deputy Tanner, that would be against the rules." Undercurrents of sarcasm colored his somber tone. "I would never–"

"Cut the garbage, will you? I know you did it. Someone followed me to try to get to you. I've run the options in my head a hundred times and they keep bringing me back to one person. You."

Bright's jaw twitched. "Maybe he was just tryin' to get your number. Ever think 'bout that?"

"We caught him. He confessed. Said he was hired to follow me to your location." Enough of this. She didn't have the energy to argue with a brick head like Bright. "You don't want to admit it, fine. Get your stuff and let's go. I'll deliver you to the courthouse, make sure you testify, then you're on your own. Good luck surviving the night."

Bright's face lightened a few shades. "Hey, hey, wait."

"When you entered the program, you signed a contract.

You broke it, so you're out. On your own."

Words tumbled from his mouth. "Look, I'm sorry, okay? That what you wanna hear?"

"Who'd you call?"

He sighed, rolled his eyes toward the ceiling. "Tessie. You got no idea what it's like bein' locked in here. I got no friends, no social life. I just needed to talk to someone."

"Tessie. Your meth addict ex-girlfriend that you met while peddling drugs. That Tessie?"

"She'd never rat me out. We're tight."

Oh, for crying out loud. Bright couldn't possibly be that naïve, could he? "She's addicted to meth. Her addiction trumps all loyalty to you or anyone else. She probably traded what she knew for a fix."

Anger flashed in his pale blue eyes. "You don't know her."

"I know her type. Now what did you tell her?"

"I just told her 'bout how you're always bustin' my chops and how Johnson's the night Nazi and makes sure lights're out by ten."

She released a measured breath. "How did you call her?"

"Waited until Johnson was in the shower, then I picked the lock to his room and took his cell. Piece a cake."

The creep actually sounded proud. She wanted to slug him.

Rubbing his scruffy hair, Bright sighed. "Look, I can't go back. The cartel's gonna spread my guts down the Florida coast if they catch up to me."

"You broke the rules. We explained the consequences–"

"Come on, ain't you never made a mistake?" He leaned forward, eyes desperate. "Gimme another chance. I'll follow the rules. Honest."

If they wanted his testimony, she really had no choice. Turning him loose now could make him change his testimony while on the stand and blow the prosecution's case.

"One more chance. Don't make me regret it."

"You got my word."

Great. Like his word was worth the oxygen he'd wasted

giving it.

She jerked her head toward the back of the house. "Let's get moving."

As Bright preceded her down the hallway, she counted down the hours. Getting Bright settled in a new life far away from here couldn't happen fast enough.

Paul shut his bedroom door and turned on the small TV sitting on top of his dresser. The local news was just starting, a booming voice introducing each of the anchors while music played in the background.

The first story was some feel good fluff; a way to ease the viewer in before smacking them with the big news.

And thanks to Lana, he knew what at least one of those stories would be.

He wasn't sure what inspired him to watch when he'd spent the last week wishing he could forget the Ripper existed. But no amount of wishful thinking could erase the facts. This wasn't going to go away, not until the Ripper was caught.

"...information on the Ripper."

The word smacked all other thoughts away. He found himself leaning forward slightly, hanging on the anchor woman's every word.

"The FBI's been brought in to help apprehend the serial killer known only as the Jacksonville Ripper. Earlier today, the police released part of the profile in a press conference."

The picture cut to a pretty, solidly-built blonde woman standing behind a podium. Lights strobed around her, but she acted as though she didn't notice. A solemn expression covered her face and matched her equally serious voice.

"The Ripper has most likely lived in this area for a while

now, possibly his whole life. We suspect him to be a white male in his twenties or thirties, with light colored hair."

A picture flashed up on the screen, blocking out the image of the blonde woman. Paul forced himself to breathe.

That was the guy! The sketch artist had captured him perfectly. Details that Paul had forgotten, such as the cowlick at the man's hairline, screamed at him from the computer generated picture.

The woman's voice went on while the network continued to show the sketch. "He has difficulty connecting with people on a deeper level and you would most likely feel uncomfortable around him. We believe he was in a serious relationship until two to four months ago, when the woman ended the relationship. The name Ana has special significance to the Ripper and is possibly the name of the woman from his relationship."

The blonde agent's face popped back on the screen as she concluded her statement. "If this sounds like someone you know or if you have any information, please call our tip line."

She rattled off the number, which also appeared at the bottom of the screen. The words filtered through his mind and he saw the numbers, but couldn't focus on them. His mind was too busy trying to banish the image of the Ripper.

"I sure hope they catch that guy soon." The news anchor's face filled the screen once again.

The camera cut to the co-anchor. "In other news, Hurricane Gino has been upgraded to a category three storm. That story and more after this break."

Like he had the patience for commercials. And much as he should care about Gino, which would probably hit Jacksonville in a few days, all he could think about was the Ripper.

He wasn't sure if the storm was deadlier than the Ripper, but the Ripper was the more terrifying of the two.

Nineteen

And here we go again.

Lana pushed open the door of her rental car with a concealed sigh. The stop at Paul's house had gone from simple to complex in the space of a few seconds. Hovering in the front yard like jackals over a carcass, reporters clamored for a shot of any of the house's occupants.

Didn't these people have better things to do with their time?

The wind whipped her ponytail into her face and she glanced at the sky. Clear for now, but if the news reports could be believed, that wouldn't last more than a day. A hurricane watch had officially been issued for the city of Jacksonville. No one was talking about evacuation – yet – but the storm was predicted to be a big one.

She crossed the street and began to thread her way through the groups of people clustered on Paul's lawn.

Children's voices drifted from the fenced back yard. Of course the kids were outside; they usually were when she stopped by on the weekend. Maybe it was best to head around the back.

"Get a few shots of the house." A woman's voice said from somewhere nearby.

In her peripheral vision, Lana saw movement to her left. She tried to get out of the way but wasn't fast enough as a wiry man turned and rammed into her. The camera in his hands betrayed him as a photographer for one of the local papers.

"Oops, sorry."

She skirted by him. "No problem."

Great. Now he'd drawn attention to her. It wouldn't take the reporters long to figure out she wasn't one of them. She had no tape recorder, no camera, no crew.

She brushed by, not at all surprised when the woman's voice sounded again behind her.

"Quick, get a picture."

So much for anonymity. She quickened her step and broke free from the group. Questions jumbled together behind her, each voice straining to be heard above the din.

"Who are you?"

"What's your relationship to Paul Van Horn?"

"Can you ask Mr. Van Horn to give us a statement?"

A hand closed around her forearm. She whirled and leveled what she hoped was a frigid glare at a man with short light brown hair.

He released her, only to promptly thrust a microphone in her face. "Ma'am, a statement? Are you a friend of Mr. Van Horn?"

Of all the boneheaded, brazen things to do. He was lucky she hadn't pulled her gun. "No comment."

Almost there. She stopped next to the six-foot gate.

Wait a second.

She couldn't ignore these people and hope they'd scram. If she went in the back yard now, they might decide to follow her lead and do the same. What she needed to do was deter them and she knew just how to do it.

She pulled her badge and held it high, but didn't identify herself. "You're all trespassing on private property. If you're going to stalk Mr. Van Horn, you'll have to do it from the sidewalk."

The words stirred disgruntled muttering, but the group

slowly moved to comply.

Hopefully that would provide Paul some peace, but she doubted it.

Man, he couldn't wait for this to be over. From the endless voicemails to the freak show in his front yard, the relentlessness of the press was exhausting.

Paul pushed his chair away from his desk and rose. It was about time to get lunch going. Most of the kids were out back playing basketball, but their stomachs kept better time than an alarm clock. If he didn't have food ready by noon, he'd likely face a revolution.

Silence blanketed the house as he entered the kitchen and headed to the sink to wash his hands. A glance out the window found Dale Webber a sweaty mess as he tried to block Trevor's shot, but the ball swished through the net no matter what he did. Several feet away, Annie twirled the tire swing for three of the younger kids.

They were so good with the kids. And definitely had more to offer than he did. With the two of them here, the kids had both a mother and a father figure.

Of course, if Lana were here, too, they'd have two sets of parents.

He shook off the thought, dropped the curtain, and turned from the window. Lunch wouldn't make itself.

Going to the refrigerator, he pulled out lunch meats, mayonnaise, mustard, and – just for Maria – ketchup. Ketchup on a ham sandwich sounded disgusting to him, but she liked it. He retrieved bread, peanut butter, and jelly from various places around the kitchen, grabbed a stack of napkins and disposable plates, and spread everything across the counter.

Sneakers squeaked on the tile behind him. He turned to

find Brittany leaning against a counter, a grin on her face.

Uh-oh. That look always meant trouble.

Brittany spoke before he had a chance to inquire. "Lana's here."

Well, that explained a lot. That look had been one of a matchmaking teenage girl.

"Really?" He tried for a casual tone.

"Really."

"I'm surprised the press didn't devour her on her way to the door."

"Lana's tough. She can do anything."

Spoken like a true teenager. He couldn't resist ribbing her. "You mean you've seen her fly? Lift cars with one hand?"

Brittany rolled her eyes. "Of course not. That's just dumb."

"But you said she could do anything."

"Well, yeah. Realistic things, anyway."

"What's realistic?" Lana's voice came from the doorway.

Although the bruising on her face had darkened since the last time he'd seen her, she looked like she was doing okay. Her hair was back in a loose ponytail and her rich turquoise tank top reminded him of the Atlantic on a hot July day.

Brittany pasted on a look of feigned ignorance. "Nothing. I'll just leave you guys. To talk. Alone." Hands stuffed in her pockets, she shot him a sly grin on her way out the door.

One eyebrow lifted, Lana turned to look at him.

"What was that about?" Laughter lined the words.

Right. Like he was really going to tell her.

He lifted his shoulders in a small shrug. "You have quite a fan club here. She thinks you can do anything."

"No kidding?" A grin spread across her lips.

"Yeah, we were discussing your many superpowers before you walked in."

"I guess I could use some pointers on maintaining a secret identity." Lana crossed the kitchen and stood on the opposite side of the island. "Anything I can do to help?"

"Not until the kids get in. Then I could use some help

assembling sandwiches for the younger ones."

"I think I can handle that."

It was good to see that relaxed smile on her face again. She'd been so tense lately. And with the car accident the other day, not to mention the fact the Ripper was still on the loose, he was a little surprised to find her so peaceful.

"How're you feeling?"

"Pretty good. A little stiff, but nothing I can't handle."

Of course not. Because Brittany had been half-right.

If there really was someone who could do anything, Lana was that person.

He kept the thought to himself. "So how bad was it out there? With the reporters, I mean?"

Leaning her back against the counter, she folded her arms loosely over her chest. "Actually, not as bad as it has been. I gave them a little incentive to keep their distance. It won't make them go away, but it should give you some breathing room."

"Yeah? What'd you do?"

"Showed my badge and told them they were trespassing. I think it'll do the trick. For a while anyway."

There was some comfort in that, but he had trouble seeing it. Would he ever get his quiet life back?

If there was one good thing about an impending storm, it was that it had finally driven away the reporters Lana had threatened the day before.

That was the only good thing about it.

Because aside from that, all it had done was create a boatload of work.

Paul felt the exhaustion deep in his bones. It had been a long day and promised to not end anytime soon.

The full force of the hurricane should hit within the next few hours. The way the wind whipped at his clothing, he found it hard to believe it wasn't here already.

While the eye of the storm wasn't expected to pass through the city, the hurricane-force winds were. Already the wind howled and clouds covered the sun, blanketing the city in a gray film. Dust particles stung his eyes and grass clippings from the freshly-mowed lawn slapped his calves.

But they were almost done.

After church, he and some of the other members had helped board up the church's windows. With so many of them, it hadn't taken long at all.

Next he'd headed to Lana's to help her do the same.

She'd fought him on it, saying he needed to worry about his own place, but he'd ignored her protests. No matter what she might think, she needed a little help sometimes.

Unfortunately, she'd insisted on returning the favor. But as the storm drew closer, the sky grew darker, and the winds grew fiercer, he wished she hadn't come.

Would she make it home in time to avoid being caught in the storm?

With the last nail pounded in, he put a hand on her shoulder and raised his voice so the words wouldn't be lost in the wind. "Why don't you wait this thing out with us?"

"They're predicting Gino won't pass us until after nine tonight. I've got plenty of time."

Several more hours of *this*?

It seemed impossible, but if that's what the experts predicted, he'd go with it. They knew more about storms than he ever wanted to know.

Okay, so she wouldn't get caught out in the storm. It would still be nice to have her around. "You sure? We have lots of room and we're going to play games."

"I'd have to stay overnight, which makes getting to work tomorrow morning complicated. It's better if I head home before this thing hits."

No point in arguing with her. When Lana made up her mind, only God could change it.

Besides, it really was safer that way. For his heart, if nothing else.

In the distance, thunder growled like a lion poised to attack.

The clouds overhead had turned from gray to black and a fat raindrop splattered on top of his head.

"Will you at least call me once you get home?"

She nodded and jogged toward her rental car. The wind whipped at her and he half expected it to pick her up and carry her away. Not like she weighed all that much.

The rain fell in visible panels now and he retreated to the shelter of the covered porch.

As her car pulled away from the curb, he turned to go inside.

Okay, time to get ready for this. He'd never actually been in a hurricane before.

What if the experts were wrong? What if the eye passed through Jacksonville and leveled half the town?

What if it leveled this old house?

Instead of worrying, he should pray.

Within five minutes, peace had replaced the fear. God was the creator of this storm and He alone controlled it.

What a cruddy time for a storm. Why did these things always happen in the middle of a big case?

Well, maybe it'd keep the Ripper off the streets. If it did, he'd weather any storm.

The phone on his desk shrilled. Arlington snatched it up on the second ring. "Yeah."

"I'm looking for the detective in charge of the Ripper case."

A woman's voice, young, with a slight tremor that told of fear.

"You got 'im." Had he told her his name? Better to play it safe. "Detective Arlington here."

"My name is Ana Cordova."

Ana. The name settled in his mind, stilled his hands. Now the question remained, was she legit or a crackpot?

"I think I know who the Ripper is."

Sure she did. So had the last two hundred and fifty callers.

Not that he'd personally taken those calls. Before any tips came to him, they went to someone at the tip line who listened to the tip, made a judgment on viability, and either thanked the caller for the information or passed the caller off to someone higher up. Him, in this case.

But if she'd made it to his desk, someone had thought she had something of interest to say. Wouldn't kill him to hear her out.

"Mind telling me how you know this guy?"

"I–I think he's my ex-boyfriend."

Great. Another one of those calls.

A couple had a bitter break up and the one with the deeper wounds called in a tip of illegal activities. Happened all the time.

He sighed. "And what makes you think that?"

"Well, the… the picture for one thing. I saw it online and it looks like Lyle. And then I heard the FBI's profile and it described him. I broke up with him back in March because he was getting all creepy and possessive on me."

March. Well, that fit with the timeline the profilers had established.

Course, anyone with half a brain could've taken that profile and dreamed up a story like this. She was going to have to do a heck of a lot better than that to convince him.

"Go on."

"Lyle was always insecure. Clingy, you know? I thought he'd get over it, but he only got worse. He had to know everything I did. I caught him following me to work, the store, even my parents' house. When I broke up with him, I had to get a restraining order because he followed me even more."

Hmmm. The guy sounded obsessive enough to be the Ripper. And that bit about the restraining order would be easy enough to confirm. "Ms. Cordova, would you mind describing yourself to me?"

A pause. "Uh, I'm twenty-six, work full time at a clothing store–"

"Sorry, I meant your appearance."

Another pause, longer this time. "You want to know what I look like?"

Maybe he should've pulled her DMV photo instead, but this was faster, easier. "Let's say I'm testing a theory."

"Um, okay. I'm Hispanic, five foot five, brown eyes, black hair–"

"Long?"

"It used to be. I cut it after breaking up with Lyle. He'd been so obsessed with it that it kinda freaked me out."

If Ana's words were true, she matched the profile of the Ripper's victims.

Or, more accurately, the Ripper's victims matched her. "You seen or spoken to him recently?"

"Not since I moved out of town. I had to. It didn't matter that I had the restraining order, he still followed me. I couldn't prove it, but I saw his car a lot."

"What kind of car?"

"I don't know. Some kind of black four door."

Another fact that lined up. Also another fact she could've gotten from the news. "And how long's it been since you moved?"

"A few months. I moved, uh... middle of April. I think."

And the murders began at the end of April. Coincidence? Not likely.

Arlington braced the phone against his shoulder and logged onto his computer. Time to pull a DMV photo and check out her story. "Mind if I ask where you're living now?"

"Hinesville."

Ah, Georgia. "You didn't go very far."

"I couldn't afford to. My cousin lives up here and she said I could crash at her place for a while."

"What's Lyle's last name?"

"Simmons. He's a photographer for the Chronicle. Or at least used to be. I don't really know what he's doing anymore."

A photo popped up on the screen and Arlington felt the first shaft of hope shoot through him. The woman staring back at him, Ana Cordova, bore a strong resemblance to the Ripper's victims, especially the first one.

"Ms. Cordova, you wouldn't happen to have a picture of Lyle, would you?"

"I threw them all out. I didn't want anything to do with him."

No biggie. Now that he had a name, he could get a DMV photo. There couldn't be that many guys in the area with a name like Lyle Simmons. Once he had a picture, he'd have Paul come down to make an ID.

"This is my fault, isn't it? Lyle's out there killing people because I broke up with him."

Technically, yes, but he'd never admit that to her. "If it is Lyle doing this, then he's a psycho. You're lucky you left him. Otherwise it coulda been you."

"Maybe if I'd found a way to prove he'd broken the restraining order instead of running away, those women would still be alive."

"Or maybe you'd be dead." Too blunt, but it was too late to do anything about it now. "It's always hard to believe that someone you know is capable of doing something like this."

"Actually, it's not. That's what makes this so hard. I knew he was capable–"

"Then what..." Arlington clamped his mouth shut. It had taken guts for Ana to call him. He'd better watch his step here.

Softening his tone, he picked his words carefully. "Why did

you wait so long to come forward?"

"I didn't know." Her voice sounded heavy, like she could barely hold back the tears. "I mean, I'd heard about the serial killer, but I don't watch the news. Then my cousin told me I should check it out 'cause the profile and picture reminded her of Lyle."

"Well, I appreciate the tip. I'm going to check it out."

"Do–do you really think it's him?"

It looked like a strong possibility, but he wouldn't confirm or deny anything. "Hard to say until I get more information, but if it is, you need to be very careful. He might come after you."

Silence greeted his warning. Seconds scraped by with nothing but the sound of her shallow breathing on the other end.

"Ms. Cordova? You okay?"

"Y–you seriously think he'll come after me?"

Much as he didn't want to get her all worked up, he had to warn her. If Simmons was the Ripper, he might've been working his way up to killing Ana. The other victims might've been a trial run of sorts. "I think it's something we need to consider. I want you to lock your doors and windows and don't let anyone in."

"But I have to work tomorrow–"

"Call out. Just for a day or two. Your life might depend on it."

"O–okay." The word shook across the line.

"Good." He reached for the pen perched on the edge of his desk. "Now let me get your number and I'll call you as soon as I know more."

Twenty

"What's next?"

Paul turned to find Dale Webber standing behind him, hands hanging loosely at his sides. "Well, we need to gather some blankets and pillows. I figured we'd wait out the storm in the main living room."

While not exactly an interior room, there weren't many options that could accommodate a group of this size. They certainly couldn't all cluster in the bathroom for the whole night.

Besides, with the covered porch running the front of the house, the second floor above them, and all the windows securely boarded over, the main room should be as secure as anywhere.

And lacking the flood danger they'd face in the basement.

"Prob'ly oughta have some water and food available, too. In case the kitchen ain't safe."

"Good idea." At least the Webbers had dealt with storms before. This was a new experience for him. "I also thought we could gather some games and activities to keep the kids entertained."

Dale turned for the door. "I'll get the bedding."

It took several trips to take all the supplies downstairs. They had just finished when his cell phone rang. It had to be Lana.

He dug the phone out of his pocket and glanced at the display on the front. No, not Lana.

"Hello?"

"Arlington here. I need you to come to the station."

"Now? Have you looked outside?"

"Storm's still several hours off. It'll take you all of five minutes to drive here."

"Can't it wait?"

"No. So what do you say?"

Aw, man. Great, just great.

The last thing he wanted was to go out in this mess. What was Arlington thinking?

Arlington's voice broke through his thoughts. "Paul, I wouldn't ask if it wasn't important. We got a lead on the Ripper. I need you to make an ID so we can get this butcher off the streets."

"What about your victim? She saw him better than I did."

"She's too beat up to drive right now and frankly, I can't spare an officer to go to her. 'Sides, you're closer. Now how 'bout it? You gonna help me out here?"

No matter how much he wanted to say no, he couldn't. If there was a chance they'd bring this maniac to justice before someone else died, he'd do whatever he could to help.

"I'll be there in ten minutes."

Driving in a storm like this ranked right up with being shot again.

Lana forcibly relaxed her rigor-mortis grip on the steering wheel and eased back on the accelerator. No point in going too fast. Like she'd told Paul, she had plenty of time before the storm was upon them.

Maybe she should've stayed at Paul's. No doubt he

could've used some help with the kids.

But she'd come too far to turn back now. Best to keep going.

Prayers for safety flashed through her mind and calmed her, in spite of the storm raging around her. Amazing how quickly God could give peace, whether in the midst of an actual physical storm, such as this one, or simply through the storms of life.

Lightning illuminated the car and the thunder rumbled so loudly she felt the vibration through the seat.

The windshield wipers moved at top speed, but couldn't keep up with the waves of rain assaulting the vehicle. Visibility was so poor she didn't dare go faster than twenty-five.

Evidently not everyone felt the same way.

Headlights bore down on her from behind, whipped to the left, and shot by her, ignoring the double yellow line down the center of the road.

What an idiot! Didn't he know that was a good way to get in an accident?

If she were a cop, she'd pull him over. And give him a ticket so big he'd have to take out a loan just to pay it.

Probably some teenager trying to get home before their parents sent out a search party.

Or maybe a tourist.

Brake lights flashed in front of her and she squinted through the rain-blurred windshield. What was he–

The car fishtailed, seemed to correct, then flew off the shoulder of the road. It went down a small embankment and came to rest in the middle of some tall wild grass.

Hopefully no one was hurt. Emergency services were likely spread pretty thin tonight.

Lana applied the brake as she steered for the shoulder.

Putting the gearshift in park, she hit the switch for her four-ways, grabbed her cell phone, and threw the door open.

Lucky for this guy she'd taken this road home or he might still be out here when the hurricane came through. She'd debated the wisdom of using side roads, knowing they were more likely to be blocked by fallen tree limbs or debris, but this was the most direct route.

A glance up the road found it deserted.

For now.

But the chance that someone else might take this route couldn't be ignored. Between the wind, debris, and rain, they might not see her car, even with the four ways blinking.

She popped open the trunk, dug around in the emergency kit she'd transferred from her own damaged car, and pulled out a few flares. After placing them on the asphalt around her car, she headed for the shoulder of the road.

She began to dial 911, but hesitated with her finger over the send key.

The emergency crews were sure to be overstressed on a day like today. Better to see if anyone needed medical attention before calling an ambulance.

Water ran from her drenched hair down her forehead and into her eyes. She blinked it away and started down the slope. Shoes sliding in the mud, she skidded to the bottom and stopped, her eyes moving across the marshy field.

Part of her wanted to hurry to the car, but the more cautious side of her forced her muscles to move slowly.

The tall grass that scratched her knees could easily hide an alligator.

That was the last thing she needed to deal with right now.

While this wasn't an area alligators frequented, during a storm there was no telling where you'd find one.

She eased forward a few steps. Then froze.

Something was wrong.

Nothing concrete that she could solidly identify, but the feeling was as vivid as a voice in her ear.

It pricked her instincts.

Warned her of danger.

Was it a gator? Snake? Some other wild animal?

Her gaze slowly worked across the field, watching for any

indication of life.

With the wind thrashing the grass, it was impossible to tell what might lurk inside. If a predator stalked her right now, she'd never hear it coming.

Weather like this should have most wild animals seeking shelter. Survival instincts.

But humans didn't always follow those instincts. What if it was a creature of a human design?

She slid her cell phone in a pocket and pulled her gun from the holster at the small of her back.

Part of her wanted to turn and run back to her vehicle, but she couldn't do it.

Checking on the occupants of the car was not only the right thing to do, but her obligation as a member of law enforcement.

There might be children inside.

Or someone who was injured. Which seemed likely since she had yet to see anyone get out of the car.

Okay. She'd check the car, then get the heck out of there.

The tinted windows made it impossible for her to see anyone inside. She inched closer.

"Hello? Are you okay?" The wind stole her words and the thunder drowned out any chance of anyone inside the car hearing her.

As she neared, she examined the car.

No visible structure damage, good. Not even a flat tire. Maybe it was still drivable.

Not likely. The mud sucking at her shoes promised that the car would sink to its axles before being driven out.

The black paint was only a shade darker than the sky above and the chrome trim…

She slowed, her hands tightening on the gun.

Black paint.

Chrome trim.

Tinted windows.

Her eyes flew to the front of the car.

Hood ornament.

This matched Paul's description of the Ripper's car. Perfectly.

She glanced around. Half expected to see a skinny white guy with a knife. But she was alone.

Or at least appeared to be.

The car had been in a big hurry. The Ripper would be eager to get his next victim to a secluded location.

Cool it. She didn't even know for sure that this was the Ripper's car.

But if it was, there might be a woman inside who needed help.

Bringing up her contact list, she selected dispatch. Someone was on the line within seconds.

"This is Deputy Milana Tanner requesting backup. Spotted possible suspect vehicle. It's a black Monte Carlo." She kept her voice low, not that anyone near the car would be able to hear her over the noise from the storm, and gave the dispatcher the license plate number.

"Copy. What is your location?"

"Ridgeview Road. About seven miles north of Lincoln Drive."

"Be advised, there are no units in your area. We're stretched pretty thin today."

Not good.

Here she was, possibly facing a serial killer on her own in the middle of a storm, and her options for backup were nonexistent.

She should leave. Now. Run while she still could.

But what if this wasn't the Ripper's car?

What if some innocent person bled to death while she acted all paranoid?

"Will you do me a favor? Call Detective Arlington at the sixth precinct and tell him what I just told you."

"Would you like to hold the line?"

What she wanted and what she needed were two different

things. She wanted to hold so that if her suspicions were correct, someone would know immediately what she'd found.

But it was overridden by the need to have both hands free, just in case.

"No. Just have him call me. As soon as possible." She ended the call and slid it into her pocket.

Most likely, she was being paranoid.

She and Arlington would laugh about this tomorrow.

But she couldn't shake the feeling that this was the Ripper's car, which meant he was sitting inside, probably watching her right now.

Rain flowed down her arms, over the Glock she gripped with both hands.

Gun up, ready, she edged closer to the car.

Her eyes darted left, right, left again, always moving, always watching for any hint of trouble.

Nothing.

Every step to the vehicle coiled her muscles tighter. Fifteen feet, twelve, ten.

She stopped.

It was all wrong.

Her instincts screamed to turn back.

The Ripper or an idiot driver? How could she tell without compromising herself?

She couldn't. No choice but to go with her gut.

This was a very distinctive car and Paul had described it precisely. How many cars could there be in the Jacksonville area that fit the description of the car in front of her?

Probably only a handful.

And what were the chances she'd just *happen* to encounter one on a sparsely traveled side road in the middle of a storm when she was all alone? Slim to none.

Unless it wasn't an accident.

It was a set up.

And the Ripper had a new target.

Her.

Lightning flashed, providing enough light for her to see through the tint covering the windows. To see the driver's seat.

Empty.

Twenty-One

Evidently the rain drove all the crazies out of hiding.

The fact that he was out, too, didn't speak well of his own sanity.

Paul stood inside the main entrance to the precinct, wiping the rain from his face. Amazing how wet he could get in the ten seconds it had taken to make it inside.

A woman with a screaming baby sat in one of the chairs, her face blotchy and her eyes swollen. A middle-aged man paced, looking every so often at the door that separated the public area from the secured ones. Several teens sat on the far side of the room, maybe taking shelter or maybe waiting for someone. Three kids under the age of ten huddled next to a girl who couldn't be any older than fourteen.

Dang. He didn't need to know the story to guess what they were doing here. Probably waiting for a relative or social services while their parent was booked for God only knew what.

Shake it off.

There were a lot of needy kids out there. He couldn't save them all.

Besides, he needed to get home to his own kids.

Paul strode across the lobby and identified himself. The officer behind the glass buzzed him through.

A bald, burly officer appeared at his side. "Arlington's been waiting for you. Not very patiently, if you know what I mean."

Paul forced a small smile.

Patience wasn't something he suspected a lot of people had on a day like today. It also wasn't something he imagined Arlington possessed in large quantities, even on a good day. "I bet."

The chaos behind the scenes was worse than what he'd encountered walking in.

Ringing phones mingled with slurred protests, loudly voiced outrage, and manic laughter.

Not the kind of laughter that made you want to join in. The creepy kind that made you want to hide.

Prostitutes, drunks, kids too high to know the difference.

Oh yeah, the storm had driven all sorts of people out in the open.

Paul's shoes squeaked on the linoleum as he followed the officer down the hall.

The officer opened a door toward the end and nodded. Arlington looked up from paperwork on his desk.

"Hey, Paul. Thanks for comin'."

Like he'd had much choice. "Sure, no problem."

Paul crossed the room and took the other chair, transferring his gaze from Arlington to half a dozen photos spread across the detective's desk. Each picture was shot on a solid blue background and contained a blonde haired man from the shoulders up.

A photo spread. He'd been called down here to make an ID from a photograph. And here he'd thought they had the Ripper in custody.

Seriously? Couldn't Arlington have emailed the pictures or something?

"See anyone familiar?" Arlington's voice made him jump.

"Uh, give me a second here."

His gaze slid past the first picture. The guy was too heavy to be the Ripper. The second picture showed a guy with curly hair. He was pretty sure the Ripper's hair wasn't curly.

The next guy had a square jaw and an expression that dared you to mess with him. Not the Ripper.

He moved to the next photo. No.

No to the fifth photo, too. His gaze slid to the final photo.

Breath lodged in his throat. It was the Ripper!

"Where'd... how did..." Paul tried to focus his thoughts but couldn't, could only stare at the man who'd terrorized the city for weeks.

The Ripper didn't look like such a monster in the picture. He actually looked pleasant.

A small smile tweaked the man's mouth, giving him a gentle, kind look.

Man, looks really were deceiving.

"I take it you found him?"

"I think so. I mean, it sure looks like him to me." Paul dragged his eyes from the photo to Arlington. "Where did this come from?"

The phone on the desk rang, but Arlington made no move to answer.

Evidently information on the Ripper trumped everything else.

"DMV." Arlington nodded at the spread. "I need you to officially point out the guy you think it is."

Paul jabbed his finger at the smiling face in the sixth photo. "That guy."

A grin, possibly the first genuine one he'd seen the detective wear, crossed Arlington's face. "That's what I wanted to hear."

"How'd you find him? I mean, what led you to this guy?"

"You're not gonna believe this, but I got a phone call. From Ana."

Ana? It took him a minute to place the name, but when he did, the implications slammed him. "As in the one connected to the Ripper?"

"As in his ex-girlfriend. Who broke up with him a few

weeks before the first murder."

No way.

It was hard to believe this nightmare might finally be over.

A sharp rap came from the door. Arlington jerked his head around, his eyes narrowing. "I'm in the middle of something–"

The officer who'd led Paul back earlier stepped into the room, a piece of paper in his hand. "You're gonna wanna see this."

Arlington snatched the paper from the officer's hand and skimmed it. "And this just came in?"

"Yeah. Dispatch called us when they couldn't reach you."

"Thanks." The words on the paper wiped the smile from Arlington's face.

Not good.

Arlington opened his top desk drawer and rummaged through it. Apparently not finding what he needed, he moved on to the next drawer. Without looking up, he said, "You don't happen to know Tanner's number off the top of your head, do you?"

Lana?

"Sure." He dug his phone out of his pocket, brought up her number, and started to read it, but Arlington cut him off.

"Call her. Tell her you're with me and see what she says."

As much as he wanted to demand more details, Paul simply obeyed.

He hit send and tried to ignore the boulder growing in his stomach. Something about Arlington's tone terrified him, although the cop's face revealed nothing.

The other end rang.

Once, twice, the ringing continued and each one seemed longer than the previous.

Why wasn't she answering? And what was all this about?

Arlington picked up his phone and hit a button. "I need to know who the closest unit is to Ridgeview Road."

Another fist to the gut. That was the road Lana would have

used to get home.

What was going on?

Paul struggled to breathe as he listened to Arlington. Then Lana's voice reached his ears.

All thoughts of Arlington's conversation fled his mind and words spewed from his lips. "Lana, praise God. What's–"

"–I can't answer right now–"

Voice mail. He terminated the call only to bring her number back up and try again. Same result.

He lowered the phone. Arlington stood behind his desk, his face contorted in a scowl.

"I don't care if they have to grow wings and fly, just get them out there now!" The phone crashed back in the receiver and Arlington fixed him with something that bordered a glare. "Well?"

"Went to voice mail. Twice."

Slamming his hand against the desk, Arlington released a string of words capable of searing the flesh off a nun's ears.

Paul's hands shook.

The tremble spread up his arms, across his chest, and through his body until it reached his feet. The soda he'd downed earlier threatened to come back for round two.

While his body fell to pieces, his voice was surprisingly steady. "What's wrong?"

Arlington swore again. "The nearest car's still a good five minutes out."

But out from what? It had something to do with Lana, that was all he knew. And Arlington was really worked up.

He had to know what was going on.

Sitting here like a log wasn't an option. And Arlington certainly wasn't volunteering the information.

Paul shot out of his chair and grabbed the paper from Arlington's desk.

Arlington didn't try to stop him.

The words impaled him. Jotted in pencil, the writing was so neat and precise it made mistaking the meaning impossible.

His knees gave out and he sank into his chair, clutching the note in a hand shaking so violently he had no idea how he could still read the message.

Call from Deputy Tanner. Requested Arlington ASAP. Ridgeview Road, seven miles off Lincoln. Found suspect vehicle.

Where was he?

The car hadn't crashed itself. Someone had been inside. But the driver's seat was vacant.

Maybe he planned an ambush from the back seat. Or the passenger side.

He couldn't disappear. He had to be here somewhere.

She glanced behind her, expected to see a shadow. No one.

That didn't mean he wasn't around. She had to get out of here.

Now.

Her gaze swept the rain-drenched grass surrounding the Ripper's car. No way to tell if the grass moved because of the wind or someone hiding there.

She could be surrounded by a group of soldiers right now and not even know it.

Gun still aimed at the vehicle, she looked behind her, saw no one, and took a step back.

Caution would keep her alive. She wouldn't turn her back on the black car. Never mind that all she wanted to do was bolt.

One more step back.

He had to be close; she hadn't seen him leave.

The man may be evil and slimy, but he wasn't as subtle as a serpent. She doubted he could move through the grass without her noticing.

As long as she had her gun, she had the advantage.

Thunder growled overhead.

She almost pulled the trigger.

Her breathing shallowed, her heart pulsed like an addict, and her mind had only one thought: get away.

No. She had to stay calm. Think rationally.

She eased back on the trigger, but kept her finger a paper's width away.

If the Ripper forced a confrontation, she'd shoot him before he got within twenty feet of her.

Lightning broke the sky and she glanced behind her again. Still no one.

She was almost to the car.

Her phone vibrated against her side. Had to be Arlington, but she couldn't answer it. Couldn't even check to be sure. She had to keep both hands on the gun, her full attention focused on her surroundings.

She let it go to voice mail.

The next step found her on the incline. With the Ripper's car now a good distance away, she turned and dashed up the hill.

She came up on the passenger side, rounded the back of the car–

Something slammed into her ribcage.

The air whooshed from her lungs. Pain shot up her spine and through her head as first her back, then her skull, crashed into the asphalt.

The gun flew from her fingers.

Numbness radiated through her body, which refused to obey the commands her brain screamed.

Until *he* filled her vision.

Gliding toward her like an angel of death, a drenched blonde man approached.

The Ripper.

An unreadable expression covered his face. His hands hung at his sides, empty.

No knife. She had a chance.

A plan formed. She waited for him to draw closer, walk past her feet.

Jackknifing her body into a crouch, she whipped her leg around. She caught him at the ankles, hit him hard enough that he teetered.

His arms flung out and he toppled backward.

On her feet in seconds, she scanned the drenched terrain for her gun. There!

She only moved two steps before a hand closed around her ankle. The pavement rushed toward her. Pain spiked through her left wrist, like barbed wire beneath the skin.

Tears blurred her vision.

Her wrist throbbed and her fingers numbed.

She blinked rapidly to clear her eyes. Stay focused. There'd be time to deal with her hand later.

If she survived that long.

She would. If for no other reason than to see the Ripper in handcuffs.

Besides, she wasn't out of options yet.

While her left leg was caught in a vise, her right one was free. She kicked at the Ripper's hand, felt her foot connect with something solid.

The Ripper cursed. His grip loosened enough for her to jerk away.

Gravel dug into her forearms, her palms, her knees. She scrambled to her feet.

Almost there.

Cold wet steel had never felt so comforting. She scooped up her gun.

Something crashed into her skull. Pain detonated inside her head, exploded fireworks behind her eyes.

Her vision dimmed and her muscles gave out.

It felt like falling down a bell tower; she even had the ringing in her ears.

The rain faded, the noise dimmed, and darkness beckoned. All thoughts ceased as she slipped into a deep black crevasse.

A fighter.

Any other time and he would've found her spunk incredibly attractive, but not now.

Not with a storm closing in. Not with the call she'd made. Not with the whole city looking for him.

His breath came in short, abrupt bursts. Muscles quivered and limbs ached, but he'd won.

On the pavement in front of him was the woman. Lana. It was like Ana, only better. Just like she would be better than Ana.

She was even prettier than he remembered.

Except for the bruises on her face, but those would heal.

Someone had beat her up good.

Had to be that Van Horn guy. Why women stayed with men like that was beyond him, but she didn't have to worry about that anymore. He'd make sure Van Horn never touched her again.

You hurt her, too.

Yeah, but that wasn't his fault. She'd made him do it.

Blood oozed from a gash on the side of her head. A gash caused by the rock still clutched in his left hand.

Why'd she have to fight him like that?

He flung the rock at the blue Nissan she'd been driving. Glass mixed with the rain as the rock shattered the rear window.

Not the most productive use of energy, but he felt better.

They had to get out of here. While he hadn't heard the call she'd made, with her line of work he was betting she'd called the cops. They were probably en route now.

He bent over her, wrapped his arms under her waist, and tried to straighten.

Limp limbs fought him, her spaghetti spine slipping from his arms. Huh. Always amazed him how someone so small could be so hard to carry.

He tried again. Her body rolled once as she dropped from his grasp.

No! He didn't have time for this!

He walked around to stand by her head. Lifting her arms, he half carried, half dragged her into the tall grass bordering the road.

This would be faster if he brought the car up to her rather than taking her to the car. He placed her arms by her sides and hurried down the incline toward his car.

His shoes slipped on the wet ground and he went down, flattening a large section of grass. Mud caked his shirt and denim shorts and promised to make a mess of his car, but he couldn't do anything about that now.

The engine roared to life. Shifting into reverse, he floored the accelerator. The car lurched but went no further.

This couldn't be happening! He'd come too far to be stopped now.

He gave it more gas. The tires spun, flung mud against the undercarriage, but went nowhere. Had to get away. Now.

Wait. This car was front wheel drive. Maybe going forward would work better.

He shifted into drive. Instead of flooring it, he applied a small amount of pressure to the accelerator.

The car jerked forward. He gave it more gas. Mud flew off both sides, the car skidded, but kept moving.

Come on, come on.

The incline loomed in front of him. He floored the accelerator. The tires spun and the car fishtailed, but he drew no closer to the road.

No, no no!

He backed up a short distance, punched the accelerator, but still lacked the traction to climb the hill.

Now what? The cops would be here any second. Then it

would all be over.

Wait. What about her car?

It sat on the pavement, waiting for him, begging to be driven.

It meant leaving his car here for the police to find, but that couldn't be helped. Besides, they'd still have to track him down and that wouldn't be easy.

Especially not with this storm.

He threw the door open, raced up the incline, and approached her prone body. A bulge in her right jeans pocket showed him where to find the car key.

Digging in the pocket, his fingers closed around something else. A cell phone.

He dropped it on the pavement next to her head. Now when the cops activated the GPS tracker that was probably inside, it'd lead them to nothing but this empty stretch of road and his abandoned car.

Time to get her in the trunk.

Popping the trunk, he picked up an emergency kit and tossed it to the side. He dragged her toward the trunk, trying not to think about how much time had passed since she'd called the police.

Drawing a deep breath, he lifted her, flopped the top half of her body into the trunk, and pushed, pulled, heaved until the rest of her followed. He slammed the trunk closed and headed for the driver's side.

No sound of sirens yet. Maybe she hadn't gotten through.

Or maybe they were making a silent approach.

He cranked the key, shifted into drive, and floored the accelerator. Now all he had to do was get out of here without passing any cops.

Because even if they saw him, he wouldn't stop.

He'd drive into a concrete median and kill himself and the woman before he let the cops take him down.

Twenty-Two

The note escaped from Paul's fingers. Thoughts battled the images in his mind.

Lana.

The Ripper.

Knife.

Blood.

Death.

He had to help her!

Pushing up, he strode toward the door. Arlington's voice stopped him before he left the room.

"You might as well wait here."

Lana was out there with a serial killer, a hurricane could hit any time, and Arlington expected him to *wait*? The man had to be nuts, certifiably crazy.

"Come on, Paul. Have a seat."

He spun around and narrowed his eyes at Arlington. "You may not care what happens to Lana, but I'm sure not gonna sit around while some lunatic guts her."

"I have officers on the way. They'll get there long before you would."

"I can't just do nothing! I saw this guy in action. What he did...."

His nightmare flashed back to him, filled his mind with things he'd rather not see. Lana being stabbed by the Ripper, her blood staining the pavement, her body void of life. "I have to try."

"Look, my guys should be there any minute. They'll call us with an update and then bring Lana here so you can see for yourself that she's fine."

One look at Arlington's face told Paul that neither of them was convinced.

But Arlington was right. Even if he did eighty, it'd still take at least ten minutes to get to Ridgeview Road.

That was assuming no one got in his way and all the traffic lights were green.

And ignoring the fact that in this weather, doing eighty was out of the question.

He returned to his chair, feeling more like a spineless rat with every minute that ticked by.

Four and a half minutes later, Arlington's phone rang. He held the receiver in his hands before the end of the first ring. "Arlington."

The blank expression on Arlington's face gave no indication whether the news was good or bad.

Not a good sign.

Lana did the same thing when she was upset or concerned. Must be a law enforcement thing.

Did they practice that in the mirror or did it come naturally?

"Paul."

He blinked Arlington into focus.

"What's Lana driving?"

"Uh..." What had she been driving? He hadn't paid much attention to it. "A rental. Two doors, dark blue. I-I didn't really notice."

But he should have. Why hadn't he noticed what kind of car it was?

"Know the rental agency?"

"No, she-"

"We'll run her credit cards."

This didn't sound promising. Not at all.

Eyes glued to Arlington's face, Paul watched for a tic, anything to hint that Lana was okay. Nothing.

Torture would be better than this. How long would it take Arlington to fill him in?

"Keep me posted." Swearing exploded through the room as Arlington slammed down the receiver. "He's got her."

A bitter taste lodged in the back of Paul's throat.

The office swirled. He closed his eyes and swallowed, neither of which alleviated the panic squatting in his mind.

The Ripper had Lana.

He could think of nothing worse. Except maybe hearing that they'd found her body.

No. He had to keep it together.

They'd find her. Alive. Without a mark on her.

Wait. Maybe they were wrong. They couldn't know that she hadn't just had car trouble, right? Sure, her rental was a newer model, but rental cars weren't infallible.

"Maybe she broke down. She could be waiting for a tow–"

"She called, remember? Said she'd found the Ripper's car." A gusty breath exploded from Arlington's mouth. "Look, I don't like it any more 'an you do, but the scene tells the story."

"What do you mean?"

"Flares in the road, a black car stuck in the mud. And broken glass on the side of the road, but no car to match it to." Arlington's narrowed eyes locked on Paul. "He busted the window and took her and her car."

"Maybe she stopped to help whoever was in the black car. They were injured and she took them to the hospital or something."

"And left her gun and cell behind?"

"You found..." The words stalled in his mouth.

She never would have left those things behind. Never.

Not willingly anyway.

"Yeah. Lying on the side of the road. 'Sides that, there were..."

Arlington's hesitation squeezed the oxygen from Paul's lungs. "What?"

"Drag marks." Arlington didn't give him a chance to reply before rushing on, "Doesn't mean she's dead. Matter of fact, I don't think she is. This guy's not one to move the bodies. 'Sides, there's no blood."

So the Ripper took her with him to kill later. Great.

No, to *try* to kill later. But try was all he'd do. Lana could handle the Ripper.

So what if the Ripper was bigger. And stronger. No way would a punk like that slow her down. Besides, she had a lot of advantages that the other women hadn't.

There was her training. And her familiarity with the FBI's profile on the Ripper.

She'd know how to figure out what the Ripper wanted and placate him long enough for them to find her.

Who was he kidding?

The Ripper was nuts. No telling what a man like that would do.

She could be dead already.

No. He couldn't think that way. He didn't think he could survive without her.

They had to stop this guy. Catch him. Dead or alive, he didn't care.

Actually, he did.

Dead, definitely dead.

"Who is this guy? Can we check his home?"

Arlington stared at him, openly debating how much information to share. "Guy named Simmons. Turns out he's a photographer for one of the papers."

Photographer for the paper. The truth was a punch to his gut.

That's how the Ripper had found Lana. He'd probably been one of the scavengers who'd haunted Paul's front yard this past week.

But how the Ripper had chosen Lana wasn't as important

as where he'd taken her. "Okay, so maybe he took her home. Or a darkroom, photographers like darkrooms. Seems like that'd be a good place to take her until this thing blows over. We could check his work."

"Okay, first of all, there's no 'we' here. You're not a cop and you're not getting involved. As for checking his work, he wouldn't take her somewhere that public."

Arlington turned to his computer and punched at the keyboard. A few seconds later he picked up a pen and muttered the address aloud as he jotted it down. "17011 Wayside Avenue."

Paul swallowed the mountain in his throat. That was a good half hour away. The only upside was that Wayside was at least forty-five minutes from Ridgeview Drive, so maybe the police could get to the house before the Ripper killed Lana.

"I'm going with you."

Arlington shot him a look that said *dream on.* "You're stayin' right here."

"But I could help."

"Forget it. And if I so much as see a glimpse of you, I'll charge you with impeding an investigation. Got it?"

Paul ground his teeth and managed a curt nod. "Can you at least give me a call the second you know anything?"

"Suppose I can manage that. I'll send an officer to escort you to a place you can wait." Arlington rushed from the office, his voice carrying down the hall as he yelled for various officers to assist him.

Paul stared at Arlington's desk, seeing nothing and at the same time seeing everything.

Ana.

The word, scrawled in bold block print, snagged his attention. A number beneath it.

He grabbed the note. It was Ana's phone number.

"Mr. Van Horn?"

He jerked, his fingers curling around the paper. Turning, he found a young officer with a shaved head standing behind him. "Yeah."

"This way."

Paul followed, realizing as he stepped through the doorway that he still held Ana's number. Well, too late now. He'd give it back to Arlington later.

Besides, maybe it would come in handy.

As the sounds of the precinct blurred around him, Paul began to pray.

Lana woke to the static of a radio. Whether it was the radio that woke her or the jackhammer going off in her head wasn't clear.

In fact, not much was clear at all.

Like why she felt so cold. Why her bed was so hard. What that awful smell was.

She tried to sit up, but her body wouldn't obey. What was going on? Memories shot through her like bullets, piercing her mind with images.

Being pushed to the ground.

Her gun flying out of her hand.

A blonde man standing over her.

The Ripper had chosen her as his latest victim!

He obviously hadn't killed her. Not yet. But if the invasion of pain in her body was an indicator of what was to come, she might wish he had.

Her head pounded with mini-explosions.

Vaguely she remembered the Ripper swinging something at her.

Was she bleeding? The way her head throbbed, she wouldn't be surprised.

She tried to reach up to touch her head, but her hands wouldn't cooperate.

The last of the fog slipped away and she became aware of pressure at her wrists. Her left wrist throbbed and she could barely feel the rope there, but there was no denying the coarseness against her right wrist.

Her eyes felt weighted by sand, but she managed to force them open.

Light assaulted her, burned her eyes, and she snapped them shut again. But she had to see where she was and, more importantly, what options she had for escape.

Wincing, she eased her eyes open.

At first just a crack, then further as she adjusted to the light. Which actually wasn't as bright as it had originally seemed.

As near as she could tell, a halogen lamp sitting on a box a few yards away was the sole light source in the room. Next to the lamp, a radio played a melody of static.

Beneath her, concrete. Above her, exposed beams.

A basement. Or maybe a storm cellar.

Not the best place to ride out a storm. Unless this place was on high ground.

Where was the Ripper? Had he dumped her here and left?

Yeah, he probably realized he forgot his knife.

Lord, help me.

She had to get out of here before he returned–

"You're awake."

A gasp slipped out and she jumped as a voice sounded from above and behind her.

Where was he? Limited movement prevented her from finding him, but she could hear him moving around.

She hated not being able to see him.

Not that she could do anything to stop him, but she at least wanted to see the knife before it sliced through her skin.

"Are you okay? I'm sorry. I didn't want to hurt you, but I heard you call the police and I knew we didn't have much time. They would've spoiled everything."

What the heck…?

The anxious, pleading tone in his voice told her all he

wanted was for her to say she understood.

And it was to her advantage to give him what he wanted. "I understand."

"So you're okay?"

She hesitated. What was the best way to play this out? A bluff? Brutal honesty?

Maybe something in between.

"My head hurts a little." And I'd kill for some aspirin.

Not that she'd accept any pills from him should he offer. No telling what kind of drugs he might give her.

Footsteps scuffed across the concrete and then he was in front of her, sitting next to the lamp. He turned down the radio and stared at her face. "I didn't want to, but you made me do it. Why did you fight back?"

Maybe because you've already killed five women. At least.

She kept the thought to herself and studied his face. Something about it struck her as familiar. Hadn't she seen him somewhere before?

The photographer who'd bumped into her in Paul's front yard.

That's who he was. And that's how he'd come into contact with her. She was here because of a stupid accidental encounter.

Was that how it'd been for all his victims? They ran into the wrong person at the store, coffeehouse, on the street?

That was certainly how it had been for Felicity.

His voice slapped her back to the present. "Why? I thought we had something special. Why'd you try to hurt me?"

The Ripper stared at her through narrow eyes, hands clenched by his side.

Her dust-dry mouth and thick tongue nearly strangled her. God help her. He was getting mad. Not just mad, working himself into a rage.

If she didn't play this right, she'd experience his savagery first hand.

Her life depended on her ability to appease him.

"I didn't recognize you. But now I remember. We met outside my friend's house, right?"

Suspicion laced his eyebrows together as he stared at her in silence. She forced herself to maintain eye contact.

This was it. If he didn't believe her, she could forget escaping or even seeing the sun rise again.

"You really didn't know it was me?"

"I didn't. I thought I was being attacked."

The fists relaxed. Anger and tension fell away, replaced by something else, something she didn't want to even try to understand.

"I knew it had to be something like that. You're not like those other girls. You're special. I knew it when we made that connection."

They'd made a connection?

The FBI's profile had nailed this one. This guy really was consumed by his own delusions. And that made him dangerous and unpredictable.

He crossed the room, crouched next to her, and brushed her hair away from her face. A finger feathered across her cheek like a large spider and she fought the urge to pull away.

Come on, sell it. Convince him you're not scared of him.

Not an easy task.

Especially when she felt so helpless lying bound on this concrete floor. Maybe she could convince him to let her sit up.

"I–" Her voice came out breathy, scratchy. Clearing her throat, she tried again. "Can you help me sit up?"

The idea of asking for his help, let alone being touched by him, moved the room's chill into her bones. A shiver shook her body as his hands settled on her arms.

"What's wrong?" The edge returned to his voice.

She needed to convince him of something other than the truth. If he knew how much he repulsed her, she was through.

"It–it's really cold in here. Where are we?"

The plan worked. Compassion flickered on his face as he helped her sit up.

"Basement. We have to wait out this storm."

She'd almost forgotten about the storm. So much for help arriving.

Most of the police's efforts would be targeted on cleaning up the mess left in Gino's wake.

Did they even know she was gone? Maybe with all the chaos of the approaching hurricane, Arlington hadn't gotten her message.

Paul expected her to call, but the kids would keep him so busy tonight he probably wouldn't notice that she hadn't. And with the cleanup efforts after the storm, it might be days before anyone knew something was wrong. Could she survive that long if she had to?

Please, God. I can't do this on my own!

The Ripper removed his hands from her arms, wiping them on his jeans. "No wonder you're cold. You're drenched."

He turned and moved toward a laundry basket sitting in the corner. When he returned a moment later, he had a thick beige blanket in his hands.

"Lean forward."

No matter how much she wanted to rebel on principle alone, she didn't dare. Cooperation was her sole means of survival.

Besides, the blanket would provide not only warmth, but an extra layer between her and the Ripper. The fact that he hadn't yet killed her brought a small measure of comfort, but also put her into new territory.

To her knowledge, she was the first one he hadn't killed in the initial attack. So now that he had her – alive – what did he intend to do with her?

The blanket settled around her shoulders and she fought the instinct to tense up as he tucked the edges around her legs. Taking a few steps back, he settled on the floor and surveyed her in silent satisfaction.

"Better?"

This was too weird. The friendly lilt in his voice and gentle smile on his face contrasted sharply with the violent nature that hid underneath.

Play along.

"Yes. Thank you."

Silence hung in the darkness. She let her gaze wander the room, but felt the way his eyes never left her.

It was creepy.

Her arms ached, but she didn't ask him to release her. Not only did she doubt he'd agree, but he'd have to touch her to do it. She'd take the ropes over that any day.

But being free would come in handy should an opportunity to escape present itself.

Even so, she couldn't bring herself to ask, not yet anyway. Maybe once she'd thought up a plan for escape, but not now.

A plan for escape. Yes, she should be working on that.

Her mind ran through scenarios.

Rush him, bite him, kick him, start up the stairs and push him down when he tried to follow.

None of the scenarios ended well for her.

Aside from that, she had no idea where she was or who else might be around.

She didn't even know how long she'd been out.

Rash actions wouldn't get her out of this mess. She'd have to outsmart him. Manipulate him into complacency.

Talk to him.

Ugh, she hated the idea of interacting with this madman.

"I never got your name." Her voice seemed loud in the room.

"Lyle."

"I'm Lana." Although he probably already knew that. If the FBI's profile was accurate, this guy knew way too much about her already.

He leaned forward, resting his elbows on his knees. "Lana. See, even your name is better than the others. I knew you were the one."

Not even ten minutes and she was already sick of being the

one. How did she intend to pull this off for the next few hours?

The air around her felt as toxic as the thoughts in her head.

What if it was more than a few hours? What if this lasted for days? Weeks?

Not an option. At least not one she could consider right now. She'd probably want to kill herself if she didn't get out of here by the end of today.

"What happened to your face?"

You happened.

Had he seriously forgotten the way he'd attacked her earlier? But pointing out that fact wouldn't be to her advantage.

"It was that guy. Van Horn. Right? He gave you those bruises, didn't he?"

Bruises? He must be talking about the steering wheel tattoo on her face. "I was in a car accident."

"You don't have to cover for him. He can't hurt you anymore."

"He'd never hurt me." While arguing might not be the wisest move, she wouldn't let him think Paul was the monster here. "I was rear-ended on my way home from work a few days ago."

"Hmm."

Impossible to tell if he believed her or not, but she doubted arguing would do her any good.

"So what's your connection with him anyway?"

She had no trouble detecting the jealousy in Lyle's voice. "He's a friend."

"Just a friend?"

"Nothing more."

Apparently satisfied, he nodded. "And the cops, how close are they? Do they know who I am?"

"How would I know?"

He jumped to his feet and stormed toward her. "Don't lie to me! I know you're one of 'em."

How did...? That's right, she'd used her badge to get the reporters to back off the other day.

Stupid, stupid! She had to remember details like that or she'd blow it.

"I'm not lying. I'm a US Marshal, not a cop. I don't work with them and I'm not a part of their investigation."

At least not officially. But no way would she tell him that.

The words settled him down and he moved to sit again. "So you really don't know?"

"No. But I'm sure they aren't that close. Why else would they have put that information on the news and asked for the public's help to find you?"

"You're right." A smile crept across his face and his teeth flashed like a viper's fangs. "That's good. I wouldn't want them to ruin us."

Was she supposed to agree with that? She couldn't, not when she prayed so desperately that the police would show up soon.

The smile slipped. "But I had to leave my car behind. They probably know my name."

That's right! The car had been half-buried in mud.

The car would lead them to him, which would lead them to her. Praise God, light did sliver through the darkness after all.

Lyle droned on, oblivious to her thoughts. "Soon as this storm's past, we'll have to leave town. The storm'll give us time to get away. It'll take 'em a while to find this place anyhow."

"Why?"

The shadows in the room made his eyes look like hollow holes.

Like looking into the abyss of hell. She stiffened her limbs to still the trembling.

Several seconds passed while those caverns studied her. "We're at my uncle's house. My name's not on the deed, so it'll be harder to track down."

For crying out loud, was his whole family in on this?

Worse yet, that meant there was at least one more person she'd have to get past when she made her escape.

It'd be good to know what she was up against. A seven-foot man built like a semi? Or a five-foot man with a cane?

"Shouldn't he be down here? I mean, with the storm and all?"

"He moved to California 'bout a year ago, but no one would buy this place. So it's just sat here empty ever since."

Judging from what little she could see of the house, she wasn't surprised.

Crack!

She whipped her head around as a groaning noise filled the room.

A small window across the room shattered. Glass sprinkled to the concrete, a rock the size of her foot sitting dead center.

On his feet now, Lyle raced to her side and clapped a hand over her mouth. The sticky hand smeared his sweat on her lips and combined with faint traces of body odor.

Ugh.

If he didn't let go soon, she was going to hurl.

Tension seeped from his body and his breathing was shallow by her ear, but he said nothing.

Several impossibly long seconds dragged by before he whispered, "I think there might be someone here. I'm going to go check it out."

Yes, go. Please go.

His hand left her mouth and he moved away only to return a second later with a roll of duct tape.

"Please, no. I'll be quiet–"

A piece of tape silenced all further pleadings.

"I've been burned too many times by people like you. Don't worry. I'll be back soon."

He crossed the room and snuck up wooden stairs that groaned with every step. The door opened and closed softly, leaving her alone in her dank prison.

Twenty-Three

The cell phone jerked in his hand. Paul accepted the call before the first ring had finished.

"She's not here."

Arlington's words were a javelin to his heart. If Lana wasn't at Lyle's house, where was she?

"But you know for sure he's the Ripper?"

"It's him, all right. Got a dark room set up in his house. We found half a dozen pictures of Tanner hanging up to dry."

Every word Arlington said twisted the javelin deeper.

It was confirmed. Not only had the Ripper picked Lana, he *had* her.

"Now what?"

Arlington let out a gusty sigh. "I guess we try the newspaper. Can't see him going there, but maybe he panicked."

"Which paper?"

"Like I'm gonna tell you. Last thing I need is you pokin' your nose in my case and beating me there."

Dang. Was he that obvious? "There has to be something I can do. Come on, waiting is killing me."

Or killing Lana, as the case may be.

Lana was smart, but the Ripper was crazy. And prone to violence.

Naïveté was a luxury Paul longed for, but couldn't have.

Lana's odds were slim. They all knew it even if no one was saying it.

Arlington's voice pulled him back. "I'll call you as soon as I know anything."

The phone went dead in his hand.

So Arlington seriously expected him to sit here and do nothing. No way.

Paul pushed himself to his feet. There had to be something he could do, some way to help locate Lana.

Oh, God. Please. You've got to help me. Lana's Yours and she needs help.

He ran out of words as ideas circulated through his head.

Maybe he'd call the newspapers, ask for Simmons, and see which paper recognized the name. Once he had the right paper, he could talk to co-workers, offer an exclusive in exchange for anything that might help lead him to wherever Simmons had taken her.

It was a long shot at best.

How many people knew enough about the people working next to them to know where that person would go to hide from the cops? Not like the topic came up in the course of normal conversation.

Heck, they hadn't even recognized him from the profile. They, of all people, should've been able to connect the dots.

Wait.

He looked down at the paper still clutched in his hand.

No one knew this guy better than Ana, the woman who had started Simmons' obsessions.

But would she talk to him? She had to be completely freaked out right now.

And she probably didn't want to talk about it to anyone, much less some stranger.

Once he told her why he'd called, he was sure she'd help, but getting her to stay on the phone long enough to explain might be tricky.

Lana's life hung in the balance. And the lead Arlington was

chasing down was likely a dead end.

He had to try. What other choice did he have?

He punched in the number, clenched his shaking fingers around the phone as the other end rang. Once. Twice. Three times.

Oh, man. She wasn't going to answer. The best chance they had at finding Lana and–

"Hello?"

"Ana?"

A long pause. "Who's this?"

Talk fast. "My name's Paul. I just got off the phone with Detective Arlington and I need to ask you a few questions."

Silence. Had he lost her?

A second later, her wary voice crossed the line. "Where's Detective Arlington?"

"He's out looking for Simmons. Which is what I need your help with. Simmons is not at his house and he's taken another woman. Do you have any idea where he might go?"

"I… give me a sec here, let me think."

One second turned into two, which rolled into five. Paul forced his mouth to remain closed.

Come on, come on. Lana didn't have time for Ana to think.

"I guess you could try the Chronicle. Lyle practically lived there some days."

"Arlington's on his way there right now, but we don't think he'll be there. We think he'll seek out someplace more secluded. Please, there must be somewhere else." As much as he tried to hide it, desperation tinged his voice.

"You're not a cop, are you?"

"No. But I witnessed one of the killings. And the woman he has now is my friend. He found her because of me."

"You're in love with her."

He didn't agree, but from the tone of Ana's voice, he didn't have to. She knew the truth.

Too bad the truth didn't get them any closer to finding Lana.

If they didn't catch up to this guy soon, Paul's feelings would be irrelevant. "Please."

Tears clogged Ana's voice. "I'm sorry. I wish I could help, but I don't know where else Lyle would go."

No! Ana had to know, even if she didn't realize she knew. This woman was his best shot at getting to Lana before it was too late.

Was there anything he could do to help jog her memory? He had to at least try.

"You're sure Lyle doesn't have a hurricane shelter at his house? Hidden somewhere maybe."

"No. His house is one level."

"Where else would he go in a storm?"

"Lyle hates storms. He was born in the Midwest and his parents moved him to Florida when he was ten. He told me about his first hurricane and how it scared him to death. It was…"

The sudden silence was almost as bad as the fear that crushed him. "What? What is it?"

She gasped. "I'm an idiot. Lyle wouldn't go to his house in a hurricane. He'd go inland, to his uncle's place!"

No way. What kind of guy would take a woman he'd kidnapped to his uncle's home? Unless his uncle was a part of this, too.

"His uncle's home? Really?"

"Yeah, yeah, that's where he'd go." Words tumbled so quickly he had trouble catching them all. "His parents lived there before they died in a car accident. Lyle was about twelve at the time. The home went to his uncle, but his uncle moved away and the house has been empty ever since. He took me out there once. It's on the edge of a swamp and there aren't any close neighbors. There's a basement and everything. We spent a few days there when a hurricane passed by Jacksonville last year."

Good enough for him. "The address. Where is it?"

She hesitated.

Oh no. She had to know the address, she just had to.

"I–I'm not sure, but I can tell you how to get there."

The directions she gave him brought a ray of hope. If the roads were clear, it sounded like he could be there in thirty minutes.

The only dilemma remaining was how he'd get the cops out there.

If Arlington knew the thoughts running through his head right now, he'd have him detained. He couldn't even tell the cops out front because they'd probably stop him, too.

But if he had Ana call, it would buy him the time he needed to get out of here.

He jumped up and strode for the door. "I need you to do me a favor. Get ahold of Arlington and tell him what you told me. I'm going out there."

Panic tinged her tone. "No, let the police–"

"The police are too far away. I can get there sooner."

"But he'll kill you!"

It was worth the risk. If anything happened to Lana, he might as well be dead.

"I'm a resourceful guy. Just make sure Arlington gets out there fast."

Rain poured through the open window and wind whistled in the room. Lana couldn't take her eyes from the hole that provided a link to the outside world.

Why, she didn't know. It wasn't like she could escape through that opening.

For one thing, the window was too high for her to reach and for another, probably too small for her to get through. But still, that window represented freedom, which gave her hope.

The basement door creaked open. Her gaze shot to the

stairs as a pair of black boots appeared.

Was it the police?

The boots clomped down the stairs.

Tears stung her eyes when she saw Lyle's face. She quickly blinked them away so he wouldn't see.

Too late.

He knelt in front of her, tipped her chin up, and surveyed the wet streaks on her cheeks. Smooth fingers touched her face and she worked to hide a shudder. He pulled up the edge of the tape and ripped it off. Pain shot across her lips and chin.

Thanks a lot, you jerk.

It wasn't like she needed that layer of skin anyway.

"Why're you crying?"

What could she say? She couldn't exactly tell him that she'd been disappointed to see him coming down the stairs.

If she said that, he'd likely chop her to pieces.

She went with the first thing that came to mind. "The wind. The cold stings my eyes."

The hand dropped and he stood. "Then I'll go board up the window. Anything to make you happy."

Anything? How about letting me go?

But of course she couldn't say that. "What happened?"

"A branch came off the big tree outside. It knocked a rock through the window."

"Why didn't you board up the house?"

"The main floor's done, but I guess I missed the basement." He shook his head. "I had other things on my mind."

Other things, huh? Like kidnapping and murder?

Maybe she could keep him out of the room longer so she could look for an escape route. "You're lucky the other window is still intact."

He studied it. "I should get it covered before this gets any worse."

"I could help you. I've already boarded up three buildings today. I think that makes me a pro."

The silence in the room was disturbed only by the howling

wind and the rain dripping to the concrete. Finally he shook his head. "I don't think our relationship has progressed that far yet. I have to be careful. I've been hurt too many times before."

He crossed the room, stopping with his foot on the bottom step. "Don't worry. I won't be gone long."

Why did he keep saying that like it was a good thing?

He mounted the stairs and disappeared from sight, leaving her alone in the darkened basement.

Leaning her head back against the wall, she allowed the tears to come.

She was as good as dead.

She couldn't keep playing along with this insanity, not for much longer anyway. Not when all she really wanted was to pick up that radio and bash his head in. Or grab a piece of that broken glass and bury it in his chest.

Wait a second.

Her gaze shot to the broken window, following the water trail to where it pooled around the glass broken on the floor.

That was it. Her ticket out of here.

She'd use one of those shards to slice through the rope then, when his guard was down, she could attack.

How long would it take him to gather the wood and nails?

Probably not long. She'd better hurry.

Bracing her back against the wall, she pushed herself up. Sharp pain shot through her wrist, a harsh reminder of her fall.

The blanket slid down a little bit and she grabbed a handful of the coarse fabric. Or at least tried to. Her right hand cooperated, but her left one felt made of clay.

Dang. She'd probably sprained her wrist when she fell.

Maybe even broken it.

No, she could move the fingers. It hurt like the dickens, but she could do it.

As much as the blanket hindered her, she had to keep it on. If he came back and it wasn't around her, he might check her hands before she'd had time to saw through the rope.

She slowed her movements to try to keep the blanket in place.

The muscles in her legs and back throbbed, but she clenched her teeth and kept going. She straightened her legs beneath her.

Okay. Now to get the glass.

She glanced at the window behind her.

Empty.

The window across the room? Also empty.

She hurried into the wind. Glass crunched beneath her feet as she turned and knelt with her back to the glass, straining to reach a shard. Careful, careful... the last thing she needed was to slice herself and leave a trail of blood across the floor.

Cold concrete brushed her fingertips and she leaned back to get her hands closer. Almost there.

Whoa!

She teetered on the balls of her feet as she tried to right herself, failed, and tumbled backwards. The blanket cushioned her fall a little, but the concrete felt especially hard against her already sore tailbone as she landed on her rear with a jarring thud.

Digging through the folds of the blanket, she gently probed the floor behind her back. Something smooth and wet met her hand. Her fingers skittered across the surface.

Angular, probably about six inches long... and a jagged edge. Perfect.

Now to get back across the room before Lyle began work on the window.

With the glass pinched carefully between two fingers, she spread her legs shoulder width apart and rocked forward.

The muscles between her shoulders protested, fresh bolts of pain flashed down her back, and her legs trembled, but she slowly rose. Glass tinkled to the ground as she lightly shook the blanket.

She began across the room, sent a backward glance at the

broken window. Still no one. The window ahead of her was clear, too. She might make it.

Now where exactly had she been sitting?

At the wall, she turned and glanced around the room. No, the view was a little off.

She took a few steps to the right. There, that looked a little more like what she remembered.

In all likelihood, he wouldn't know exactly where she'd sat anyway.

Then again, the man was crazy and obsessed. He might know her exact location.

Shoulders against the wall, she quickly slid down, being careful not to stab herself with the glass. The wall pushed the blanket up, bunching it across her shoulders, but she doubted the Ripper would remember exactly how the blanket had been positioned.

On the floor once again, she looked at both windows, didn't see Lyle watching her from either one.

Okay, now to look defeated.

She leaned her head back against the wall and closed her eyes. Now when he looked in, which she was certain he'd do, maybe he would believe she'd given up.

But she wasn't out of the game yet.

Far from it.

With her eyes still closed, she turned the glass and began to work on the rope.

She'd get out of this and make him regret the things he'd done.

Crash!

She jumped. The glass slipped, sliced the side of her left arm.

Ooh, did that hurt. She blinked rapidly, trying to clear the tears that collected in her eyes and blurred her vision.

Lyle's face appeared briefly in the opening where the window had once been. Apparently satisfied that she hadn't escaped in his absence, he pulled back, held up a board, and hammered it into place.

The pain dulled. Her fingers felt slimy, sticky. Blood.

And from the feel of things, quite a bit of it.

Perfect. It looked like she'd done the hard work for him.

He couldn't kill her if she'd already slit her own wrists.

No time to worry about that now. She continued to saw through the rope. The blood coated the glass shard and it slid from her fingers.

Great, now where was it?

With all the folds in the blanket, it might be impossible for her to find it without looking.

Her glance darted to the window, but his face hadn't reappeared.

Carefully, deliberately, she dug her fingers into the fabric collected on the floor. It couldn't have gone far.

There!

She picked up the glass and tried to wipe it off on the blanket. Hopefully that would keep it from getting away from her again.

How much farther did she have to go?

Hammering came from the other side now. He was on the second – and last – window.

Time was almost up.

Twenty~Four

Rain fell so heavily it obscured Arlington's vision and the water on the road made driving at high speeds dangerous.

He did it anyway.

A few more blocks and he'd be at the newspaper office. Somehow he had a hard time believing the Ripper would take a victim there, but it was the best lead he had at the moment.

The only lead.

Several officers had stayed behind to tear the Ripper's house apart, searching for any clue as to where he might have taken Tanner, but time was against them.

No matter how unlikely, he had no choice but to follow up with what they had.

Sitting back while one of his own was stabbed by a maniac wasn't an option.

Although technically, Tanner wasn't one of his own.

But close enough.

Even if she hadn't been, she was a victim in need of his help. That was reason enough for him.

The siren announcing his approach wailed loudly. Part of him wanted to silence it on principle alone, but these streets were dangerous enough as it was.

Speeding around silently in weather like this could only be termed as reckless.

Besides, sirens were hardly unusual on a day like today, so

the Ripper probably wouldn't think anything of it if he heard them approaching. Assuming the Ripper was even anywhere in the neighborhood.

His phone rang and he snatched it up. "Arlington."

"Yeah, it's Murphy."

What the heck was someone at the station doing calling him right now? They all knew he was chasing the Ripper.

"What?"

"You've got a call here. She says it's urgent."

For crying out loud, he didn't have time for this. "Who?"

"Ana Cordova."

An urgent call from Ana? Not good, not at all.

"She say what it's about?"

"The Ripper."

Maybe she had a better lead. Couldn't be any worse than the one he was following up on right now.

Or maybe Simmons had killed Tanner and grabbed Ana.

No, it defied the timeline. In this weather, it would take Simmons at least two hours to drive to Hinesville.

"Give her my cell. Have her call me."

"Will do." Murphy hung up.

Arlington hit the off button but kept the phone in his hand. A minute later, it rang.

A slightly hysterical female voice that he vaguely recognized as Ana's screeched in his ear. "You've gotta go after him! I couldn't stop him and he's gone after Lyle and I told him it was dangerous but he wouldn't listen."

"Whoa, whoa, slow down. What the heck are you talking about?"

"That guy. The witness."

There was only one person who fit that description.

But it wasn't possible. Ana and Paul had never met; how could she know he'd gone after the Ripper? More than that, how could he know where to go to find the Ripper?

"You talkin' about Paul?"

"Yes. We were talking and then he said he was going after

Lyle and you should get out there *now*."

Dread slithered through his blood. "Out where?"

"Lyle's uncle's place. I remembered it and told him and he freaked out. He said he was going after him and I tried to stop him but he wouldn't listen. He just wouldn't!"

The pieces clicked into place. He swore. "Where?"

The area she described sparked images of gator infested bayous.

The Ripper had gone there. Arlington was sure of it. If he were a serial killer bent on taking his victims to a secluded place, that's where he'd choose to go.

And he was driving the wrong direction.

He slammed on the brakes, made a tight right at the next intersection. The tires slid on the wet pavement, but he pulled out if it before crossing the yellow line.

The rearview mirror confirmed the black and white behind him was following his lead. Good; he'd need the backup.

Ana rattled on about something else, but he had no time to listen. "Ana! Slow down."

Silence greeted his demand.

Finally. It was hard to get a word in with this woman. "How long since you hung up with Paul?"

She let out a shaky breath. "I don't know. Five minutes? Maybe."

Five minutes. And since the station was at least fifteen minutes closer to the Ripper than Arlington was right now, that meant Paul had a pretty good head start.

"Thanks for letting me know. I'll be in touch." He ended the call, snatched up the radio handset, and called in their new destination.

If the Ripper didn't kill Van Horn, maybe he'd do it.

What was the idiot thinking barreling in there like some kind of superhero? Unless he could bounce bullets off his body, he had no business doing what he was doing.

But in all honesty, he knew why Van Horn was acting the way he was.

If their positions were reversed, he'd probably do the same thing, gun or no gun. Wasn't the smartest thing in the world, but guys didn't always use their brains where a pretty woman was concerned.

Especially one who acted so tough and carried a gun. There was something pretty hot about that.

None of that mattered now.

Van Horn was running on emotion and fear. Not a good combination.

Arlington swore again. He just hoped he made it there before someone died.

Paul snugged the baseball cap lower on his head.

Rain pelted the top of the hat, but the bill kept it out of his eyes, which was about the only dry part of him. Water streamed down his neck, under his shirt, between his shoulder blades. His flip flops sunk in the mud, wild grass scratched his legs, and at least an inch of water covered his feet.

If he'd known what this afternoon would bring, he would've worn better shoes.

Tree bark scraped his arm, but he didn't move.

The tree provided meager protection against the wind and the driving rain, but it shielded him from any watching eyes at the house in front of him.

Lana was inside. Somewhere.

Didn't matter that he had yet to see her, he knew she was in there. She had to be.

The house appeared to be a square shaped, one-story unit with a basement. Peeling blue paint, a porch that sagged, and a roof missing more shingles than he could count made it the perfect place for a killer to hide out.

Why anyone had even bothered to hang boards over the windows was a mystery Paul didn't care to solve.

And yet, a lone man knelt in the mud, nailing one last board over a basement window. At least twenty-five feet separated them and all Paul could see was the man's back, but he knew he was looking at the killer who'd tormented his dreams for the last week and a half.

The Ripper. Simmons.

He wanted to sneak up behind the Ripper, take the hammer from his hand, and bash his head in.

But he had to be smart.

He had one shot at the Ripper, one shot only. If he blew it, he didn't just fail himself, he failed Lana.

That wasn't an option.

The Ripper collected his tools, jogged up the porch steps, and entered the house.

Everything in Paul said to rush in there and save Lana before the Ripper could do any more damage, but he refrained. He had to give the Ripper plenty of time to get inside and settled into whatever place he'd chosen to ride out the storm if he wanted to maintain the element of surprise.

He glanced at his watch.

5:39.

He'd give it until 5:45, then he was going in.

Wind howled around him. Above him, branches groaned.

He looked up. Limbs thicker than his body swayed like party girls in a club.

Maybe the tree wasn't the best place for him to seek shelter.

Too late now. He checked the time.

5:41.

Really? Only two minutes had passed?

Don't think about the time.

He surveyed the front of the house. What was his best course of approach? The front door? Maybe something around back? A window?

No, the windows were all boarded over. So then, a door.

The front. It was close and direct. Logically, the Ripper shouldn't be in the front room, anyway.

Although nothing about this guy was necessarily logical.

Where would the Ripper and Lana be waiting out the storm? It looked like a small house. With the state of disrepair, the safest place might be the basement, in spite of the risk from flooding.

His eyes strayed to his watch again.

5:44. Close enough. Time to stop the Ripper.

Permanently.

Lana fingered the rope. Who'd have guessed cutting with glass would be such a slow task?

At least it felt like she was over halfway through. A little more work and she could probably snap free.

Floorboards creaked overhead. He was coming back.

Hurry, hurry!

Once he was in the room, she'd have to concentrate on keeping her movements hidden. It would be much more difficult to free herself.

The door opened and he tromped down the stairs.

Mud caked his boots and the knees of his jeans, and his white t-shirt clung to his scrawny body.

What a shrimp. How the heck had he gotten the better of her earlier?

Maybe she needed to put in more time at the gym.

He unfolded a cat-puke orange towel and patted down his face, neck, and arms before rubbing his hair.

Settling on the crate, he turned those dark eyes her direction and stared.

The silence unnerved her, but she wasn't about to break it. She wanted nothing to do with this man, let alone to begin a conversation with him.

"Would you like a chair?" The storm raging outside nearly drowned out his voice.

As much as she wanted to get off the floor, she couldn't. She couldn't move from this spot until she was ready to take him down.

Not with the blood that undoubtedly coated her arm, back, the blanket, and the floor.

He'd see the cut, find the glass, and kill her for trying to escape.

"No."

Unreadable eyes lingered on her face. What she wouldn't give to know what he was thinking.

"The electricity has been off in this house for months. It could get cold. I think we'll need to keep each other warm."

No way. They could be in a blizzard in the middle of Alaska and she wouldn't let him near her. If she had to choose between being anywhere close to him and freezing, she'd take the latter.

He pushed off the crate.

"No." The word came out sounding more panicked than she'd intended.

A twitch in his jaw was the first warning that she'd upset him. Then his hands clenched and he pulled himself up to full height.

If she didn't do some damage control in a hurry, she wouldn't live long enough to finish cutting the rope.

"I–I just need more time. This is all happening so fast and I didn't expect any of it."

"When two people belong together, they shouldn't need more time. It shouldn't matter how fast it happens."

His tone contained an edge that made the hairs on her arm stand at attention.

Not good. How could she bring him back around–?

From above, a long, low creak. Just like the sound she'd heard before the Ripper had come downstairs.

He heard it, too. Tension crackled from him like sparks off a fire as he turned to face the stairs.

Was someone there? Someone who would help her?

Hope made it hard to breathe.

Another thought crashed through her mind, snuffed out the hope sparked there. If someone was up there, it wasn't necessarily a good thing. The Ripper could have an accomplice.

No, a man like the Ripper would work alone. Wouldn't he?

Besides, he looked alarmed. If he had an accomplice, he wouldn't be concerned, right?

Neither of them moved. Seconds turned to a minute with no further sounds from upstairs.

The Ripper crossed to her, knelt down and spoke, his voice a snake-like hiss. "I'm gonna check it out. You so much as breathe wrong and you'll wish I'd killed you like the others."

She expected him to pull out the duct tape, but he turned and began up the stairs.

Why hadn't he taped her mouth? Maybe he forgot.

Or maybe he had a weapon and planned to kill whoever was up there.

If someone was up there.

Listening carefully, her mind filtered out the wind and rain. Still no noise from the main floor. Could they have been hearing things?

Not likely.

They wouldn't both have imagined it. But maybe it had been caused by the house shifting in the wind.

Maybe this whole place was getting ready to cave in on their heads.

Well, there were worse things. Like being raped. Or stabbed in a violent outburst. At least if the house collapsed, it would take down the Ripper, too.

The door squealed as the Ripper pushed it open and disappeared from sight.

At the moment, whether or not someone hid upstairs was

immaterial.

Maybe they'd help her, maybe they wouldn't, maybe they didn't even exist, but one thing was blindingly clear. She'd been given another chance to finish what she'd started.

One last chance to break free and fight back.

Hinges squealed. The sound rang through the still house, seemingly louder than the storm outside.

Finally. It had taken the creep long enough to get up here.

Paul flattened himself against the wall.

Entering the house had been easier than he'd expected. The complete stillness on the main floor, not to mention the lack of response at his entry, had confirmed his theory that the Ripper and Lana were in the basement.

Which only left the quandary of how to get down there.

If he opened the door and walked right in, the Ripper would see him coming long before he was in a position to fight back.

What if the Ripper had a gun? There had to be a better option than walking into a bullet.

Worse yet, the Ripper might use Lana as a shield.

Might even hurt her to distract him.

And then the floorboards had creaked as he'd crossed the room. It presented the perfect solution. All he'd had to do was stay still and wait for the Ripper to come to him.

Part of him wanted to attack the Ripper. Hit him hard and fast.

Make Simmons' blood flow like all the women who'd already died.

But would that make him any better than the Ripper?

Besides, the best thing he could do was get downstairs and put himself between that monster and Lana.

A blonde man emerged from the hallway.

Slowly. Cautiously.

Crouched behind a sheet-covered sofa, Paul watched as the man moved toward the center of the room.

The Ripper's head never stopped moving as he scanned the room.

Paul resisted the urge to duck lower. Any extra movement might draw the Ripper's attention.

Keep going. Don't stop now.

Simmons took three more steps and stopped.

No, not there!

Simmons turned. Anger narrowed his eyes as they locked with Paul's.

Paul launched himself at the smaller man.

Simmons jumped backward.

A fist sailed over Paul's head. He twisted aside as another whistled past his ear. A tennis shoe connected with his shin.

Paul threw a punch of his own, but Simmons darted aside.

Dang. The little runt was fast.

A book smacked the wall behind him, exploding a cloud of dust around his head.

Paul coughed, barely catching sight of another book flying his direction. He wrenched to the left and the book thudded to the floor.

Two more sailed toward him. He dove.

The worn carpet chafed his arm and his shoulder bumped against an end table.

Enough defense! He had to get on the offensive and stop this whack job.

A thick hard-backed book filled his vision. Even as he yanked back, he knew he wouldn't make it.

The book glanced off his shoulder as he lost his balance and fell, his head smacking a sheet-covered coffee table.

Sparklers exploded behind his eyes. He collapsed to the floor, fought his way through the daze.

Footsteps retreated. A door slammed.

Simmons was going after Lana!

Twenty-Five

What the...?

Lana glanced at the ceiling. What she wouldn't give for x-ray vision right about now.

The thumping, crashing, banging, and pounding footsteps sent particles and dust floating through the basement. It even drowned out the storm.

The noises could only mean one thing. Help had arrived.

Please, God, let whoever it is have a gun.

What if it was just someone seeking solace from the hurricane? If no one had lived here for years, the house probably looked abandoned. It'd be a perfect place for the unprepared to wait out the storm.

If that was the case, she wasn't the only one in danger.

She couldn't wait and hope to be rescued. Besides, that whole damsel in distress routine had never been her style.

She sawed at the ropes. She might have minutes or maybe only seconds, but she'd make use of whatever time she'd been given.

Footsteps echoed above her, growing distant as they moved away.

At the far end of the room, the basement door opened and slammed shut. The Ripper ran down the stairs, taking them two or three at a time, and raced across the basement floor.

Face pale, breathing hard, he glared at her with granite

eyes.

No trace of affection. Not even the compassion she'd witnessed earlier.

This was bad.

The thought barely registered before his hand shot out. It spanned her neck, lifted her to her feet.

He slammed her against the wall.

Fire exploded in her head and shot down her back.

Black invaded her vision.

"You lying, filthy little tramp!" The scream ricocheted off the bare concrete walls.

The fury in his voice chased the blackness away and his narrowed eyes and flaring nostrils filled her vision.

What was he talking about?

She swallowed hard, the action difficult against the crushing force on her throat.

"You said you were just friends." Spittle hit her forehead as he spat the words at her. "You said there was nothing between you. I should've known you were lying. Now both of you will pay."

Paul blinked the haze away and pushed himself to his feet.

The first few steps were unsteady, but by the time he arrived at the basement door he'd reached a full run.

A man's voice drifted through the closed door.

Paul couldn't make out the words, but the tone told him all he needed to know.

That kind of anger, coming from the Ripper, meant nothing but bloodshed and death. And Lana was in the line of fire.

He threw open the door and barreled down the stairs.

He might be walking right into a trap. Maybe a bullet with his name. Or the tip of a knife.

It didn't matter.

The Ripper could have a Samurai sword ready to take off his head for all he cared. As long as Lana was okay.

He'd gladly take whatever violence the Ripper wanted to dish out if it would spare her.

The darkness swallowed him as he rushed into it.

But the further down he went, the lighter it became. A halogen lantern sat in the center of the basement, pushing the shadows to the corners of the room.

Which was exactly where the Ripper stood, pinning Lana against a wall.

Arms behind her back, her feet barely touched the floor as the Ripper used both hands to choke her.

"Let her go!"

One hand left Lana's neck as the Ripper half-turned toward him. "Stay back! I'll kill her. I swear I'll do it."

Of that, Paul had no doubt. He jerked to a stop.

How could he separate Lana from that maniac? There had to be a way–

Lana's hands shot out from behind her back.

A flash of red from something in her hands, but she moved too fast for him to see what it was.

The Ripper howled.

The noise had a wild sound to it, like a pack of coyotes on a clear winter night.

It spoke of pain and promised vengeance.

Which wouldn't happen, not as long as he was around to stop it.

The hand around her neck loosened and she dropped to the floor. A bloody, jagged chunk of glass slid from her fingers, shattering at her feet.

Paul hurled himself across the room.

He swung his fist at the Ripper's head, put all his fear and anger and hate into the punch. The blow caught the Ripper in the jaw.

The Ripper collapsed on the floor and Paul followed him

down, landing another hit to the blond man's head.

Yeah. And how do you like that, big man?

He struck the prone man again.

For Lana. Carmela. Ana. All of the women he'd tormented.

"Paul." A hand caught his arm. "Stop. He's out."

"He wouldn't have stopped. He deserves whatever he gets."

"That's not for you to decide." A tremor rocked her words. "Please. You're better than him. Don't sink to his level."

She was right.

How was beating on an unconscious man any different than the way the Ripper had preyed on women weaker than himself?

Her hand fell away. "We need to tie him up."

Turning, Paul found her cloaked in shadows a few feet away. Not even the darkness could hide the blood staining her arms and clothes.

Had he arrived too late? Had the Ripper stabbed her? In the stomach?

"Are you okay?"

"I'm fine. But we need to tie him up. Before he comes to."

Was she really okay? The blood said otherwise. Then again, she'd stabbed the Ripper. Maybe the was all his blood, not hers.

And she was right. First he had to tie up the Ripper.

The stinging in Paul's hand confirmed the hits had been solid, but on the off chance the Ripper surprised him by waking up soon, he wanted to make sure the killer wasn't going anywhere.

Aside from that, Lana would feel more secure if he was tied up.

That duct tape ought to do the trick. He picked it up, ripped off a large strip, and twisted the Ripper's arms behind his back, winding the tape around his wrists several times. He wrapped some tape around the Ripper's feet next, then attached the man's hands to his feet with a final piece of tape.

Even if he woke up before the police arrived, there was zero chance the Ripper could break free from that.

Paul stood and looked back at Lana. Or at least, where Lana had been.

The spot was empty.

A glance around the basement confirmed his suspicion. She wasn't down here any longer.

Not that he could blame her.

He glanced at the Ripper.

What he wouldn't give to have a gun in his hands right now. He'd use it. He'd empty the whole cartridge into that pathetic slime.

It was probably a good thing he was unarmed.

Maybe he'd take the lantern.

The storm had blocked out most of the natural light upstairs and besides, part of him liked the idea of the Ripper being in darkness if he woke up.

The door to the main floor was open and he stepped into the hallway. Which way would Lana have gone?

Somehow he doubted she'd move further into the house.

No, it seemed much more likely she'd head for the front room. She'd want a clear escape route if they needed to get out of the house fast.

The carpet, worn and frayed as it was, absorbed his footsteps as he walked into the living room. There, sitting on the sofa he'd hidden behind earlier, sat Lana. Elbows on her knees, she rested her forehead in the palm of her right hand and cradled her left hand in her lap.

Wind battered the house, which moaned around them. He glanced up at the ceiling. Would this building survive the storm?

Downstairs was the safest place right now.

But he couldn't ask her to do that.

He tried to shut the sound of the wind from his mind by concentrating on her instead.

"Lana?"

She jumped and whipped her head around to look at him. One hand quickly ran across her face as she tried to hide the evidence of tears while the other rested limply in her lap.

A forced, shaky smile appeared. "I'm sorry. I couldn't stay down there any longer."

"Hey, don't worry about it. I'm just glad you're okay."

"How did you find me?"

"Ana told me. She remembered this place and I came to check it out." While that didn't nearly cover all that had happened, he didn't think she had the energy to deal with the whole story right now.

Besides, something wasn't right.

Of course it wasn't. Nothing about this afternoon had been right.

Still, there was something else. It was more a nagging instinct than anything solid he could nail down. A gut reaction to… something.

He studied her more closely.

Although pale, her face looked unharmed. No busted nose, split lip, or black eye.

Her red throat looked raw and would probably bruise, and although that bothered him, it wasn't what nagged at him right now. The tight ponytail that had held her hair back earlier had sagged, but still held most of her hair out of her face.

Wait a minute…

The hair on her left side, right by her ear, was plastered to her head. It also looked slimy and maybe a little darker, although her black hair made it hard to tell for sure.

He brought the light closer. Definitely blood.

"What happened to your head?"

One of her hands, streaked with dried blood, gingerly touched the matted hair. "The Ripper knocked me out. I don't know what he used."

Forget the gun.

He wanted to stomp back down those stairs and kill the

Ripper with his bare hands.

He should've done it earlier.

No one would know what had really happened. He could say the Ripper had escaped and come after them. Self defense.

Heck, the city would probably give him a medal for stopping the Ripper.

But Lana would know. And she'd have to choose between telling the truth or lying to protect him.

The thought curbed his urge to exact revenge.

No way would he put Lana in a position to make such a choice, especially since she would blame herself for his actions.

She rubbed her bare arms. As she did, he caught a glimpse of a dark stain on the back of her shirt. It started toward her lower back and ran in streaks to a pool at the bottom of her shirt.

He didn't need a closer look to know what it was – more blood.

The log caught in his throat refused to budge.

How much damage had that butcher done to her?

His mind blanked as he stared at the blood. On her back, her arms, her shirt and jeans. He tried to ask her where it had come from, how many cuts she had, where the Ripper had left the knife, but his tongue froze to the roof of his mouth.

Words finally exploded from his lips. *"What happened?"*

Confusion flickered on her face as she looked up at him. "He tricked me, okay? But I had to check, to make sure–"

"No. There's blood on your back."

Now that he thought about it, she had way too much blood on her hands and arms for all of it to be from stabbing Simmons. She'd hit the man in the bicep. There'd been some blood, but not a lot.

She stared at him as if she didn't understand what he was asking.

Could she have a concussion? Or some other serious head injury?

Setting the lantern on the table, he dropped onto the sofa beside her. "Lana. Where did all this blood come from?"

She looked down at her hands as if seeing them for the first time. "I forgot. I cut myself on the glass. My hands were behind me."

"Is it still bleeding?"

Eyes clouded with pain met his. "I don't think so."

Not good enough. He had to know for sure. "Which arm?"

"Left."

He gently captured her left arm, which felt like a twig in his hand. How had he never noticed how delicate she was? Even though the arm was swollen to almost twice its normal size, his fingers wrapped around it easily.

A cut ran halfway from her wrist to her elbow. Blood smeared the skin around it, but the congealed blood covering the cut revealed that she was right. It'd stopped bleeding.

"And that's it?"

"I think my wrist is sprained."

That explained the swelling. "Anything else?"

"I don't think so."

Thank you, Jesus.

His hand shook as he carefully set her arm back in her lap. Tears burned his eyes, but he wouldn't let them fall.

That had been too close. He'd almost lost her.

If the storm had moved any faster, if the Ripper had set his sights on her earlier, things could've turned out very differently. And he never would have seen her again.

"Paul, I'm okay."

He met her eyes and almost lost all composure.

That she saw his battle for control was evident as tears drowned her dark eyes.

Scooting closer, he put an arm around her shoulders and drew her to him, cradled her gently like the precious treasure she was. Occasional shudders wracked her body, but she made no sounds. He had no idea if she was crying or just shaky.

Outside, the wind howled and rain lashed the roof, but inside silence ruled.

Several minutes passed before Lana's voice broke the quiet. "He's a photographer for one of the papers."

How did she know that? The Ripper must have told her. "That's what Ana said."

"I can't believe no one noticed anything off about him. I mean, the journalists or the people he worked with should've noticed something. A guy like that can't just blend in."

Sure he could.

Paul had been blending in for years and no one, not even Lana, knew about his past.

Fresh guilt crushed his chest and he labored to draw in air. "You'd be surprised how easy it is to act normal."

"Still someone should've seen something. I can't believe... Wait, did you say Ana told you?"

His arms had never felt emptier than when Lana pulled back to look at him.

Eyes dry now, she looked more like her usual self and certainly sounded more like the US Marshal he knew her to be.

"Yeah. She saw the news and called Arlington this afternoon to tell him about her ex-boyfriend. Thank God she did. If it weren't for her, I wouldn't have found you."

"I'll have to thank her later."

It was such a Lana thing to say.

With cuts on her arms, blood on her clothes, and bruises on her neck, she'd survived a nightmare too horrible for words and she was already thinking about the other people involved. A small smile even graced her lips.

He leaned in and kissed her.

It wasn't something he'd intended to do.

His brain screamed at him, called him every kind of fool, accused him of ruining the best thing in his life, but he couldn't help it.

His heart had taken control of his body.

Then he felt her hand cradle his cheek as she responded. Was it simply the emotions of the day? Or had she wanted this for as long as he had?

Bang!

From somewhere in the house, something slammed, splintered.

The Ripper!

Paul jumped up, positioned himself in front of Lana, and scanned the room for a weapon. A lamp, a fireplace poker, anything he could use to fight back.

Nothing. Except for furniture, the lantern, and the books the Ripper had thrown at him earlier.

Well, if that was all he had, he'd use them.

Footsteps thundered toward them and thin beams of light cut through the dim room.

Wait, multiple beams?

Now that he thought about it, there were too many footsteps to be from one man.

A gun crossed the room's threshold, followed by a uniformed cop. Paul's legs shook. Backup had finally arrived.

The officer flicked the light in Paul's eyes. "Got 'em."

More footsteps. Arlington stepped into the room a few seconds later. The detective scanned the area before lowering his gun.

"You two okay?"

"All things considered." Lana's voice came from Paul's right and he realized she hadn't remained behind him like he'd intended.

Which shouldn't surprise him.

Had she ever been one to willingly let someone else fight her battles?

Just like she rarely admitted that she needed help. But he would not let her pass herself off as fine. "You got an ambulance coming? Lana took a few good blows before I got here."

"You think I could find a free ambulance on a day like

today, you're crazier than I thought." Arlington stepped closer to see the damage for himself.

Lana shifted under his professional scrutiny. "It's no big deal. Just a few cuts and bruises."

"Not as bad as it coulda been, but Van Horn and I are on the same page on this one. Soon as we wrap this up, I'm gonna drop you by the hospital."

Arlington shifted his focus to Paul and hardened his look. "And you. You got any idea how stupid comin' here was? Like the Ripper needed another reason to want you dead. I should haul you in for impeding an investigation. A night in lockup oughta kill your hero complex."

The bluff was empty; they all knew it.

The media would fry Arlington for locking up the man who'd stopped the Ripper.

Paul shifted the attention away from his own actions. "What took you so long to get down here?"

Arlington snorted. "Case you hadn't noticed, we got a storm rollin' in out there. One of the roads was blocked and we had to take the long way around."

It must've had something to do with the direction Arlington had come, because Paul hadn't encountered any blocked roads. Unless it happened just after he went through, always a possibility on a day like today.

Paul breathed a silent thank you to God before returning his attention to Arlington. "The Ripper's in the basement. We tied him up."

Arlington got on his radio. "Guess Simmons is downstairs. Anyone find him yet?"

The radio crackled in response. "Headed down there now."

What if the Ripper had somehow escaped? He might take Lana again.

No way. He'd tied that killer up securely. He wasn't going anywhere.

But what if he had? Stranger things had happened. Paul tried to stamp down the fear that swallowed him, but all he could think was that the Ripper would go after Lana again and kill her this time.

He felt every agonizingly long second tick by as he waited for Arlington's radio to come to life again.

Come on, tell us something.

Above them, the roof groaned under the force of the wind.

They needed to leave, the sooner the better. This place felt about as secure as a house of cards on a rollercoaster.

Crackle. "We got him. He's out cold."

"Good. Bring him up and let's get outta here. Don't want this place to come down on our heads."

Within five minutes, Paul was in his car, following Arlington as the detective sped toward the hospital. The US Marshal in Lana had taken over and she'd decided to ride with Arlington so she could brief him on what had happened.

Too bad he had his own car.

Not only did Paul want to hear her side of the story, he needed to have her close. He'd come too close to losing her today.

As the swamps were replaced by suburbs, Paul couldn't shake the feeling that life as he knew it had been inalterably changed.

Twenty–Six

The waiting room in the ER didn't have a single seat available. Some people sat on the floor.

Whether it was the head wound, the blood coating Lana's arms, her status as law enforcement, or the news that she'd almost been the Ripper's latest victim, Paul wasn't sure, but the nurses bumped Lana to the top of the list and took her right back.

Man. Had it really only been a few hours since all this started?

It felt like days had passed.

He should try to call home. Let Dale and Annie know not to expect him anytime soon.

Although, realistically, he'd probably have a hard time getting through. Nothing like a natural disaster to clog communications.

He stepped into the hallway leading to the bathrooms, where it was marginally quieter, and brought up Dale's cell number. Call quality was poor, but he managed to get the message across.

Turning, he found Arlington leaning against the wall a few feet away. "Still need to get your statement."

Did they have to do this now?

Paul dropped his phone in his pocket and sighed. "Whenever you're ready."

"Run through what happened. Start at the part where you went all superhero on me." Arlington pulled a notepad and pen from his pocket.

Summarizing as much as he could, Paul hit the high points.

An occasional nod and the movement of the pen were the only indicators Arlington heard him.

Paul finished his story, hesitated, then asked the question that had smoldered in him since hearing the Ripper had Lana. "Did the Ripper do anything to her?"

The notepad and pen back in his pocket, Arlington met Paul's eyes. "Depends on your definition. She remembers fighting the guy in the rain and then she woke up in the basement. Said she tried to play along with what he said, that she set him off a few times, but he didn't hurt her."

Yeah, right. Evidently getting hit on the head no longer counted as being hurt.

"But he didn't, uh…" Man. Was there a good way to ask this?

Arlington saved him from having to put it into words. "She says it didn't happen."

"And you believe her, right?"

"Yeah. She had no problem saying it point blank, didn't display any signs of emotional trauma, even said the doctor could do an exam. When a woman wants to hide a sexual assault, she normally refuses medical treatment."

Okay. So the physical damage was minimal, but what about the psychological?

How long would it be before he saw the usual fearless Lana again?

Arlington straightened. "Lucky for you, catchin' the Ripper's put me in a good mood. I'm gonna let your interference in my case go. But if you ever do somethin' that stupid again, I'll haul your sorry butt in and charge you, we clear?"

"Don't worry. I don't plan to make it a habit." Paul tried to work up a smile, but was too tired.

"I need to get back to the station and wrap this up before the storm hits. You might wanna get outta here, too."

"Not until I hear how Lana is doing."

It was obviously the answer Arlington expected. The detective offered his hand. "Thanks. It's good to have the Ripper behind bars."

He followed Arlington back to the waiting room. As the detective walked out the door, Paul slid down the wall and sat on the cold tile floor.

Man, what a mess.

Sure, he'd saved the day, and the girl, but it was his fault Lana had gotten caught in the middle in the first place. The Ripper was off the streets, but at what cost?

Around him, the room bustled and life moved on, but he felt death crowding him on all sides. After all that'd happened, he couldn't help wondering if violence trailed certain people around, haunted their moves, dogged their steps.

People like him.

What if it was true? What if the things he'd done in the past, though unrelated to everything that had happened today, were a result of the bad choices he'd made when he was younger?

Not like Karma getting revenge, more like the sins of his past catching up with him. If he'd been honest with Lana from the start, maybe none of this would've happened.

How many more people would be hurt because of what he'd done so many years ago?

But God had forgiven all that, hadn't He?

Paul had studied the Bible, spoken to many pastors and theologians who had assured him that nothing he'd done would separate him from God if he truly confessed and repented.

Which he had. The past was just that – past.

But the effects of his actions could still be felt. There were consequences with which he must deal. Consequences he'd spent years avoiding.

"Paul Van Horn?"

The sound of his name from an unfamiliar source threw him to his feet. A nurse stood by the swinging doors that led into the ER, a lined piece of paper in her hand.

"I'm Paul."

She gave him a quick, tight smile. "I was asked to give this to you."

The note was in his hand, the doors swinging shut in front of his face, before he could blink. His leg muscles shrunk as he stared at the folded piece of paper.

Not good, not at all.

The note had to be from Lana.

She was going to tell him that she hadn't meant it, that it'd been nothing more than the heat of the moment, that the kiss had been an easy way to release the stress built up from what she'd experienced. Maybe she'd even chew him out for taking advantage of the situation, and her weakness, and tell him that she needed her space.

Kind of like a Dear John letter.

Which was ridiculous. Had anyone actually gotten a Dear John letter from someone they'd never dated?

No. That would make this a flat out rejection.

Thanks but no thanks. We were good friends until you had to go and screw it all up. See ya around. Or not.

Acid bubbled in the back of his throat and his muscles threatened to drop him to the floor.

Had to sit. Now.

A few chairs had opened up. His legs barely carried him to the closest one.

It wasn't until he'd sat down that he began to unfold the note.

The first thing to register was that it was short. Three lines. But a rejection letter didn't have to be long, did it? In fact, it probably would be short. How many words did it take to say "get lost"?

He blinked the lines into focus.

Paul, I'm in for a long night. The doctor hasn't been in to see me yet but with a head injury, I suspect he'll keep me overnight. Go on home before this storm hits. Your kids need you. I'll call you tomorrow. Lana.

Not a rejection.

His hand shook as he reread her familiar writing. Nothing at all to indicate that what'd happened earlier would negatively impact their relationship.

But of course it would. Even if she didn't know it yet, things would never be the same.

He refolded the note and stood, stuffing it in his pocket as he moved for the door.

Leaving lingered at the bottom of the list of things he wanted to do, especially given what had happened earlier, but she was right. Even if he stayed, no guarantee existed that he'd be able to see her.

Or that she wanted him to. Besides, she needed to rest.

And the kids did need him more than she did right now. The storm would probably shake up the older kids, not to mention what it would do to the younger, less stable ones like Maria.

The wind and rain blasted him as he stepped outside, but his thoughts strayed time and again to the kiss.

Where did he stand with Lana now?

That kiss had changed everything and their relationship – platonic or otherwise – would have to be redefined.

He could try to pass it off as a spontaneous reaction to the stress and grief of the day, but she'd never buy it. Even the kids could tell how he felt about her; after today, Lana undoubtedly knew it, too.

Which meant he had to make a decision.

Tell her about his past or leave it buried. He was covered by grace, forgiven in God's sight; couldn't that be enough? Why bring it all to light and hurt a lot of people over things that were best left in the past?

Because grace or no grace, the law required justice for what he'd done. And with her profession, Lana would expect it, too.

He could try to keep the secret from her, but if their relationship did progress further, he'd spend every minute of every day feeling like the worst kind of fraud. And if he said or did something and accidentally revealed the truth, it would hurt her more than if he just leveled with her now.

But telling the truth would land him in jail. No question. How could he help the kids from prison?

Trust.

That's what it really boiled down to. Did he trust God to take care of him if he told the truth?

The truth was important to God, the Bible made that blindingly clear.

The Bible even said that truth and freedom went together. *And the truth will set you free.*

While not quite the context Christ had meant when He'd originally said it, it still applied.

Paul's hand shook as he fumbled to unlock the car door.

He knew what he should do. But could he find the courage to do it?

The storm hadn't done as much damage as he'd expected. Paul jerked another nail from the board and dropped it into the bucket by his feet.

Well, at least the sun was out today.

It had rained the last two days, preventing him from getting any of the boards removed from the windows. And did this house ever have a lot of windows. It hadn't seemed like a lot before, but after boarding over every one on Sunday, it now felt like hundreds.

At least he had plenty of help.

Dale and Annie were both hard at work, hammers and crowbars in hand. A few of the older kids had also been entrusted with tools while the younger ones were tasked with picking up the debris scattered around the yard.

He removed another nail, his mind straying to Lana. Not that he'd thought about much else since Sunday. Had it really only been three days since all that had happened?

Thinking about that day haunted him.

Memories of the kiss consumed him.

And questions about the future plagued him.

A fool. That's what he was. He threw away the best thing in his life over a compulsive decision. Could he have done anything more stupid?

Sure. He could have told her how he felt. That would have changed things even more.

They hadn't spoken since the kiss. Which was part blissful relief, part torture.

Mostly torture.

True to her word, Lana had tried to call him the day after it happened. The message she'd left said she was okay, had been released from the hospital, and would probably be busy most of the day. He'd called her back, but had only gotten her voicemail.

"I think that about does it." Dale's voice broke into his thoughts.

He looked at the house and discovered Dale was right. All the windows were uncovered with the exception of the one in front of him.

Which meant it was time to have a serious discussion with Dale and Annie.

They cleaned up the boards, nails, and tools, and stored them in the locked shed on the corner of the property. A game of basketball started up in the back yard, but Paul caught Dale before he could join in.

"Can I talk to you and Annie for a minute?"

Dale's brow wrinkled. "Sure, let me grab her."

"I'll meet you in my office."

His muscles stiffened as he walked up the porch stairs and through the back door. Was he sure about this? He hadn't said anything to anyone yet. He could still back out.

No. He couldn't. He was doing the right thing.

The peace he'd felt since he'd reached the decision Monday night couldn't be ignored. Yes, with the peace had come a mountain of sadness. He'd be leaving his kids. His life. Lana.

He couldn't do this! He just couldn't.

Who would comfort Maria? Take care of this place? Love his kids? Keep Lana safe?

Right. Like he'd be able to do anything about that last one.

Still, he was doing good work here. Why should the past have any impact? He was a different man now.

Come on, God. Really? Isn't there any other way?

Silence.

The stillness settled over him like a dead body. God had already told him what he needed to do, but obedience was his choice to make.

Why did it have to be so hard?

The sound of Annie's sandals smacking against the flesh of her heels made Paul blink. The time was now. For once in his life, he was going to do the right thing.

The Webbers stepped into his office.

"Come on in." Okay, that was dumb. They were already inside the room. "Would you mind closing the door?"

Dale arched an eyebrow before pushing the door closed. Both he and Annie seemed reluctant to come any further into the room. Not that he could blame them. Uncertainty scented the air. After what felt like an eternity, Dale put a hand on Annie's back and nudged her toward a chair.

Once they were seated, Paul couldn't do anything but look at them.

He knew he should say something. But he had no idea how to say what needed to be said.

Yeah, I really screwed up and am going to jail for the rest of my natural life. Can I sign this place over to you?

There had to be a better way.

"So..." Dale cleared his throat. "Uh, what's up?"

A glance at Annie found her watching him, eyes wide in her usually cheery face.

Paul sighed. This was harder than he'd imagined.

Just do it. Putting this off wouldn't make it any easier. "How would you guys feel about taking over this place?"

The silence that descended made him want to crack a smile and say he was joking.

But he wasn't. And if he said that, he'd probably never find the strength to go down this road again.

Before they could say anything, he continued, "And I'm not just talking for a week or a month. It'd be permanent. The house is paid for and there's a trust, so money won't be an issue–"

"You're leavin'?" Annie found her voice first. "What about these kids?"

"I don't want to, trust me."

"Then why?"

"There are some things in my past..." He lifted his shoulders in a limp shrug. "I can't do this anymore. I can't live a lie. I need to own up to what I've done and face the consequences."

"What kinda consequences are we talking about here?" Dale's sharp eyes locked on Paul.

"Prison."

"P-prison?" A squeak highlighted Annie's voice.

"Yeah. It was a long time ago, but God's telling me to set it right."

"If it was a long time ago, you might be past the statute of limitations." Dale rested his elbows on his knees. "What'd you do? It's probably not as bad as you think it is."

Wouldn't he be surprised.

Paul shook his head slightly. "I think it's better if you didn't know the details. But trust me when I say that statute of limitations won't apply."

"Is there anything we can do? I don't know any lawyers, but I'll do whatever I can to help."

That was exactly the response he'd expected. "Thanks, but no. I think it's best all the way around if I turn myself in, confess, and take whatever the system gives me."

Dale didn't even look at his wife before answering. "In that case, the answer is yes. We'd love to run this place."

"This is a huge decision. You need time to talk it through, pray, really think about it. There're unbelievable pressures. The kids look up to you and expect you to take care of them and these are kids who don't trust a lot of people so that's huge–"

"Paul." Annie's calm voice stopped him. "We know. We've lived here long enough to see what you go through. We can handle it."

Of course they could. Probably better than he had.

"You're sure about this?" Dale asked.

Paul nodded before he could talk himself out of it. "I'll call Jason and have him draw up all the necessary papers. Thanks. You guys are an answer to prayer."

And so much more.

Not only did it calm his fears about leaving the kids, it served as God's confirmation that he was doing the right thing.

"I hate that the kids have to lose you, but we love these kids. We'll do anything we can to help them."

Which was precisely why he'd asked the Webbers to take over for him. Not only did the kids already know and love them, he'd know the kids were in good hands.

"When do you have to leave?" Annie's soft question brought his thoughts into clear focus.

He hesitated. "As soon as Jason gets the paperwork ready. Maybe tomorrow."

"So soon?" Annie's words came out with a gasp.

If he waited any longer, he might lose his nerve. But he

didn't tell her that. "I can find someone to help you until you find your footing–"

"Just show us what we need to know. You can count on us." Dale's voice was thick, the emotion on his face unchecked.

"Thanks. You have no idea how much easier you're making this transition, not just for the kids, but for me." He swallowed hard. "And you won't have to worry about money. Some comes from the government, but there's also a trust established for this house so if you ever find yourself short, you can access that. We'll go over all that tomorrow."

"We have time today if you wanted to do it now." Compassion laced Dale's tone.

"Thanks, but I need to go visit Austin. It'll probably be the last time I see him and I feel like I need to give him some kind of explanation."

Dale hesitated. "What are you going to tell the kids?"

That was the question, wasn't it?

When his thoughts hadn't been consumed by Lana, they'd been focused on that very question. In the end, he'd finally decided that the simpler his explanation, the better. "I'm going to tell them that there are some things from my past that I have to deal with. That I made some mistakes and don't have a choice. I think the older kids will figure it out, but the younger ones probably won't."

"I think that's good. We'll try to field any other questions after you're gone without giving them the details." Annie uncrossed and re-crossed her legs. "When are you going to tell them?"

"Tonight. After dinner."

It meant the next twenty-four hours would be spent with teary, clingy kids, but they each deserved the time they needed to say good-bye in their own way.

He wasn't looking forward to it.

It'd be much cleaner and easier for him if he just walked out the door and never looked back, but he couldn't do that to his kids.

Many of them had already had adults do that to them. He would not join those ranks.

It would be hard, very hard, and he would have to try to rein in his emotions as much as possible, but he would do it. It was the least he could do for the kids. The last gift he had to give.

Twenty–Seven

If someone rang a gong to signal his death, Paul imagined it would sound just like Lana's doorbell.

He shifted his weight and glanced around Lana's quiet neighborhood. No sign of life anywhere.

Kind of like how he felt inside right now.

Wednesday had been jammed full of tears and promises to write or email or call, not that he thought he'd have many chances to use a phone or computer.

But he couldn't tell the kids that.

Somewhere between all that, he'd found the time to go over the house's finances and operations with Dale and Annie. With Jason's expertise, they'd created legal documents that would hopefully keep the government from trying to confiscate the house or the money that kept it running.

After all that, Paul had packed up his things and put them in the attic. Why he'd held onto them, he wasn't sure, but on the off chance he ever did see the light of day again, he might need some of those things.

Funny. He'd never before thought of himself as an optimist.

By the time he'd finished all that, it'd been so late he'd decided to wait until the following day to face Lana.

Might have been cowardice. He honestly wasn't sure.

Now here he was. The final leg of his journey. And the hardest one to complete.

The deadbolt slid, a chain rattled, and the door opened to reveal Lana in a green v-neck top and jeans. Her hair was loose around her shoulders and a soft smile made her face glow.

Closer examination found stress lines around her eyes, a brace on her left wrist, and her Glock clutched in her right hand. Did she usually bring her gun with her to answer the door or was this a new development, the result of facing the Ripper on Sunday?

He wasn't sure, but he hated seeing her afraid. All he could do was pray she'd return to her old self soon.

Not that he'd be around to see it.

"Hi." Her surprised voice broke the silence.

Was it his imagination or was her voice different than usual? It sounded almost a little... shy? He tried not to dwell on what that could mean because every scenario that came to mind ended with her returning the feelings he'd worked so hard to hide.

Which would've been a good thing any other time, but not today.

"Come on in." Her voice drew him from his thoughts.

He stepped inside, turning to watch as she locked the door and deadbolt. Slipping past him, she led the way into the living room and took a seat on the couch.

Every muscle in his body wanted to join her, but he couldn't. He didn't trust his emotions now, much less in close proximity. The chair across from her didn't give as much distance as he would have liked, but it would do.

"How are you feeling?" The strain in his voice caused her smile to slip a little.

"Fine."

The quick reply sounded more like autopilot than the truth. Besides that, there was no way anyone, not even Lana, could be fine after what had happened. "No kidding."

The skepticism had the desired effect.

She hesitated briefly. "I've been better, but I'll be okay."

That sounded closer to the truth. "Look, I'm sorry to stop by like this, especially when you're getting ready for work-"

A short laugh that contained no trace of humor burst from her. "I wish. I'm on mandatory leave until I get cleared by a psychologist."

"Oh. Well, that's not such a bad thing."

"Easy for you to say."

"Hey, what happened to there being no shame in that, huh? Isn't that what you told me?"

"I just want things to get back to normal. Work is normal. This–" She flung her uninjured hand out and gestured to the room around her, "me being here, not doing anything, isn't. It just reminds me of everything that happened."

"Well, you were attacked by a serial killer. It's gonna take time to come back from that."

Her eyes narrowed. "If you're going to treat me like I'm some kind of victim, you can leave now."

Whoa! What had he said? It wasn't like her to be so testy.

She curled her legs up under her and looked away.

Time to do some damage control.

"Lana." He waited for her to look at him before continuing, "I'm sorry. I didn't mean to... I don't think of you as a victim. Not now or ever. You're one of the strongest, most capable people I know."

Pink flushed her face. Her chin trembled. A few tears escaped her eyes and she swiped them away. "No, I'm sorry. You didn't do anything wrong. I haven't been sleeping well and I'm cranky."

"All the more reason why a little time off work is a good thing for you right now."

She gave a curt nod before clearing her throat. "Well, anyway. Enough about me. I'm sure you didn't come over here just to check up on me. What's up?"

He wished that was why he'd come. He wished he didn't have to drop another bomb on her right now. Not after all she'd already been through the last few days. "You're right.

There's something I need to tell you."

But where to begin? He couldn't even seem to come up with how to say this, much less the exact words to convey the truth.

"I didn't see your car out there." Her voice seemed loud in the wake of the silence.

"Jason dropped me off."

There was so much more he could say, needed to say, but the words wouldn't come.

He leaned forward with his elbows on his knees and for several seconds couldn't do anything but look at her.

Man, was she beautiful. Bruises and all.

And hands down the kindest, most selfless woman he'd ever met.

What was he doing, slamming the door like this when she might return his feelings? Was he crazy?

Yes, he was. Crazy for ever thinking this could work out to begin with.

"So you're really okay?"

He was pretty sure she recognized the distraction for what it was, but she didn't point out the obvious. "I am. My wrist is only sprained, not broken. I had a headache yesterday and the cuts on my arm still burn a little, but all in all, I'm fine."

Sure she was.

No matter what happened, Lana always seemed to bounce back stronger than before. And she'd recover from the blow he was about to deal her, too. She'd be fine long before he was.

"Lana, I…"

The words fled his mind.

Maybe he shouldn't have come. He could've written her a letter, had Dale or Annie deliver it once he was in prison. That would've been much easier.

It also would've been the coward's way.

No, she deserved to hear the truth from him. In person. It was the least he could do.

But how? How did he do this? There had to be a better way than blurting out the truth.

She leaned across the coffee table and touched his hand.

Gently. Not like one friend to another, but like something potentially stronger.

Great.

"Hey, it's okay. I get it–"

If only.

"No. No, you don't." He sighed and forced himself to hold her eyes with his own. "There's something I need to tell you. I haven't been completely honest."

Completely? Heck, he hadn't been remotely honest.

Her eyebrows knit together. "I'm sure we can work through it. That's what friends do."

"You may not feel that way after you hear what I have to say." His voice was so soft he wouldn't have been surprised if she hadn't heard him.

But of course, she had.

She pulled back. The absence of her touch left him feeling very alone.

Well, here went nothing. "There are some things in my past that I need to come clean about."

The words made it sound so minor, like all he was going to tell her was that he'd been married before or had five kids with five different women, but something in his tone must've tipped her off. Her smile faded into a look of concern.

"You can talk to me about anything. You know that, right?"

She made it sound so simple.

"There are things about me… I'm not who you think I am." He fell silent, his mind racing from one rotten way to break the news to another. Why hadn't he scripted this prior to coming?

"Paul?"

"My name's not Paul."

An expressionless façade fell into place as she leaned against the back of the sofa.

And there was the work face. The one that revealed nothing about what was going through her mind. While he'd expected it, it still hurt to see her defenses come up.

"You're worrying me. What's going on?"

Even her tone was unemotional.

"Remember when we met?"

"Sure. At church. You were sitting in the back row by yourself and I stopped to talk to you."

He shook his head slowly. "That wasn't the first time."

"What do you mean?"

"We met before, in Oregon. I was going by–"

"Nate Miller." The words came out in a breath. She stared at him, lips parted, eyes wide and unblinking. "I–I can't believe I didn't see it before."

"I've had plastic surgery since then. It's no wonder you didn't recognize me."

"No, no. It's impossible. You can't be–"

"Nate Miller."

A stony mask slipped across her face. She crossed her arms over her chest but said nothing. Dark eyes glittered in the early morning light and the corners of her mouth twitched down.

The silence in the room smothered him.

"Why are you here?" Her tone had the warmth of a rocky Alpine cliff in a blizzard.

He wanted to reach for her, but kept his hands where they were.

If possible, he hated himself more at that moment than he ever had in his whole miserable life.

Receiving the work mask was the hardest part. It denied him any glimpse into how the truth had affected her. "Lana, don't do that. Please."

"What do you want me to do? Say what a selfish pig you are? Do you have any idea what this will do to your kids? Or the position you've put me in here?"

"I know! I know." His voice broke. The burning behind his

eyes rivaled the fire in his throat that blocked the words he knew he needed to say. Clearing his throat, he forced the words past his thick tongue. "I want you to take me in."

The mask cracked and Lana's eyes drowned in moisture.

He wished there was something he could do to take those tears away. "I'm sorry. I never meant... this wasn't supposed to happen."

"Just what did you think would happen?"

"I never thought it through that far. I thought grace was enough and I could leave the past behind."

He leaned back, his eyes locked on her face. "After you were shot, I took a serious look at my life. I ended up in some hick town in Montana and stayed there for almost two months. There was this church and the pastor, well, I guess you could say he finished what you started. He even helped me find a purpose – helping kids like me."

"And Stevens? What about him?"

"I talked to him about God, but he never really bought into my new lifestyle."

"Not that. Is he really dead?"

"Yeah." That day was seared into his memory. This day would no doubt tie it for worst day ever. "We both went to Montana. Matt bought some land and a few ATVs. He was out riding one day and flipped it. I found him the next day."

"And that's it?"

Did she believe him? With her carefully masked emotions, it was difficult to tell. "If you want to search death records, he was going by Logan Haskill and died on October 8, three years ago. He left everything to me. I couldn't stay there so I sold the ranch."

"Why Jacksonville? Out of all the places you could've chosen, why here?"

Her eyes told him she already knew the answer, begged him to deny it, but he couldn't. Lies and secrecy had dominated this last year, his whole life, actually, and he was done. It was time for the truth.

"I'd lost the only person who cared that I existed. You were the next closest thing I had to a friend and I guess I wanted to be close by." A humorless laugh escaped from his lips. "I told myself it was in case you got into trouble and needed my help."

Right. Like *he* could help *her*. What a joke.

"So you came to my Dad's church to spy on me." Her flat tone belied her expression, which revealed a storm of emotions that her words would never betray.

"I didn't know it was your Dad's church. You've gotta believe me. I was shocked when you came over and introduced yourself to me."

The day flashed back with vivid clarity. He even remembered what she'd been wearing. A light purple shirt and gray skirt that hit just above her knees, sandals, silver fish necklace.

He sighed. "I told myself I'd never go back to your church, but I really liked it. Every Sunday I'd go and tell myself it was the last time and before I knew it, you were coming to help with the kids."

The hard set to her mouth softened. "I knew there was something familiar about you, but I was never able to place it. It's probably why I was so comfortable with you from day one."

Every word peeled back another layer of his heart.

This was so hard; why had God asked him to do this?

Things had been going fine and he'd been doing good work. If God had wanted him to turn himself in, why not a year ago? Before he'd gotten so emotionally invested?

"Why now?"

Lana's question so closely mimicked his own it took him by surprise. "Huh?"

"You've been here for what a year, year and a half. Why are you telling me this now?"

"I thought I could put it all behind me. God knew the truth and had forgiven me and I thought that'd be enough. But I felt like a hypocrite every time I told the kids to do the right thing. More than that, I couldn't stand lying to you any longer." He sighed and raked his fingers through his hair. "I can't explain it, but I feel like I have to do this. I can't run from who I was. Not anymore."

"If you're turning yourself in, why not just do it? Why're you here?"

"You deserved to hear the truth. From me." His throat closed and he tried to retain some semblance of control. Lana swirled into a blur of colors and he blinked her into focus, sending a tear escaping down his cheek. "I need you to take me in."

"Why me? Why not go down yourself and tell the FBI the whole thing?"

That was the easiest question she'd asked yet. "I trust *you*. I know you're mad at me right now and I deserve it. But I also know you'll do everything you can to make sure I don't disappear in the system. You'll keep them accountable."

Even though he'd never killed anyone personally, he'd be going to prison as an accomplice to Stevens' murders.

Stevens had a lot of enemies. Some that may be willing to take him as a substitute.

What if one of them – heck, it could even be someone in law enforcement – made him disappear? If the person was powerful enough, they could cover up the fact that he'd ever existed, much less been incarcerated.

Acid surged through his stomach. His muscles ached from the constant tension, but he couldn't get them to relax.

What would he do if Lana refused to help him?

Not that he'd blame her if she did. She was right; this put her in an awkward position.

What would her boss say when he learned that she'd spent the last year hanging out with a man who was both a thief and the closest friend of a hit man? Not to mention what her friends, family, and the people at church would think.

He was a jerk.

How could he think of asking her to do this? It wasn't right and it certainly wasn't fair.

He pushed himself to his feet. "I'm sorry, I shouldn't have asked. I'll go talk to Arlington and do this myself–"

A hand on his arm stopped him from turning.

"Did I say I wouldn't help?" A ragged sigh escaped her lips. "You're right. I'm mad and I'm hurt and part of me wants to slug you, but you're still my friend."

The words were ointment to his seared heart. Even after all he'd done, she still called him a friend. It wouldn't change the facts, but it made what was left of his life more bearable.

His mind couldn't focus on anything but that one word.

Friend.

Never anything more, but Lana would get over it and move on. He wouldn't, but he could handle that. As long as she was happy, he could live with anything.

"Thanks."

"What exactly are you confessing to?"

"I guess it'll be accessory to murder." Acid pricked his eyes and he didn't know how much longer he could impede the tears that threatened. "And theft."

"Theft?"

"Let's just say I was really good at getting into highly secure places. Came in handy for Matt's work."

The silence that engulfed the room was laced with a sadness so tangible it seemed to have a distinct personality. It lasted for several impossibly long seconds before Lana finally broke it.

"What about your kids? And the house?"

"I signed it over to the Webbers. Jason drew up the paperwork yesterday."

"They'll take good care of the place."

More silence. He released a shuddery breath. "You know why I chose the name Paul? Because in a small way, I feel like I can relate to the Apostle Paul."

Wait, that wasn't quite what he meant. He rushed on before

she could misunderstand. "Not that I think I'm some great apostle changing the world or anything. I just meant with our pasts. He killed people and God still used him. I guess I liked the idea that God could use me, too."

But he should've known better. At least the apostle's intentions had been good. When the Apostle Paul had killed the Christians, he'd thought he was doing the right thing.

And though he'd never personally killed anyone, he'd known what Matt was doing and had done nothing to stop him. Condoning the acts made him a passive participant.

He might as well have pulled the trigger himself.

"God did use you." Lana's soft words filtered through the harsh self-loathing. "And I don't think He's done yet."

Did she really believe that or was she just being Lana?

He met her eyes and saw the sincerity there.

The desire to hold her almost overwhelmed him. If he didn't go now, he might do something to make this even harder.

He blew out a long breath. "I'd better go before I lose my nerve."

"I'll grab my keys." Her voice was so soft he almost missed the words. Turning, she headed toward the kitchen.

"Lana."

She stopped but didn't turn to face him.

"I'm sorry. Really. If I could take it all back, I would."

A nod. The only response she gave, but it was enough.

This was it. The end of the road.

His hands began to shake. The trembling moved from his hands, up his arms, and down his body until he felt like a skyscraper in an earthquake.

Sinking back into the chair, he clenched his hands to keep them still.

Come on, suck it up.

"Do you know a good defense attorney?" Lana's voice brought his head around. Standing in the kitchen doorway, she leaned against the jamb with her arms crossed loosely over her chest.

Didn't she get it? There wouldn't be a trial. He'd confess and deal with the consequences.

"Didn't figure I'd need one. I'll accept whatever they give me. We both know this won't go to trial."

"Maybe not, but an attorney can insure there's a deal in place before you tell the FBI anything. Maybe make life inside a little better for you. At least make sure the Webbers and your kids are insulated from all this."

"I didn't think about that." But she was right, wasn't she? The authorities might seek the death penalty, regardless of the fact that he'd come to them. "I can call Jason. He'd offered to set me up with someone."

Lana gave a curt nod. "Do it. We need an expert to negotiate our way through this."

Our.

He couldn't believe she'd stand by his side after all he'd done.

Five minutes later it was set up. Jason had arranged an emergency meeting with one of his friends, a criminal attorney with an office on Broadmoor Drive, at nine. That gave them a little over an hour to get there.

He followed Lana out the back door and to the garage, climbing into the passenger side of yet another rental car.

The car shrunk around him as fear crushed him from every side.

Life as he knew it was about to change forever.

It overwhelmed him. Terrified him. And in some strange way that he couldn't understand, relieved him.

He was done lying. It was time to live in the truth.

Epilogue

The cell door clanged shut behind him. The sound bounced down the hall, fading with the guard's footfalls.

He surveyed the cell that would be his home, probably for the rest of his life. The room contained next to nothing. A toilet. A sink. Two cots with thin mattresses that would take some getting used to.

If he had a cellmate, the other man was out.

Securing the services of a lawyer had been a smart move. The lawyer had thought of details that Paul hadn't even considered. Like placing him in a minimum security prison outside of Jacksonville and guaranteeing that he would remain there and wouldn't be transferred from one location to another.

And allowing Lana almost unrestricted visiting privileges.

Assuming she even wanted to see him.

She'd made no promises, but the lawyer had insisted the legal paperwork be put in place for her to visit as often as she wanted.

If she wanted.

Not that he'd blame her if she didn't. How would that look to her friends, her coworkers, if she visited an inmate on a regular basis?

He sat on the cot. At least it wasn't quite as uncomfortable as it looked.

Right. Who was he kidding?

His eyes roved the small room. In less than four weeks, he'd lost everything he'd worked for, everyone he cared about.

His freedom.

His kids.

Lana.

And yet, amidst all that, he'd found something else, something that amazed him more than words could say.

Peace. True peace that permeated through every fiber of his body.

With the steel door locked behind him, the barren walls in front of him, the armed guards in the hall, he'd never been more confined. But for the first time in years, possibly his whole life, he was truly free.

A note from the author

Thank you for joining me on Paul's journey. His character captivated me from the start and I knew he needed a story all his own.

Don't be fooled; his story is far from over! I hope you'll pick up the final book in the Deadly Alliances series, Deadly Redemption, and see what happens with Paul and Lana next. Check out the following pages for a sneak peek at that novel...

Obedience. Scripture clearly tells us that it is the proof that we love God and are God's people (John 14:15-24, 1 John 2:3-6).

I love the Old Testament, especially the prophets, and it's absolutely amazing how often obedience – or lack thereof – is mentioned in those books. Is it easy? Sometimes, but oftentimes the things God asks of us are hard, really hard.

So why does He ask us to do things that are so hard? I think the answer to that question is two-fold: one, because it gives solid evidence to our faith and trust in Him, and two, because it forces us to rely upon Him.

Face it, if God asks you to do something you want to do anyway, does it take any great degree of faith to do it? No way. But when He calls you to do something you don't want to do, something that requires great sacrifice or suffering, you have a choice to make. Trust God and obey or do your own thing?

I hope you'll join me in seeking God's will and responding in obedience. If you feel God telling you to set something right, do it. It may revolutionize your life and give you a peace that you've never experienced before.

And if it's been a while since you cracked open the word of God, I can't encourage you enough to shake off the dust and get reading. God's word will change your life, if you'll let it. If you're up for a challenge in obedience, maybe start with the book of Jonah, one of my personal favorites. It's so much more than a man getting swallowed by a fish! You'll see Jonah's struggle with disobedience, his reluctant eventual obedience, and – if you're anything like me – be challenged by his bad attitudes and selfishness. Jonah is a relatable prophet. We see his humanity, his sin and flaws, and how God uses him anyway. What an encouragement to us all!

Thanks for reading. If you enjoyed this story, I hope you'll tell the other readers in your life about it... and maybe consider writing a brief review.

I'd love to hear from you; comments, suggestions, constructive criticism – they're all helpful. Feel free to email me at candle.sutton@outlook.com or message me on facebook (facebook.com/candlesutton).

I pray you'll seek God and obey Him with a faith that will challenge the world and change a culture.

Excerpt from Deadly Redemption

Prologue

Rain battered the windshield. The wipers whipped water from the glass, but couldn't keep up with the onslaught.

Brody gripped the wheel. The storm outside paled compared to the one raging within.

He'd found a traitor.

Even now, with irrefutable proof, he could hardly believe it. That Judas had been in their midst for weeks; how could none of them have seen it?

Tim would be furious.

Headlights bore down in his rearview mirror. Brody didn't need to see the car to know who it was. That treacherous leach would do anything to stop him from telling Tim the truth.

Because once Tim knew, he'd take care of the problem. He always did.

The car drew closer. Brody pressured the accelerator.

The Hemi in his truck responded with a power that usually thrilled him. But not tonight.

Wind threw rainwater against his truck in waves. Going this fast was foolish, but what choice did he have? He had to get back to headquarters before they could stop him.

If only his phone hadn't gotten crushed in the struggle. Then he could've called Tim and wouldn't be driving in the storm like some kind of maniac.

The wind increased as his truck crossed the threshold to the

Wappoo Creek Bridge.

Flashing lights glimmered through his rain-spattered windshield. An accident?

He slammed the brakes. The wheels screamed on the sodden asphalt, the truck's bed whipping like a pendulum.

The guardrail filled his vision.

The crunch of metal, the tinkle of glass, and the lurch of sudden impact registered seconds before he felt himself freefalling into darkness.

The truck hit the water with a jolt.

The airbag exploded against his chest and face. He twisted to the side to see around it. Then he wished he hadn't. Liquid blackness encased him.

Water rushed in.

The cold shocked his limbs. He couldn't move. All he could do was stare at the black liquid as it filled the floorboards and crawled up his legs.

Do something!

He punched the airbag out of the way as he felt the truck lazily tip backward.

His fingers fumbled with the seatbelt release. Jammed!

Jerking at the strap did no good. The accident had locked it up.

He strained for the glove box and the knife he kept inside.

The water reached the bottom of his ribcage, plastering his t-shirt against his stomach. Shivers rocked his body.

Cool metal met his searching fingers. He flipped the blade open.

The vehicle pivoted. His body fell forward, the seatbelt cutting into his chest and stomach.

He was headed to the bottom. Fast.

Water splashed his face. He turned his head and sucked in a breath. The water level climbed higher.

He couldn't see, but he put the knife against the seatbelt and sawed.

Fire engulfed his lungs. His movements slowed.

It was no use.

He couldn't hold his breath any longer. But he had to or he'd drown. Even as he commanded his body to obey, his mouth opened and sucked in a lungful of liquid salt.

He coughed, but only drew in more saltwater.

Blackness lurked at the edges of his mind.

He'd failed. And his friends would pay the price.

One

"You 'fraid ta take me on?"

Nate Miller stared at the pipsqueak in front of him. The kid stood at least six inches shorter and a good fifty pounds lighter. From the looks of things, he had more ego than muscle.

"Just walk away."

A handful of guys noticed the tension in the kid's stance and came over, smelling a fight.

The things that passed for entertainment in the yard.

The kid fisted his fingers and stepped forward. "Whatsa matter, old man?"

Old? Okay, so he had twenty years on the kid. Forty-three hardly made him old.

Well, so much for the fresh air. Nate pushed himself up. Sometimes it was easier to just stay in his cell, no matter how nice the sun felt on his face.

"Not so tough without Stevens watchin' your back, are you?"

Nate paused and turned, spearing the kid with his eyes. "Who do you think taught him to shoot?"

Okay, so maybe the kid wasn't the only one whose ego got the better of him sometimes.

Silence descended as Nate strode away.

No wonder. He'd never told anyone that piece of

information before. Completely true, but not something he was particularly proud of, especially considering the body count Stevens had accumulated with the training Nate had given him.

That blood was on his hands.

Nate crossed to an empty bench and sank down, scanning the yard. Orange jumpsuits and razor wire as far as the eye could see. Some days it seemed unbelievable that his life had come to this.

Several furtive glances angled his direction.

Yep, the rumor mill was active and healthy. By the end of the day, what he'd said would probably be exaggerated to the point that everyone would believe he'd not only trained Stevens, but that he *was* Stevens.

Funny how being associated with Stevens had given him instant street cred in this place.

It had also made him a target for the new guys looking to prove something. Like the kid who'd tried to get in his face just a few minutes ago.

He leaned his head back and stared at the storm clouds building overhead.

The sky might open up any time. In fact, he could smell the rain on the wind.

"Miller."

Now what?

Nate turned his head to find not an inmate, but a guard, walking toward him. "Hey Abrams. What's up?"

"You got a visitor."

Weird. Lana was the only one who ever came to see him and she only came on Saturdays. Never on a Tuesday afternoon.

Unless something was wrong.

He pushed up from the bench and followed Abrams inside. The former Marine fell into step beside him as the door closed.

"Know who it is?"

"Negative." Abrams' voice contained its usual note of steel.

"But don't get too excited. It wasn't that hot deputy friend of yours."

Darn. Although a part of him was glad since a break in her routine would signify trouble.

"You ask me, the guy looked like one of those cookie-cutter Fed types."

A Fed? Even weirder.

Well, he'd find out soon enough.

Nate angled his eyes toward Abrams. "How were your days off?"

"Too short. But I caught the game so it wasn't a total waste."

"How're the Jags looking this season?" The season had just started, but from everything he'd heard, the team was strong this year.

Abrams shrugged. "Okay. But I'm a Cowboys fan, myself."

"Traitor."

"Hey, I may live here, but I'll always be a Texan at heart."

Movement caught Nate's attention and he glanced over to find Kirk, the newest guard on the team, leaning against a door with his arms crossed over his chest. The kid said nothing, but he didn't have to. His look said more than enough.

Well, at least he was keeping his snide remarks to himself this time. For once.

As the newest and youngest guard, the kid displayed his superiority complex as proudly as he did his badge.

Abrams opened the door to the private visitation room and waved Nate inside. An abused wooden table sat in the center of the room, all four legs bolted to the floor. On either side of the table, wooden chairs faced off.

The room's lone occupant looked up as Nate approached the table.

Drawn features, piercing eyes, and short brown hair gave the man a hawk-like appearance. The gray pinstriped suit, white shirt, and gray tie screamed federal agent. Or public defender, but since Nate had no need of a defense, that seemed unlikely. A cheap briefcase sat closed on the corner of the table.

Pale eyes stared out of an equally pale face. The man's pinched eyebrows lowered and his mouth looked like he'd just crunched a Granny Smith apple.

Obviously coming here to talk to him hadn't been this guy's first choice.

Yeah, buddy? Well, that makes two of us.

Nate pulled out the chair across from the agent and eased down.

The man cleared his throat. "Nate Miller?"

What, he thought the guards would bring back the wrong man? "Yeah."

"Agent Underwood, FBI."

In spite of the curiosity roiling inside him, Nate remained silent. This meeting was Underwood's idea; let him get it started.

"Tell me about yourself." A condescending tone colored the demand.

Other than arching his eyebrow, Nate didn't move. No way had this Fed driven all the way down here just to get to know him. Something was up. "You've got my file."

"It doesn't say why you turned yourself in."

So that was it. He should've known.

"Freedom was boring. Thought I'd see what life was like on the inside."

Underwood leaned in, his hands clenching. "I cleared my day for this. I'm not leaving until I get some answers."

"Suit yourself. I'm not going anywhere."

Underwood stared him down.

Nate bit back a chuckle. Did this pinstriped pipsqueak really think he could intimidate him?

A minute passed before Underwood spoke, his tone cold. "Look, you wanna know why I'm here, right? Level with me and I'll tell you."

Something compelled him to honesty. Experience told Nate it was probably the Holy Spirit. "I had to. There were some people in my life who deserved to know the truth."

"So they suspected you."

"No, but I had to..." Breath hissed from between Nate's teeth. "I don't expect you to understand. But when you hear God telling–"

"Aw, man. Don't tell me you're one of those who found God while locked inside."

"I found Him before."

"Sure you did."

Ignoring the sarcasm, Nate kept his eyes locked on Underwood. "Believe me or not, I don't care, but I held up my end. Tell me why you're here."

Underwood leaned his elbows on the table, interlaced his fingers, and ground out words that he apparently would have rather kept locked away. "You're being given a chance to serve your country."

"Think I'm a little too old to join the Army."

A muscle in Underwood's jaw twitched.

"A killer with a sense of humor. Great."

"I've never killed anyone."

"In the law's eyes, you did. Accomplice to murder is the same as pulling the trigger." He didn't wait for Nate to respond before pushing forward. "We need your help."

Out of the scenarios Nate could have imagined, this one never would've crossed his mind. "The FBI?"

A curt nod answered his question. "We need you to infiltrate a militant group."

"You want me to do undercover work for the FBI?" The absurdity of the request almost made him laugh. "Whose sick idea of a joke is this?"

An abrupt chuckle burst from Underwood's lips. "Don't I wish. It's no joke."

If it wasn't a joke, then it was some kind of trap. There was no way the FBI wanted him on their payroll. "Well, gee.

Thanks for the asking me to join J. Edgar Hoover's finest, but I'll pass. I'm not exactly FBI material."

"You wouldn't be joining. Think of it more as consulting."

Unbelievable. "Why me?"

"They just lost their system's expert in a car accident."

So he was good with computers and had hacked many high-level systems in order to get into places that he shouldn't. He wasn't the only one who could do that. "Come on. The FBI has their own computer geeks. People better than me, I'm sure."

"None with your reputation. It'd take too long to get one of our agents correctly positioned. You're already well known in certain circles. Plus you're acquainted with one of this group's members."

Really? He couldn't think of anyone he knew who was part of a militia. "Who?"

"Edward Carson."

Edward Carson? Nate racked his memory to place the name. It didn't sound familiar...

"Also goes by Eddie. He's in here with you right now."

An image of the twenty-something guy with a shaved head and plugs in his ears flashed through Nate's mind. The guy had been here about six months and had attached himself to Nate for some reason that Nate had yet to figure out. They'd talked a bit, but had Eddie ever mentioned being in a militia? If so, Nate had missed that detail. "What group is he with?"

"They call themselves White Fire. They're well-funded, well-armed, and growing more deadly."

White Fire. Sounded like an acid rock band from the '80s. But with a name like that, they had to be a white supremacist group. "What are they into?"

"Lots of things. They've been around for years, but have escalated in the last few months."

"Into what?"

"Most recently, bio-toxins. They've already killed forty people with it and our intel tells us they have a lot more where that came from."

"Where do you get your intel?"

Underwood hesitated. "I'm not at liberty to say, but I can tell you it's accurate."

Sure it was. Because snitches never gave bad information. "I don't know what you think I can do from in here."

"You wouldn't be in here." Underwood opened the briefcase, removed a stack of papers, and slid them across the table. "You're being offered a full pardon for your assistance in bringing these guys to justice."

No way.

Nate couldn't help skimming the letter attached to the top of the stack. The signature at the bottom snagged his attention.

The president. Of the United States.

Man, this was big.

"All you have to do is help us dismantle the group from the inside. We want everyone involved with them behind bars. After that, you're a free man."

Free. No more being treated like the second-class citizen he was.

He'd be able to see his kids.

Better yet, he'd be able to see Lana. Any time he wanted. An ache settled deep in his chest. No matter how much he looked forward to them, weekly visits weren't enough.

But to get there, he'd have to return to a life he swore to leave behind forever. "And if they want me to hack into someplace important? Like the FBI's database or the Pentagon? What if they expect me to steal several million credit card numbers? What then?"

"String them along. Fake the information. Whatever you have to do. We want them stopped."

"So what, the ends justify the means?"

Underwood's silence provided all the confirmation he needed.

Wow. Freedom. What he wouldn't give to be out of this place. But at what cost? What if he gained freedom only to imprison his soul?

He shoved the papers back across the table. "I can't."

"You got any idea how lucky you are? Things like this are *never* handed out, especially not to scum like you. Why the heck wouldn't you do it?"

"I left that life behind. I won't go back to being a criminal."

"It may not come to that. All we need is an in, then we can take them down."

"And if I can't get what you need without breaking the law? What then?"

Underwood's snort sounded loud in the barren room. "You've gotta be kidding me. All the laws you've broken and you're worried about one more?"

"I'm not the guy I used to be."

Pushing back his chair, Underwood stood. "Fine. Sit here in your little cell and rot."

Nate never moved as Underwood tossed the file into a briefcase and stalked by him.

He'd just turned down a one-way ticket out of here. What had he been thinking?

Like what you see? Deadly Redemption is available now in print or ebook format exclusively at Amazon.com.

Victory is June
His hope is a sunrise
How Great Thou art
Jesus loves me

Made in the USA
Coppell, TX
12 May 2020

25124226R10192